The Truth,
So Let It Be Told

DERRICK SPIVEY

PAGE PUBLISHING, INC.
Conneaut Lake, PA

First originally published by Page Publishing 2021

ISBN 978-1-64544-595-1 (pbk)
ISBN 978-1-64544-596-8 (digital)

Printed in the United States of America

INTRODUCTION

L et's just say that I know the hell I'm talking about, or let's just say
that I don't. Let's even say that my master's degree, along with
this PhD I possess gives me the right to spin this tale. Or we can
just say that I'm another high school dropout who has a ghostwriter
and a half of a plan.

See, you just opened this book, and already you want to know
what the deal is with me. Is he black or white? Is he educated? Or is
he just another damn fool that's hoping to sign a book deal or two
before it's all over with? Well, Dear Reader, trust me when I tell you
that I am all these things and a whole lot more. I'm the *truth*! So let
the truth be told.

My name is Jonathan "The Truth" Locklord. Okay, I won't beat
around the bush, I know you want to know why they call me The
Truth, and I'm going to tell you. But don't expect me to go into some
long, in-depth, detailed analysis, because this and other things you're
about to find out really ain't none of your business. Feel me?

Nevertheless, my mother was somewhat of a high-class call girl.
The long and the short of her story must be told in order to get to
the heart of mine.

Rose, as this was what she always told me to call her, was in
trouble from the get-go. And on her eighth birthday, that same trouble sought her out and looked to destroy. Here's the whole get-down,
according to how I got the story over the years. My grandmother,
whom I've never met in my entire life, simply walked Rose down
to the Greyhound bus station and told the little girl that she was on
her own. However, after years of vicious child neglect, sometimes

going for days without eating, and along with being left to her own the whole day and often on through the night, Rose simply said, "Well then, that might be better for us both." The years of alcohol and crack-cocaine usage had a walking dead woman standing before Rose, so as Rose often put it, it wasn't hard for her to take her show on the road.

So after hanging out in the Greyhound bus station for a day and a half, without anything to eat for the whole time, you—even being the reader of this story—can see why it was so easy for Rose to accompany the strange man, even as she was a little black girl, with him being a full-grown white man.

Yes! I know just what you're thinking, and you're very right in doing so. So in order to save you, Dear Reader, from having to endure some real sick shit, I'll rate it PG-13 censor, the remainder of this introduction. But as the book goes on, know that I can't make any more such promises.

Let's just say that Cruz stole Rose, and depending on how you're looking at it, maybe even rescued her in a criminal type of way. If you've ever been on the mean streets of downtown LA, then you might have some type of understanding for where I'm coming from

In any event, Cruz treated Rose (in the beginning) as well as any kidnapper could. He homeschooled her, fed and clothed her, and then groomed her in every way to become one of his top-notch girls. It has been told to me that by the time Rose was twelve years old, she was already turning high-class tricks from LA to the Bay Area up north. But be it a high-class or low bottom, we all know a whore is still a whore!

It should go without being said, but I'll say it anyway: Cruz was my mother's everything! She lived and would have died for that son of a bitch. Again, keep it in mind, he was the only one who had shown Rose any type of love, so it was no real big surprise when at the tender age of fourteen years old, Rose would give birth to his firstborn son. Nevertheless, when Cruz informed Rose that he didn't want her son named after him, nor given his last name too, I believe that that was the beginning of the end of one error and the treacherous start of another.

It has been told to me that I went without a full name for the first two years of my life. See, Rose got it in her mind that she wouldn't name me anything if she couldn't name me after the father. However, the hospital had to put something on the birth certificate, so they simply put "Baby Locklord," seeing as that was my mother's last name.

Soon after I was born, Cruz became very indifferent toward Rose. He no longer approached nor touched her with the same love he used to. He began to treat her even worse than he did the rest of his whores. Even when he did have sex with her, it wasn't with the same care he once took. It was now a ruthless act and a vicious conflict that usually left her busted up in one way or another.

Even so, Rose (not knowing any better) still put up with whatever Cruz dished out; that is, until the day Cruz came home with a beautiful Puerto Rican girl name Maria who was thirteen years old. Rose could remember thinking about how much of a bitch life really was. Here it was eight years later almost to the day when Cruz brought her home as an eight-year-old girl, and now here he was again. Now at the sweet age of sixteen, Rose would begin to see things a little more clearly. The very next day would be the day I got my full name, Jonathan "The Truth" Locklord, as Rose said I would forever be the truth to remind her of just how treacherous white people really are.

So there you have it, Dear Reader. Yes! I know you're thinking there just has to be more to Rose's story than that, and you're right! But first of all, didn't I tell you that this was the long and sort of her story in order to get to mine? All you need to do is kick back, and if I were you, I'd buckle my seat belt, because the rest of this ride is going to be bumpy!

CHAPTER ONE

As Conrad Cruz pulled off the Harbor 110 Freeway into the Downtown District of South Los Angeles, he was very pleased with himself. Not only was his business booming both in the drug game as well as the pimp game, but the top dogs in the criminal world were also starting to recognize him as being the big dog on the block. He smiled to himself for being one of a handful of white boys that could even cut a corner in South Central, Los Angeles. Having been truly born and raised in the City of Compton a.k.a "The Hub City." Cruz did it, moving as if he were black as coal.

Now there were many mistakes that one could make in this man's company that would cost the person their life, but none as deadly as calling him a white boy. Don't get it wrong, he knew he was a white boy, just like black males knew that the powers that be saw them as being niggas. But just like a white man couldn't call a black man a nigga and get away with it, nor could a black man call Cruz a white boy and get away with it.

See, this went back to the days of his childhood, growing up on the Eastside of Compton, California. His family was one of the last white families to move out, once the blacks started to move in during the sixties. Conrad would hear some of the little black kids using the N-word and thought it was okay to do, until he got his little ass kicked one day for doing so. When his mother explained why the word was not to be used by him, he questioned her about the words the little black kids used concerning him.

"Mother, why do they keep calling me a white boy?"

"Well, baby, maybe that's because you are a white boy. You must understand that that's not as bad as using the N-word, son."

"Well, it sure sounds like it, the way they be saying it, so if I can't call them the N-word I'm not going to let them call me a white boy no more."

"And if they do, baby?" his mother asked playfully.

"I'm going to do them like they do me," he said angrily.

"And how is that?" his mother asked, as she tickled little Conrad until he laughed hard.

"Like this!" he said as he pulled away from her and started swinging at the air wildly. His mother took it as a joke, but she would later on find out that the little boy she loved so dearly would grow into a monster that made it hard even for a mother to love.

As Cruz pulled to a stop in front of the Wine Gardens Hotel in his 2007 SL55 drop-top Benz, which sat on Lowenhart 20s, he revved the engine one more time on the two-seater Mercedes to really make sure that everyone in the perimeter knew that he was there, just in case some standing around did not notice him pull up. As he opened the door of the car, Roger Troutman and Zapp's, "I Heard It Through The Grapevine" spilled out of the car, filling the ghetto night with old-school funk. Cruz hopped out of the Mercedes Benz and started Crip-walkin' in time with the beat, right in the middle of the San Pedro street like the gangsta that he was. K-Loc could only stand there looking at his boss with hate and contempt, as Cruz received the honor from his peers that he felt he should be receiving.

K-Loc was from a gang called the downtown Gangsta Crips or DTGs if you will. See, at first this gang was made up of niggas that couldn't cut it in their own hoods for one reason or another, but don't get it twisted, this was not to say that they were bustas. The truth be told, they were more like a set full of cutthroats that you didn't want to cross paths with if you didn't have to. However, K-Loc was a BG (baby gangster) that was put on when he was a kid. But now at the age of twenty years old, he had his own crew as ideals on how to turn the DTGs into one of LA's finest. The only problem was he didn't have the money it would take to do so, and that's where Cruz came in.

In any event, Cruz wasn't sleeping on K-Loc, the streets were talking, and you could bet that they were talking to Cruz. K-Loc didn't like the fact that this white boy "and from Compton no less," had a lock on the downtown drug trade. But K-Loc was no fool either; he knew crossin' Cruz was in the making of bring two cities together in order to form one big ass gang. It's like this: Compton and Watts, a.k.a the Hub & the Dub, have always rolled together in prison, at least the Crips did. They had to, as the sets were too small to go it alone. But once they came together, it was like one wicked-ass machine in motion. Them niggas hooked up and started pushing unreasonable lines in the joint; whether it be pens down south or ones up north, they was always on some low-key bully shit. And now here it was, this white Crip was trying to get it popping on the streets. He wasn't only trying to unite the Compton and Watts Crips, but the Bloods as well in the pen and on the streets. K-Loc knew that he didn't want that kind of beef, so he would just have to bide his time and strike when the time was right. Maybe the deal wouldn't go down, he didn't know, but until he knew something one way or the other, he was just going to get his money right and keep his eyes and ears open to what the streets had to say.

"What's up, Cruz?" K-Loc called out.

"My muthfuckin' money is what's up, nigga, you got it?" Cruz called back as he kept C-walking in the middle of San Pedro street.

"Aw nigga got yo' money, cuzz! You ain't got to get at a gangsta like that," K-Loc said with larceny in his tone.

Cruz stopped dancing on the spot and stormed into K-Loc's direction.

Once in the young man's face, Cruz spoke in a deadly tone and said, "Then separate mine from yours, muthafucka, before I flatline your smart-mouth ass right here on the spot."

K-Loc looked into the eyes of a man that he knew wasn't play-ing, so he tried to take some of the sting off his words, saying, "Damn, playa! It's like that?" He said this as he handed Cruz his money in a brown paper bag.

Cruz looked at the brown paper bag and then back to K-Loc and said, "Yeah, you low-budget-ass muthafucka! It's just like that, so now what, nigga?"

At this point, K-Loc wanted to pull his gun out and dismiss Cruz, but his heart was not of the same mind. "Look, cuzz, I don't have no beef with you," K-Loc said.

"Then step down, Crip, before you get knocked the fuck down," Cruz shot back at the younger man. They both stood there eye to eye for a long moment, until K-Loc finally lost the stare off and looked away and walked off.

"That's what you do, Loco!" Cruz shouted at K-Loc as he walked away. "And my money better be right!'

"Damn, Cruz!" Sandy said as she walked up. "That's how you get at these niggas on a solo tip? Coming down here checking mutha-fuckas on their own turf and shit?"

Sandy was one of the home girls from the hood. She was hood rat fine and our baller hit it here and there. But as of lately, Cruz didn't see it that way with all the shit he had on his mind. He had put her down town to be his eyes and ears, and as he saw it, sex would only get in the way of the business at hand. Nevertheless, Sandy didn't see it that way and was pissed off about it.

"Hey, San, what's the get-down, baby?" asked Cruz.

"You the get-down, Daddy. When you going to hit this hot-ass pussy of your number-one girl? Oh! It's like that, Cruz? I guess a bitch has to be ten, eleven, or twelve years old in order to get some of that dick."

The words barely got out of Sandy's mouth before Cruz knocked her the fuck out. Her body crumbled to the ground as if she had just been shot down by a sniper. It took Cruz damn near ten minutes to bring her back to consciousness, and when she did wake up, she found herself sitting inside of Cruz's Benz.

"Sandy, let me make this crystal clear to you one time and one time only. The next time you put my business out in the street, I'm going to kill your kids, your sister's kids, and then I'm going to kill your mother. And then I'll give you a shot of this dick, that is, right before I kill you. Now do we have an understanding, Sandy?"

Sandy looked at Cruz more unconscious than conscious, and barely said, "Yes, Daddy, I understand."

"Now, get the fuck out of my car."

But before Sandy could completely get out of the car, Cruz pulled off, causing her to fall out, making her roll on the ground three or four times like a stuntwoman before she staggered to her feet in a feeble attempt to compose herself. Cruz laughed as he looked through his rearview mirror, only to see a sober woman stumbling back and forth like a drunk that had one Cisco too many. He laughed even harder as she got smaller and smaller in his mirror, until he realized he had forgotten to get his ten grand from her. "GODDAMN IT!"

*****

As Rose walked into the principal's office, his mouth flew slightly open as he zeroed in on the fullness of her beauty. It was true that she was three shades lighter than charcoal; however, her skin was smoother then Chinese silk. She stood five feet eleven at 141 pounds, which was all in the right places, with a shape that could stop traffic going in either direction. Her hair was a clear sign of her Indian heritage, as it cascaded down the middle of her back, touching the upper part of her round, beefy ass. But the first thing that anyone would notice about her when they encountered her face-to-face would be her money green eyes. And if that wasn't good enough, God even had the audacity to give them an Asian shape. She was simply stunning!

Rose could see that he was clearly moved by her beauty, as he was speechless, so she spoke first. "Good morning, I'm Ms. Locklord."

"Yes! Yes, you're Jonathan's mother. Please have a seat."

My God, she is beautiful, he damn near wanted to say out loud. "Ms. Locklord, if I said I knew where to start, I would only be lying to you. It's not just the fights I am hearing about your son having—"

"Your hearing about him having?" Rose said with an attitude as she cut him off. "You mean to tell me you don't know? And that you're just hearing? Mr. whatever-you-said-your-name-was-again?"

"Stanton, Mr. Stanton."

"Well, Mr. Stanton, you do know that just hearing about fights is not reason enough to kick my boy out of school, don't you?"

"Ms. Locklord! Who said anything about kicking your kid out of school? I'm an educator, and I can't do my job if the kids I'm supposed to be teaching are out on the streets, now can I?" he said, with the tone of someone who had a little gangster in him. "Now if you will allow me to finish, we can try to get past the problem in order to find a solution."

What? (She said this in her head.) *I know that this pretty-ass nigga ain't trying to put me in check, and look at him sitting there all sexy, caring about what happens to my son*, she thought to herself. "Okay, Mr. Stanton, you got my undivided attention."

"Look, Ms. Locklord, your son is a very smart young man. He hasn't been caught doing anything as of yet. Nevertheless, there are students that don't like him for one reason or another. Maybe they owe him money or something, I don't know. But I do know that more than one has been in my office talking about your son, even though as if they're doing it in code."

Rose raised her hand as if she was one of his students.

"Yes, Ms. Locklord?" Mr. Stanton said with a smile on his face. "You raised your hand?"

"Yes, sir, now let me get this right. He hadn't been caught? But his name is popping? Is that what you're saying?"

"I'm saying that his name is popping like Pop-Tarts, Ms. Locklord. They call your son 'The Truth' around here, and it's said that the truth is pushing drugs in my school, promoting prostitution in my school, loan-sharking in my school, and the list goes on, Ms. Locklord! Now know this, if even one of these things is the truth about the The Truth, then we got a big problem on our hands. He could go to jail for a very long time for just one of these things, if not for all of them. Is this what we want, Ms. Locklord?"

Rose knew he was telling the truth about her son, and still she looked at him as if to say, "*Not my baby.*"

"Look, Ms. Locklord, I'm not the bad guy here, I'm just passing on to you what I've been hearing about Jonathan, and not the police. If it's not true, then we have nothing to worry about. But if it is true, let us do whatever we need to do to put a stop to it before it gets out of control."

"Are you finished, Mr. Stanton?"

"Yes, Ms. Locklord. Here's my card, you can call me if you need my help with anything."

"Anything?" Rose said as she took his whole hand into hers along with his card.

"Anything!" he said, as the two were feeling one another.

Just as the heat was beginning to turn up, Jonathan walked through the door. "You may want to give my mother's hand back to her, Mr. Stanton, before I lose my muthafuckin' mind up in this bitch!"

Mr. Stanton looked deeply into Rose's money-green eyes and said, "You may be right, young man, you got enough worries. We don't need you to lose your muthfuckin' mind up in here."

"Well, Mr. Stanton," Rose said, "I'll keep in touch."

"I do hope so, Ms. Locklord. I do hope so."

As Rose and Jonathan walked back to the car, no one said a word, until both entered the car. Rose looked over at her son and said, "Dude! Yo' shit is really starting to get raggedy! You're really starting to fuck up, man!"

"And you, Rose," Jonathan said with just as much stank in his tone. "You look like you want to fuck the principal."

Rose took off on Jonathan as if it was on, onsite! But her son warded off her attempts to do so as he laughed at her playfully. "Come on, Rose! It's not this serious."

Rose just stopped and looked at him, and as tears began to roll down her face, she thought back. Here it was 2007, twenty years later to the day Cruz walked into her life and one sixteen-year-old-son later that didn't even know Cruz was his daddy. The boy didn't even know the entirety of his mother's situation, and the worst part about it all was that he didn't seem to care to know.

"Damn, Rose, come on now, you don't have to cry. I know I'm fucking up, but I'm going to get it together, and I'm still going to get you that high school degree you be on your boy about. So wipe them tears away, girl, I got you," He said, trying to cheer his mother up, but she still cried. "What's the matter, Rose? Has that white mutha-fucka been putting his hands on you again? I done told his ass—"

"Dude! Just shut the fuck up, 'cause you don't know what you're talking about."

"Then, what's up with you, Rose? I said I was going to get my stuff together."

She looked at her son with soft eyes and said, "Baby, we need to talk."

"Okay, Rose, let's talk."

"Jonathan, do you even know what I do for a living? I mean really *know*, man?"

Jonathan looked at his mother with her own green eyes and returned the same softness he had seen in her eyes and said, "Rose, I know you do what you got to do in order to make things happen for us. But that's why I've been putting my own thang down, Rose. In a minute you want have to work them suckas out of their cheese, I got you."

"Jonathan, is that what you think I do, baby?" she said, looking like she was going to cry again.

"Okay, Rose, you want it butt-ass naked, then here it is. No! That's not what I think you do. I'm no fool, Rose. But hell! I look at it like this, there are bitches out there running around fucking for free. And then there are others that think they're getting paid, but in reality they getting played. But you, Rose, everybody know that you that bitch! Yo shit tighter than turtle pussy. All your clothing is the top-of-the-line designer shit, not that swap-meet knockoff shit. You pushing a brand-new fully loaded Jaguar, and you got a brand-new Range Rover, even though I drive it all the time."

"I got it for you anyway, Jonathan," Rose said as she wiped her tears away.

"That's the shit I'm talking about, Rose, you down for me. Now, I want to be down for you. We live up in Westwood, and we got a hideout on the beach in Venice, so what's up, Rose? Are you asking me if I like you fucking them born-to-be-trick muthafuckas, then the answer is, FUCK NO! But am I complaining and knockin' you for keeping our heads above water, Rose? That answer is hell no as well! How can I?"

"Because," she said as she smiled at her son, who had made her happy for not judging her, "I'm your mother!" Then she started kissing him all over his face as he playfully fought her off him.

"See, this is why I can't say anything nice to you, yo' ass always got to get all soft on a nigga."

"Shut up, boy, and let your mother kiss you."

They both shared a heartfelt laugh, then Jonathan said, "So now that we all soft and shit, does that mean I can start calling you Mommy?"

"Hell to the no, boy! Don't be playing with me, I'm not old enough to be yo' mommy or anybody else mommy. And anyway, you know we look more like brother and sister, boy."

"Yeah, brother and old-ass stepsister," Jonathan said as he laughed hard at his mother, as she once again tried to beat him up, playfully. Then without warning, Jonathan became very serious. "Rose, I'm going to ask you something and I'm going to need you to keep it real with me."

"Okay, Daddy, what is it?" she said, still playing with him.

"Rose, I don't want you to screw my principal. I really don't need that kind of shit in my life right now."

Rose looked into his eyes and could see he was not playing. "All right, Jonathan, is there anything else?"

"Yes, as a matter of fact there is."

"And what would that be, son?"

"Rose, is Cruz my real father or not?"

*****

As Cruz hit the Century 105 Freeway bound for LAX to pick up Maria, he couldn't help but think out loud. *Damn! This hoe money is almost better than the dope money, if you ask me. I guess that's what happens when you get them bitches super young, their worth is three times the norm*, he thought to himself. *Less problems too.* \

He had fourteen girls that were grossing twenty thousand dollars apiece monthly, apart from the money that them bitches was holding out on him, of course, like all hookers did. Nevertheless, at the end of the month, that was 280,000 dollars. At the end of the year that was 3,360,000 dollars!

"Pimp, muthafucka, pimp on!" he bragged to himself.

Then at the same time he really didn't want this street shit to blow up in his face. He would get out if he could, but once you're in, it's like having your feet stuck in quicksand. He thought to himself that there was really no way out of the game other than death. So if you're going to live just in order to die, then do what the fuck you want to do, shit! The Crips should have been as big as the Mafia by now, if not then bigger. But niggas are truly like crabs in a barrel. If they see one trying to climb out, they'll kill him. This just because they wish it was them getting out.

The Crips started back in sixty-eight or sixty-nine, I don't know, but here it is 2007, and they are damn near in every state, coast to coast. He smiled to himself not because he had that knowledge, but because a white Crip was about to put the Hub and the Dub on the map in a major way!

When the Crips and the Bloods from Compton & Watts are united, then them LA niggas would have to follow suit and get on board.

If not, we will have to swallow their asses up too. In the end, it will be one big ass black crime family, and it will spread across the US of A like the fuckin AISA virus, one big-ass money-making machine and one leader of that army!

That leader is him! His smile got much bigger at the thought of that, as he pulled up to the Delta Airlines terminal at LAX to pick up Maria.

"Hey, Papi! Is that big-ass smile 'cuz you miss me?" Maria was hoping.

"Bitch! This smile's way bigger than any smile I'd ever give to the likes of your ass," he said before pulling into traffic.

"Well, Daddy, maybe this will make your smile a little bigger for your number-one girl."

She handed Cruz forty thousand dollars in cash.

Cruz was thinking to himself, *This bitch is not only to model fine, but she is a flat-backin', money-makin' machine.* "Now that's my girl," he told Maria as she snuggled to him.

Rose and Maria were making twice as much as the rest of his call girls. They were fuckin' everything from pro ball players to senators and anything in between that had big money. Cruz had a black book with so many high-profile names in it, that the book alone was worth more than his hoes made in a year. The book alone would cash any check that trouble could bring his way. Yes, it was all coming together like sweaty ass cheeks in the summertime. Coincidentally, Sandy calls at that very moment to let Cruz know that he forgot to collect his ten Gs from her.

"Daddy, I'm sorry fo' puttin' yo' business in the streets last night. It won't happen again."

"I'll be there in the morning to pick up my money, Sandy," Cruz replied. "You need to know that I got mad love for you, boo. We go way back, just stick to the goddamn plan, Mommy, okay?"

"Aight, Daddy," Sandy acknowledged before he hung up in her face. As he looked over to Maria, he simply told her, "It's all comin' together, little mama."

"As well as it should be, Daddy, as well as it should," Maria agreed. Cruz slapped a Carlos Santana CD in and the song "Europa," filling the cabin of the Benz as they drove down the road.

CHAPTER TWO

A s Sandy sat in her apartment, she really didn't know what to make of her situation. She had known Conrad Cruz ever since she was in the third grade. They lived three houses away from one another in the old neighborhood. She even recalled having his back against some of the other blacks when they were growing up. She always like Conrad, even though he was much older than she was. He was so sweet once upon a time, but that was then, and this is now. Maybe the years and/or the streets, maybe the money; most likely the game had changed him. Nevertheless, Conrad was turning into someone she didn't really know anymore. Deep down, she wanted to betray him for the shit he had done to her last night. But how could she, after all he had done for her? He was the one that had put her through college. He was the one who had come to her mother's aid when they were going to lose their house back in the day, and he was the first man she had known sexually. Sandy knew deep down that Cruz cared for her, but how much has always been the question at hand. Here she was living in downtown LA, yes, down muthafuckin' town LA but livin' comfortably nonetheless. She was drivin' a ragtop Corvette C6, with a top-notch wardrobe to match. And her spot was laid the fuck out! On top of that, all of the above was paid for by Mr. Conrad Cruz.

On the other hand, she ain't livin' half as good as them younger bitches he's got set up, one in Malibu and the other in Westwood.

What's that shit all about? she thought to herself, *and as of lately, he won't even bone a bitch like he used to. Oh, hell no! This shit is not cool.* Sandy marinated in her own stew. *I may not be able to do this good* by myself, *but I can sure as hell be happier* by myself. *I'm thirty-four now, and I am not satisfied with sharing the father of my children with two other bitches.*

Just then the doorbell rang. *Who the hell could that be?* Sandy thought to herself. *Conrad got his own key, so it can't be him.*

"Who the hell is it?' she called out as she walked to the door.

"It's K-Loc, Sandy! I need to holla at you."

"What is it, K-Loc?" Sandy replied, as she opened the door.

"This is not a good time."

"What, it's like that now, Sandy?"

"Nigga, what chu mean is it like that now? I gave you the pussy one time in a moment of weakness, and now you actin' as if we got some real shit goin' on! Now, nigga! WHAT DO YOU WANT?"

"Sandy, the only reason why I'm pushin' up on you right now is cos' I'm really feelin' you," K-Loc said with a tender tone to his voice.

"Really, *feelin'* me? Dude, you don't even know me, cos' if you did you'd be trying to stay clear of me."

"I know you well enough to know that you not feelin' that white muthafucka beatin' up on you like you some nigga in the streets," he said as he tried to touch the bruise on the side of her face from the night before.

"Man, you don't even know what's goin' on," she said as she pulled her face away from his hand. This shit's way too deep for you to understand."

"Look, K-Loc, just get on up outa here before Cruz roll up on you for being up in his spot."

"And? Then what? The nigga is never here with you anyway," K-Loc said, as brave as he could.

"Boy, I saw your young ass bow down last night when Cruz pushed up on you, so don't be trying to go big now," Sandy said.

"Sandy, that wasn't bowing down. I may just be twenty years old, but even that's old enough to know that I can't stand up under the shit that could pop off, if I rub that fool the wrong way."

Sandy looked deep into K-Loc's eyes and saw that there was no fear there, though there should have been. "Okay, big man, so you're not afraid of Mr. Conrad Cruz. Now what?" Sandy said flirtatiously.

He walked into the apartment and pulled her close to himself. She wanted to stop him, but at the same time she wanted to feel his tender touch again, so instead of fighting it, she let her walls down and gave in to him without confrontation. He picked her up and carried her to the bedroom then made passionate love to her. She gave him all of herself, fully and wholeheartedly in every way he wanted her, until they both ran out of gas.

As they lay in one another's arms face-to-face, K-Loc pulled Sandy even closer into himself and whispered, "Sandy, would it be so wrong for me to love the woman I know you really are?"

"Look boo—" Sandy tried to speak, but K-Loc cut her off.

"No, Sandy, let me finish. I have been feeling you ever since you moved down here. I just didn't know how to get at you nor how to be what you truly needed in a man. See, you're so far out of our league," K-Loc said.

"Our league?" she asked, not understanding what he was trying to say.

"Well niggas like Cruz and myself, you've got to know that you deserve better than this, so much better than just another gangsta," K-Loc said with concern.

"Look, baby, a lot of shit is about to go down. Trust me when I tell you that we can never be. And please trust me when I tell you that it's very unsafe for you or anyone else to be down here."

"Just what are you talkin' about, Sandy?"

"Look, K-Loc, I really can't explain it to you. Not this, because of my loyalty to Conrad."

"Conrad? Who the fuck is that?" K-Loc asked with a puzzled look on his face.

"Cruz, K-Loc. Cruz! That's his first name. Nevertheless, you just made me see my situation so much clearer. But how can I be sure that you mean the things you just said, K-Loc?"

"Sandy, I'm not really big with words, and I don't know how to use them to make a woman fall all over me, but when I open my mouth, I say what I mean and mean what I say!" he assured her.

"Then come with me, K-Loc."

"Come with you where, Sandy?"

"I don't know yet, boo, but let's just get the fuck on the highway and figure it out once we get there."

K-Loc just looked at her like she was crazy.

"Look, man! I'm trying to tell you that Cruz is about to put down some category-six shit up here, and if you don't want to believe that to be true, then just stay here and see what happens. Look, if Cruz finds out I told you even this much, I'm dead! Dead, I tell you! So I'm up out of here, dude," Sandy said.

As she tried to get dressed, he stopped her. "Hold up, baby. All right, I know there's a lot of truth in what you're saying. I just didn't know the madness was already upon us."

She knew his eyes were asking for more information, so she tried to reassure him. "I've known Cruz all my life, and he trusts me with more of his business than he should," Sandy said as she pulled out the ten grand. "Here, Daddy," she said as she handed the money to K-Loc. Now he knew she was for real.

"Okay, Sandy, what's the plan?"

"Look, boo, you need to follow me to this address in Long Beach," she told K-Loc as she wrote the information down on a piece of paper.

"And then what, Sandy?"

"And then we hit Cruz's safe house and skip town. That's what, Daddy."

"What?" K-Loc cried. "You mean to tell me that you know where that muthafucka keeps his dope?"

"Yes, baby, but you got to think bigger than that. See, we can't push across state lines with no dope, but we can, however, push with three-fourths of a million dollars if we bust that shit down into traveler's checks," said Sandy.

"Yes, you're more than right," he said as he tried to hand her the ten grand back.

"No, Daddy, when I give my man something it's his, and on top of that why should that white muthafucka make all the money in your hood?"

Upon hearing that, K-Loc smiled with a new understanding.

"Now, we don't have much time, Boo. Conrad is coming over to pick that money up today. Nevertheless, we will be in traffic by the time he gets here, so let's get to movin'."

"What time do you want to meet, Sandy?"

She smiled because he seemed to be all for her plan. "Meet me out in front at 6:00 p.m. tonight, Daddy."

"Okay shorty, don't be late."

"I won't, Big Daddy," she said and kissed him fully on his mouth as if it would be their last kiss ever. They looked deep into one another's eyes, and then K-Loc walked away with some swagger in his step as if he had just hit the lotto. He had finally bust Cruz's girl, he had ten grand of Cruz's money in his possession, and would soon have three quarters of a meal ticket in his hands. Now all he had to do was lie low in another state and flip the money for a year or two then come back to Cali as the muthafuckin' man!

*****

Ring… Ring… Ring! Cruz answered the phone. "Cruz here."

"This me, Daddy, Sandy. Where you at?"

"I'm on the way to your spot, Mommy."

"Well, Daddy, I think you might want to put that trip on hold."

"What are you saying, Sandy? And make sure you choose your words wisely over this phone, you hear?"

"Yeah, Daddy, I hear you."

"Then speak, Mommy."

"I caught the rat ahead of time. He'll be in the trap around 6:00 p.m."

"Damn, Momma. See, now that's shit I'm talkin' about. That there is the shit that makes you more important to me than the other bitches," Cruz said with satisfaction. "Which trap is the rat going to be in?

"The one in Long Beach, Daddy!"

"That's hella cool, baby, hella cool."

"By the way, Daddy, I had to use the ten Gs as bait to get the job done."

"That's aight, Mommy, sometimes it takes money to make money. Nevertheless, whatever the rat has left on his person is yours, for a job well done."

"Thank you, Daddy."

"Sandy?"

"Yes, Conrad?"

"You know I love you, don't you?"

"Yes, Conrad, I know. However, it would be nice if you'd get around to showing me physically as well as emotionally more often."

"And I shall, as soon as this business of ours is taken care of, Mommy."

"I love you, Cruz."

"Okay, Mommy, I'll see you at six."

Click.

*****

"Jonathan. Why all of a sudden you wanna know about that shit?"

Jonathan looked out the window as if she had just betrayed him. Rose, sensing that he got hurt from what she had said, turned his face toward hers.

"Okay," she said as she pulled away from the curb, "you're old enough for me to put you up on some of the ugly things that life has to offer." Rose took him back to the beginning and told him the whole story. Finally, she was able to let it all out. Finally, the burden that was in her soul would be transferred to another soul. Someone else would finally feel her pain. Finally, she ain't gotta bear this hell alone. Now, her only sorrow (if you could call it that) would be that her son would have to suffer alongside her truth.

By the time she finished her whole story, they were sitting in front of their beach home in Venice. This was the spot that no one knew about but them, a place they could lie low at or hide out in case a time came when they had to. Jonathan looked over at his mother and spoke for the first time in an hour.

"Mom." The word came out of his mouth easily as if he had been using it all along. It was still very unfamiliar to Rose's ears.

Before he could say another word, Rose spoke. "I really haven't been much of a mother to you, now, have I?" Rose uttered sadly.

Jonathan looked at her with kind eyes and said, "No, Mom, you haven't, but in all fairness I really haven't been much of a son to you either, now, have I? However, you have been my best friend, Mom, and no matter what comes or what may, know that I'll always love you in spite of whatever the deal is with you."

Rose looked at her son and said, "Thank you, baby."

"Don't trip. We're Locklords, and you know we're all we got. Right, Rose?"

"You're right, baby."

"Then I got a question for you, Rose. How much is Cruz worth?"

She took a long look at her son. The sixteen-year-old young man already stood at six feet even and was 210 pounds. The boy should have been playing some kind of ball, but no! And when one would look at him, one could not escape the beauty that surpassed ordinary handsomeness. The boy could have been a movie star, but no! This one was a gangsta without a gang and a leader without any to follow him yet. And now here he was asking about a man that would kill him as soon as he looked at him. The last time Cruz even saw him was three and a half years ago. Jonathan was thirteen years old when he walked in on Cruz roughin' Rose up over some money that she had spent on the boy. Instantly, Jonathan had Rose's gun in hand, pointing it at Cruz, and before Rose could have stopped him, he let off a shot that barely missed Cruz. This caused Cruz to react by pulling out his own gun and shooting Jonathan in the shoulder. He could have killed Jonathan and probably would have if the boy weren't his own son.

Jonathan. The Truth. Locklord.

"My one and only son, trust me when I tell you that you're in no ways ready to go up against a monster like Cruz!" his mother exclaimed. As the young man looked at her with her own green eyes, she saw something in them that was different. The quiet rage that she saw in his eyes belonged to his father. This was just one more characteristic, like many others displayed by the boy over the years, that told Rose that he was more his father's son than he was hers.

"Okay, Rose, that may be so, but you know as well as I know that it's just going to be a matter of time before me and that dude face off."

"Yes, baby, trust me that I know. And when that time comes, you'll be ready. But now is not that time, Jonathan, and I trust that you understand that as well."

His eyes now told her that he did understand where she was coming from. Nevertheless, it was time to school the boy. She had to make sure he was ready to do what he already had a mind to do, because he had already made up his mind to do it, with or without her help.

*****

K-Loc couldn't believe his luck. His whole life had been an uphill battle, but now his ship had finally come in. He couldn't help but reflect back to how it came to this. His mother gave birth to him in a porta-potty in downtown Los Angeles. She was smoking crack cocaine the night he slipped out of her drug-infested uterus, onto the filthy piss-soaked floor of the porta-potty. Later on, it had been told to him that she finished smoking her last few crumbs before collecting the newborn baby off the floor.

"It's a wonder that I'm even alive today!" K-Loc thought out loud.

His mother walked back with the newborn to the mission where she was living on Sixth and San Pedro. She lay down with the baby still attached to her umbilical cord. When they tried to pry him out of her bloody hands, K-Loc was told that she fought with everything she had to keep it from happening. However, she was deemed an unfit mother, and K-Loc became a ward of the state. It took her two years to clean up her act. Nevertheless she did, and soon after she came to get him.

K-Loc thought to himself, *I don't really remember these things, nor do I remember some of the other things said about her over the years. All I know is, while most of my homeboys' mothers were still getting high, mine wasn't. However, I did ask why and what made her stop gettin' high, but the answer I received wasn't the one I expected. She explained how she lost a child eight years back before she had me and how drugs were the reason why.*

K-Loc's mother simply told him that she didn't want to go through that same kind of hurt again. K-Loc wanted the reason to be more about him. Nevertheless, it was what it was, and he'll have to live with that.

Sometimes, I can still see the pain of whatever happened, in my mother's eyes. A deep hurt that can't be fixed by anyone, the kind of hurt that stays with a person for a lifetime, thought K-Loc.

"Things are going to change," K-Loc pondered as he fired up a Newport, inhaled deeply, and blew out a cloud of smoke.

It has been said that money isn't a cure-all, but my mother never had any money, so now that she will, let's just see if that statement is really the truth or not. I figure, Sandy and I will go down South for a year or two, maybe my mom and baby bro will come with us too. Then, when my money is right, my baby bro and I will go back to LA, reassemble the crew, and really get it jumpin'. The Downtown area is under somewhat of an overhaul or a facelift, so to speak. The old way of life is passing away, and the city is under construction. The homeless are being moved out, and the rich white folks are setting up shop, driving the cost of living down here up higher than it used to be. Soon, there will be big money to be made in the downtown area, but by the time I get back, there will be even more to be made. K-Loc smiled at that very thought, as he took his last hit on his cigarette, and flicked the butt onto oncoming traffic.

K-Loc continued to contemplate. After I beat Cruz out of his money, I'll slip in and out of Los Angeles with payments for my crew to show 'em that I'm still stickin' to the plan. Maybe I should put the boys up on the latest events… NAH! One should never let his left hand know what the right hand is doing.

But could he really trust Sandy? He remembered when they first met, how they used to "just" kick it and talk all hours into the night. How she used to call him her little brother even when she knew he wanted to tap dat ass. Then one night, it happens! They were kickin' back, getting drunk, and one thing led to another, and the rest is hot sexual history.

I just feel like I can trust her, she knows everything about me. She even knows my plans to take the young DTGs to the next level of the game, makin' us the new face of Los Angeles, K-Loc reasoned with himself. *Hell! She just gave me ten grand and about to put three quarters of a million more in my hands to fulfill my plans. Hell yah, I can trust her!* he tried to convince himself. *Nevertheless, I'll have my little brother follow us in his car in order to make sure this shit goes according to the plan.*

Solo picked up his phone on the first ring. "Solo here."

"What's up, baby bro?" K-Loc asked. "Damn, big dog, I thought you was this little honey I've been waitin' to hear from."

"Sorry to disappoint you, my nigga, but I got some real shit that's about to pop off, and I need you to have my back."

"What's the get-down, big bro, we finally goin' to rock that white boy to sleep?" Solo asked with eagerness.

"Something like that, but I can't fill you in with all the details right now. But know this, our shop has finally come in. I need you to bring the Tech-9 and just follow my car while I'm following Sandy's car to this spot in Long Beach."

"K-Loc. Cuzz. I really don't trust that bitch Sandy. There's just something about her that rubs me the wrong way."

"Look, Solo, she's not like you think. She cool. She got yo' nigga's back. However, if the shit goes bad, I need to know that you got my back, little bro," K-Loc said.

"Nigga, you know I do! That's on Moms," Solo reassured his big bro.

"Aight, I need you to get to Sandy's spot a half an hour before I get there, park somewhere where she can't spot you, and just wait until I get there," K-Loc instructed.

"When you pull up, do you want me to get out or what?" Solo asked.

"Na'uh. Just lie low, but when you see me pull off after her, follow me. Aight, little bro?" K-Loc told his little brother.

"Okay, bro, I got you!" Solo responded.

"I know that you don't trust her, but trust me when I tell you that it's all good," K-Loc emphasized. "But at any point that it starts lookin' bad, just get out of the car and start gunnin'."

"If it looks like it's funny, I'm going to get out blazin' and that's on DTG, cuzz!" Solo said with confidence.

"You do that, bro. By the way, you know I love you, man."

"Don't be getting all soft on me, big bro, we Locklords. Family comes before anything else."

"True that, little bro, we all we got, gangsta. Crip out!"

Click!

As K-Loc hung up the phone after speaking to his brother, Solo's last words echoed in his ears. "We Locklords, family comes before anything else."

Solo was only sixteen, but he had more heart than most grown men. K-Loc made one more call before he left.

"Hey, Mom?"

"Kenny, is that you, baby?"

"Yes, Mom, it's your favorite son!"

"Well, this must not be my son Kenny because he knows that I don't have favorite children. He knows I love both my boys equally. So who is this again?"

"Stop playin', Mom."

"No, boy, you stop playing!"

"Did you get that money I sent you, Mom?"

"Yes, baby, I got it. How come you just didn't bring it by, you out of town or something?"

"No, Mom." *Not yet, at least,* he thought to himself. "I was just handlin' some business and decided to send you some money."

"Well, thank you, baby! It's not like I didn't need it. By the way, have you seen you brother? You know, he moved out last week. He's most likely shacking up with that little whore of his."

K-Loc just laughed to himself. His mother couldn't stand no girl his brother Derrick go with. "She cool, Mom, maybe you just need to give her a chance."

"I am not going to give her shit but a black eye if she hurts my baby."

"Stop it, Momma, and to answer your question, I'll be seeing Derrick today. But, Mom, I called to let you know that I will be going out of town for a little while."

"You're not in trouble are you, Kenny?" his mom said with concern.

"No, Momma, everything is cool. And don't worry, I'll keep in touch. I'm just going to handle some business that will make things better for us all."

"I got a bad feeling about this, Kenny."

"Momma, don't start."

"Okay, Kenny, if you want me to get off your back, I'm going to need you and your brother to get over here tonight, especially seeing as you're going out of town."

"What's the deal, Momma?"

"The deal is that I have something to tell you that I should have told you a long time ago."

"Mom, I don't have time for this."

"Well son, you better make some time because you boys have an older sister that you don't know about, and it's time that you learn the truth about that situation."

"You have got to be shittin' me, Mom!"

"No, Kenny, I wish I was, but I'm not. So will I be seeing you both?"

He looked at his watch and said, "Mom, this really is bad timing, but I guess we had better make it our business to get there."

"Yes, son, I think you had better do just that."

"Okay, Mom, we'll be there as soon as we can."

"Good, Kenny!" Her voice sounded kinda sad.

"You know that I love you no matter what, Mom?"

"Well, son, we'll soon see, we'll soon see." She said as she hung the phone up.

*****

As Cruz bent the corner on Long Beach Boulevard, he slowed down for the dip on Greenleaf, so he wouldn't tear his car up. He then pulled the safety off his 9 mm and placed his finger on the trigger. The neighborhood Compton Crips (that being the set he was from) and the Southside Compton Crips had a full-scale war going on. Yes! There was a peace treaty at this time because of the plan Cruz was trying to put down of uniting the Hub and the Dub, but Cruz would be foolish to think niggas wouldn't take a shot at him despite that. There's always someone looking to fill your shoes, be it a homey or a foe. When he cut the corner on Cuzco Stree and saw the homeboys standing out, he became a little more comfortable. However, he did not pull his finger off the trigger cos' nine times out of ten, it's someone close to you that does you in. Cruz had the hood tight, anybody that wanted to get paid got paid in full, but niggas always want more no matter how much you had fed them already. As he pulled his black 300C sitting on Armano VIP 22's to a stop in the middle of Cuzco St., The Outlaw Bandit Loc and his road dog Gangsta Bam made their way to the car without a word and hopped in. Cruz had already phoned them and put them up on game, so no other words were needed. As they pulled off one of the baby wolves from the hood called out, "Big Cruz! What's up, dog? You can't get at the wolf pack before you roll out?" Cruz slowed down to see tomcat and about twelve of the tiny hood boys standing behind him.

"Fuck them little niggas, Cruz, keep on rollin'!" Gangsta Bam called out from the back seat, but Cruz paid the man no mind as if he never even spoke. As he pulled the car to a stop, he looked at the one that was doing all the talkin' and called out to no one in particular, "What's up hoodsta?"

Tomcat stepped off the curb and said with a little sting in his voice, "This peace treaty sho' ain't the fuck what's up!"

Cruz looked at the man with "warning" eyes but at the same time nodding his head, giving Tomcat the go-ahead to continue. "Cruz. You the one that told us to make them niggas pay and with their firstborn if necessary."

"And?" Cruz said with hostility in his voice, still pissed about the tone the little homeboy was using.

"Well, Little Loc's car got shot up last night, and we all know who did it!" Tomcat complained.

"Did anybody see who done it?" Cruz asked.

"Naw, dog."

"Well, then, you don't know who did it, do you, cuzz?"

"Oh, we know and you know too, big dog."

"How old are you, Tomcat?"

"I'm sixteen, Loco."

"So you runnin' those wild dogs behind you?"

Tomcat looked at the young men on both sides of him and said, "Something like that, Cruz."

"Then, get you bad ass in."

At the sound of Cruz's words, Gangsta Bam popped open the back door. Tomcat looked at Cruz as if it were going to be his last ride. Now the young man spoke with a little more respect.

"But this still neighborhood Crip, big Cruz."

"Then get yo' ass in, cuzz!"

Tomcat nodded to two of his boys, and all three young men started toward the car, but before they got halfway there, Cruz hopped out of the car with his gun still in his hand.

"What the fuck is this shit?" Cruz asked.

The two young men stepped back up on the curb much faster than they stepped down. Although Tomcat stood his ground even if it was with more fear than courage. "Why the fuck is you still standing there for? Get yo' ass in fo' the last time, cuzz!" Cruz demanded. Shaking like a leaf on a tree, Tomcat made his way to the car and got in.

As the men dipped through traffic with Westside Connection banging in the background, Tomcat wondered what the fuck he had gotten himself into as no one said a word. He looked over to Gangsta

Bam and then to Outlaw Bandit Loc who was sitting in the front seat with Cruz, only to see Cruz looking at him with murderous eyes through the rearview mirror. Quickly looking away, the young man realized that he was rolling with three of the most deadly mutha-fuckas from the hood. This was no joyride, somebody was going to die tonight, and Tomcat could only pray that it would not be him

*****

As Sandy sat in her Corvette trying not to think about K-Loc's fate, she told herself that it's all business. The only thing is, she really found herself starting to have feelings for the young man. Nevertheless, she had played her hands as well as her part, and now the chips would have to fall where they may. Just then, her phone went off as K-Loc's car pulled up behind hers.

"Hey you!" Sandy said.

"What's up, boo, you ready to do this, shorty?" K-Loc asked.

"Yes, boo, let's go get paid," she said, as she pulled off into traffic with K-Loc on her bumper.

*****

K-Loc and his brother made eye contact as he followed Sandy to the 710 Long Beach Freeway. Solo didn't like this at all as he had a sinking feeling in the pit of his stomach. Nevertheless, he thought to himself as he touched the barrel of the TEC-9: *I'll play my roll and back my brother's play until the very end, no matter the circumstances.*

K-Loc seen his brother's car fall about three cars length behind and phoned him on his hands-free.

"What's up, big bro, is everything cool?"

"Fo' sho, Solo. I'm just calling to make sure that you cool."

"I'm cool, cuzz."

"Aight, little bro, just stick to the plan. I need you to keep your eyes open for anything that don't look right."

"Don't worry, K-Loc, cuzz. I got yo' back, nigga!"

"Aight, Solo. By the way, Mom's got some deep shit she wants to holla at us about."

"What now, my nigga?"

"Don't trip, I'll fill you in after this shit is over with."

"Aight, doggy-dog, but I'll tell you this right now… I ain't moving back there!"

K-Loc just laughed and hung the phone up.

*****

Cruz and the boys got to the safe house fifteen minutes earlier than Sandy and K-Loc did. Cruz popped the truck open on the 300C, and Gangsta Bam pulled out a big black bag. Cruz looked in the rearview mirror at Tomcat and saw that the young man was sweating even though the AC was on. When Cruz told The Outlaw Bandit Loc to go and set the trap up in the house with Gangsta Bam, Tomcat wanted to get out of the car and run down the street, calling for help. Just then, Cruz turned around and spoke for the first time to the young man. "Do you believe in this Crippin'? I mean, really believe in it?"

All the young man could say was "Yeah, it's do or die on mine."

Then Cruz said, "Would you die for this Crippin', or would you be the type that is only willing to kill for this Crippin'?

Before Tomcat could answer, Cruz continued. "This shit's way bigger than us, so we got to let it grow to the monster it was meant to be. Look, cuzz, I know you don't really understand right now what I'm talkin' about, but by the time it's time for you to run the whole Eastside of Compton, Crips and the Bloods"—Cruz paused to let his words sink and continued—"by then I'm sure you will."

"Now, do you think you can control them wild dogs of yours until I put this shit in motion?" Cruz asked demandingly.

"Big homey, I can control my side of Long Beach Boulevard, but who's going to control them muthafuckas on the other side of the Boulevard?"

"I got a meeting with Little C. tomorrow, trust me, he'll get a handle on the BGs over there. Now, there's some really ugly shit about to go down over here. I need you to take my car and pick up someone you can trust, then go pick up Sandy's car from the beach and park both cars in the hood. Can you handle that?"

"Fa' sho, but what's goin' on, big homey?"

"That's none of yo' damn business," Cruz said as he peeled off a C-note, handing it to the young man. "Just do the job," he said before handing Tomcat the keys and walked in the house.

*****

When Sandy pulled into the beach parking lot, K-Loc wondered what was going on. She got out of her car with an empty black bag and got in to K-Loc's car. "There's no need for us to take two cars boo, feel me?" Sandy said.

"Why?" he asked.

"Well, let's see. Maybe Cruz got someone spying out the spot. If so, we don't want to tip them off now, do we?" she said smilingly, to win him over, and continued, "I'm always in and out of this place, so no one will really pay any mind, but if two cars pull up we might draw a gang of attention. You understand?"

"Aight, I feel you, Sandy, let's roll."

Before K-Loc could drive up outa there, Sandy said, "Tell whoever that is you got following us to park at least a block away from the spot."

"What are you talkin' about, Sandy?"

"I'm talking about you startin' to make it real hard fo' me to trust you?" she questioned him with her eyes. "K-Loc, we don't have time for all this bullshit."

He didn't say a word and pulled up next to his brother's car. He simply said, "It ain't goin' down after all, Solo."

He then handed Solo a thousand-dollar bill with the address clearly written on the note. He eyed his brother then the note he had just handed him and pulled off. Their eye contact did not get past Sandy; nevertheless, she acted as if she didn't catch it at all.

When they pulled into the driveway of the stash house on the Eastside of Long Beach, K-Loc surveyed the neighborhood instinctively. It was a quiet spot. Kids were playing in the street, and one man was watering his lawn as his old lady was working in the garden. There was no sight of bullshit a foot within eyes' view.

"Come on, baby, let's get this over with," Sandy said as she grabbed the black bag. K-Loc looked into her eyes to see if they would tell him something, but he only saw in them what appeared to be love. He pulled his 9 mm from under the seat and said, "Show me the way, boo."

Once they made their way to the door, Sandy pulled out a set of keys to both doors, first the steel-bar gate and then the big wooden one. Once inside, K-Loc pulled out the weapon he had concealed in the small of his back. The living room was empty; other than the wall-to-wall mirror that reached the roof, there was nothing else in sight. K-Loc went from room to room with his pistol drawn like he was Five-0. All seemed to be clear. Sandy walked up beside him and said, "Damn, boo! Chill. Let's get this money and get up out of this muthafucka."

As they walked into the master's bedroom, K-Loc noticed this room had the same mirror as the living room had. He thought to himself how he would like to have sex with Sandy in a room such as this. Just then, Sandy opened the closed door, revealing not only her ass but a four-by-three-foot safe mounted in the wall. As she opened it, K-Loc's dick hardened. He didn't know if it was because of the ass shot she was showing or 'cuz of all the fuckin' money that was about to be his.

"Here it is, baby! Let's get it and bounce up outa here," Sandy said in haste. K-Loc walked over to see the money up close. The safe had wall-to-wall money in it, he couldn't believe his eyes as he bent down to help Sandy pull the money out of the safe. Placing his gun on the hardwood floor, he began to help Sandy fill the bag, which at that moment Sandy's phone rang, causing K-Loc to jump. "Hello?" She covered the phone's mouthpiece and whispered to K-Loc, "It's Cruz, baby."

She directed her conversation to Cruz. "It's all over, Cruz! I just can't take your shit no more… I'm not at my house, and I am never coming back! Don't worry where I'm at! It's over."

"Give me the phone!" K-Loc demanded as he looked over his shoulder while transferring the money in to the bag. "Look, white boy! Sandy is with me now."

"And who the hell is this?" Cruz said over the line. "This K-Loc, muthafucka, now what?" he said as he walked away from the money and his gun to look at himself in front of the mirror and gave Cruz an earful.

"Is that right?" Cruz answered back on the phone.

"Yeah that's right! You wanna be black, peckerwood-ass mutha-fucka! Oh, and another thang! It's going to be me and you real soon, so watch yo' back, Cruz!"

K-Loc was still admiring himself when that same mirror began to spit open like the Red Sea.

"What the fuck?" K-Loc cried out in a high-pitched voice as he ran to retrieve his gun, only to see Sandy pointing his own weapon at him. "No! What the fuck is goin' on, Sandy?"

He turned back at the big mirror and saw Cruz and two other men walking out of the little room in between the two mirrors he had noticed earlier.

They're two-way mirrors, I should have known, he thought to himself as he tried to run for the door, only to have Outlaw Bandit Loc hit him with a two piece (biscuit included) that slid him halfway across the hardwood floor.

Half dazed, K-Loc looked up at Sandy who had a single tear rolling down her face and asked, "Why? Why would you do this to me, Sandy?"

But there was no answer that she could give him. Instead his statement was met with the barrel of Cruz's 9 millimeter that knocked out four of K-Loc's front teeth.

"Look at you now, you smart-mouth mutherfucka. How's this bitch made nickel and dime getting part-time hustla going to act, Bandit?" Cruz asked his homeboy, not really looking for an answer, nor did he get one. "This dude got balls! First he fucks my bitch and then he tries to steal my money!"

"I'm sorry, Cruz. Please, man, don't kill me," K-Loc said with blood pouring out of his mouth.

"Don't worry about it, K-Loc. It ain't about the bitch *or* the money."

K-Loc's eyes pleaded with despair to know the real reason why he was about to die, so Cruz told him. "Besides you calling me a white boy, the reason you're about to die is strictly business related. See, I need that downtown area, and you're simply in the way, my friend."

"Man, you can have that shit!" K-Loc cried out.

Before he could say another word, Cruz shot him in his right kneecap. The scream that came out of the man's mouth sounded like it came from some kind of wild animal! "Aaaaaaaaaahhhhwwwww!"

Gangsta Bam came with the duct tape and taped the man's mouth shut. With tears running down his face, K-Loc tried to buy himself some mercy, but Cruz wasn't selling any and shot him in his other kneecap. The more the man pleaded for mercy with his eyes, the more ruthless Cruz became. Before it was over, along with the gunshot wounds to the knees, Cruz also shot K-Loc in both of his shoulders.

"You try'na say something, K-Loc?" Cruz said, knowing the man could not talk with the duct tape over his mouth. "Pull that shit off his mouth, Sandy, you see yo' little man try'na say sum'thin!"

Sandy looked at Cruz with a bit of hate in her eyes but did not waste any time doing what he had asked her to do.

"Cruz, cuzz! You gotta give me a chance," K-Loc begged.

"Give you a chance? Now, why would I give a gangsta a chance? If I give you a pass, you could come back later and kill me. If not, your son or something."

K-Loc looked over at Outlaw Bandit Loc, who was putting together some type of bomb. He tried to speak again, but the words just wouldn't come out of his mouth. Deep down, he knew it was over for his ass, so he looked up at Sandy and told her, "You cold bitch!"

The men in the room all laughed because they knew that it was the truth; a bitch would get you killed.

"Sandy, tell me, should I give him a chance?" Cruz asked sarcastically.

"Cruz, he already gave himself a chance!" she said as she looked out the window to see his brother pull up in his car.

"Is that right?" Cruz was surprised but not shocked. Bandit and Sandy's eyes met, and Bandit winked at her and said to her, "Thatta girl! Show this nigga who you really rollin' with!"

As Cruz walked to look out the window, he saw Bandit wink at Sandy and wondered what that shit was all about, but that thought was pushed out of his head when K-Loc managed to cry out, "Don't hurt him, Cruz. He's just a kid."

"Muthafucka, you better watch out for yo'self. In any event, this is yo' chance! How much time does he have, Bandit?"

"Sixty seconds, Cruz!"

"Aight, K-Loc! If you can crawl yo' ass up out of here in sixty seconds, then you win. But if you can't, then you lose."

Cruz nodded in Gangsta Bam's direction to duct-tape K-Loc's mouth up again. K-Loc watched the four put on motorcycle leather jackets on along with helmets. As they walked out the back door, K-Loc's mind told his legs to follow them, but his legs would not obey his mind's command! He tried to drag himself, but his shoulder wounds made that impossible. The clock was at thirty-five seconds, and from afar he could hear a knock on the door. However, the roar from the motorcycles drowned it out.

"Oh god, oh god!" K-Loc moaned through the duct tape as the clock ticked down to ten seconds, nine seconds… He wondered who his sister was… Seven seconds… Six seconds… Five seconds… *Please, God, forgive me for my sins…* Two seconds… One second… Boooom!

*****

Solo couldn't take it anymore, so he got out the car with the TEC-9 in hand, almost running to the door. Just as he was knocking and about to kick the door down, four Kawasaki Ninja ZX14s passed by slowly, looking in his direction. Something made him want to get a better look at them, so he quickly began to make his way back to the street as the blast from the house sent him airborne. Dazed and somewhat confused about what had just happened, he looked up just in time to see the four Kawasaki Ninjas barreling down on him. He tried to reach for the TEC-9, which was out of reach, but the lead rider of the foursome scooped the gun up as the bike sped by. As he looked at them bend the corner, Solo's thoughts rushed back to his brother Kenny. He cried out to the blazing fireball that used to be a house. "KENNY! KENNNNNY!"

CHAPTER THREE

As Maria looked out over the water from the deck of her Malibu beachfront property, she was unable to control her anger. It had been two days to the last time she had seen or heard from Conrad, and to her this was unacceptable.

It's my twenty-seventh birthday, and this white muthafucka don't call nor show up or nothin', she thought out loud as she walked back in to the house. *Okay, that's cool, cos' a bitch gon' do what a bitch do best.*

As she looked at herself in the full-length mirror, she shook her head with satisfaction, as she was happy with herself for being a dime piece. Maria only stood at five feet four in height, but she was built like the fantasy that can only be created in the mind of a master storyteller. She wore her hair in that classic Halle Berry short cut, which only accentuated the despair that a common man felt when looking at such an uncommon face such as hers, and having to know that he could never touch or possess such a creature, which made most men burn with hate for her inside. She had a shape that was almost cartoonish, you know, the one that's so perfect that not one flaw or defect could be found on it. Her measurements were 38-22-38, and when she walked, you didn't want her to stop. But if she did stop, you'd be almost willing to pay her to strut again. "Cruz can kiss my ass!" she said as she grabbed the keys to her Harley Davidson motorcycle. "I'm getting the fuck outa here."

*****

As Jonathan entered the World on Wheels parking lot in his Range Rover, some nigga from the Rolling '60s Crip Gang hit him up. "What's that Rich Rollin Neighborhood 60 Crip like, cuzz?" Jonathan wondered if this stupid muthafucka wanted war or peace. Not wanting the shit to snowball downhill, Jonathan hit the banger up with a peace sign: nevertheless, the Desert Eagle that sat on his lap would introduce the gangbanger to war if peace didn't work out.

"It's yo' world, big baby, I'm just runnin' around in it try'na chase the short money," Jonathan said with half of a smile on his face.

"Where you from, cuzz?" the banger asked from his low rider.

"Look homey, I'm from being fresh off a bitch's ass about my money. I'm from looking to get rich in unusual places, and when it's all said and done I'm from rolling solo, so I know you can see that I don't bang."

The banger looked at his passenger place the gun back in its stash spot. The banger looked back at Jonathan and said, "What they call you, youngsta?"

"I'm The Truth, big dog," Jonathan said as he kept his eye on the passenger.

"Nigga! Them yo' bitches down in the skating ring?" Jonathan didn't answer.

"How old are you?" the man curiously asked.

"Shit, no disrespect, but what the fuck does that have to do with anything?" Jonathan said with his finger on the trigger of his Desert Eagle.

"The Truth, is it?" The driver looked at his passenger and said, "I like this nigga."

Then, he looked back at Jonathan and said, "We don' give you a pass this time but if them young hoes of yours are up here next week, we gonna have to get a cut of your take. You feel me, pimp?"

The two men's eyes locked, but no more words were said as the driver locked up his six-four and smashed out. Jonathan didn't foresee this kind of trouble coming; nevertheless, it was time to take his show on the road. Deep down he knew, in order for him to make big money, he'd have to get the girls' they own spot instead of postin' them around different places. Rose had been schooling him on that part of the game and was going to help him get tricks from a better class of soft-dick muthafuckas.

As the girls got into the truck, Tammy got in the front with a big-ass frown on her face, but Shannon got in the back with a big smile on hers. Tammy spoke first. "This ain't happenin'. Baby Locklord—"

Shannon cut her off before she could finish and said, "Come on, Tammy, it ain't that bad."

"Bitch!" Tammy shot back. "You'd fuck for peanuts if Baby Locklord told you to."

Shannon smiled as she almost jumped over the seat to kiss Jonathan on the lips and said, "Bitch, you got that right! I sure would."

Tammy twisted up her face even more as she continued, "We only made a thousand dollars between the two of us, Baby Locklord shit! We may as well be street whores."

Jonathan looked over at Tammy. She was fine even with her face all screwed up, almost too fine to be selling pussy. Nevertheless, she liked to fuck, and if she weren't getting paid, she'd most likely would be fucking for free.

"Let me tell you what sweet thing. This is what I'm going to do for you. I'm going to let you keep that grand, seeing as I'm not a pimp, because if I was my shoe, I'd already be up your ass! However, along with that grand, I'm going to have to ask you to take your show down the road."

Now Tammy spoke with much more respect in her voice.

"What are you talkin' about, Baby Locklord?"

"Tammy, I got a lot of shit going on right now and a lot of shit I need to do. However, I don't have all the resources to complete nor finish any of the shit I need to do. On top of all that, I'm try'na finish school as well as dress, feed, and keep you high-maintenance bitches in school. Now! If you're not working with me, that could only mean you're working against me. And if that's the case, bitch," he said with a cold calmness in his voice, "I want you to take that money, as well as that act and/or drama down the muthafuckin' road! Now what's it goin' to be?" He asked as if ice was hanging on each and every word.

Tammy looked at Jonathan in all kinds of love, nevertheless at the same time, having a newfound respect and fear for him.

"Baby Locklord…"

"No words, Tammy! Just make your choice."

Tammy dropped her eyes from his gaze and handed him the money.

"Keep the money, Tammy. I want you to spit it with Shannon and buy some new shit for the house I'll be buying for us all!"

Both girls went crazy at the sound of his words. They jumped all over him and yelled as if it were Christmas time. They had finally got what they had always wanted!

"Get y'all asses off me," he said playfully. "A nigga gave y'all a little good news and everything's all good, but wait till a nigga give you bitches a little bad news and see how you act! Get the fuck off me."

As the girls bounced up and down in their seats, singing a little song, talkin' about "We got a house, we got a house," Jonathan started up the Range Rover with Dr. Dre's "What's the Difference" featuring Eminem bumpin' in the background. Deep inside he felt their joy cos' he wasn't feeling' that roach motel he put them in for five and a half months, but that was where the money they were making put them, so it was what it was.

"What we gon' do tonight, Baby Locklord?" Shannon inquired from the back seat of the Rover.

"I don't know what I'm going to do yet. But y'all got a meeting with Rose.

"Oh shit," Shannon said. "We got a meeting with the queen bee, shit must really about to jump off!"

*****

As Maria pulled into Rose's driveway, Rose couldn't believe her eyes.

"What the fuck is this bitch doing at my house?" she uttered under her breath.

They had never been cool. From day one, it's been a competition to possess Cruz's love between the two, and now Rose was tired of playing this game. Maria got off her bike, but before she could get to the door, Rose made her way to the door. Just then, Jonathan pulled up blocking Maria in, so Rose decided to play it cool.

"Rose!" Maria shouted at the tip of her voice.

"Yeah, bitch, I'm right here!" Rose answered as she stepped out of the door. "What the hell are you doin' at my house?"

"I didn't come here to start no bullshit, I'm just lookin' for my man."

"Bitch, you bullshitted the minute you hopped your wide ass off that tricycle of yours, now! If you were referring to Cruz when you said 'your man.' Well, he's not here. On top of that, after I fuck him don't I always send him back to you?"

At that shot, Tammy and Shannon, who had just got out the truck, started to burst out laughing.

"Okay, bitch! Maria said. I'm going to need that fade."

But before the words got out of her mouth, Rose had jumped off her porch and was running up on Maria. Jonathan stepped between the two ladies, grabbing his mother off her feet, walking her back to the door as he whispered in her ear, "Rose, you know damn well we don't need these white folks seeing this kind of shit coming from our spot, now get a hold of yourself."

"Jonathan, you better get that bitch gone then."

"Don't trip. I got this, Rose. Tammy! Shannon! Get in the house!"

Tammy twisted her face up but did what she was told. Maria laughed out loud, then mumbled something under her breath as she tried to start her Harley Davidson.

"Now what?" Maria cried out in anger as her bike wouldn't start.

Jonathan looked at her with lust in his heart. If he had ever seen a Puerto Rican bitch finer than Maria he couldn't remember when.

"Are you just going to stand there, Papi? Help a bitch out."

"Do I look old enough to be your daddy?" Jonathan said with a big-ass smile on his face.

"Okay, Mr. Funny Man, my shit won't start as you can see, so can I get some help so I can get the fuck out of here?"

Jonathan hit her off with what he called his sexy smile before he said, "Now a nigga a lot of things, but a grease monkey for damn sure not one of them."

Maria tried to start the bike one more time then said, "Fuck it."

She then pulled out her phone and started to walk down the street with the phone to her ear. As she walked away in her tight-ass leathers, showing a man everything he wanted to see and more, Jonathan's dick instantly got hard.

"Hold the fuck up, Mami!"

Maria turned around and said, "Nigga! Do I look old enough to be your mother?"

"Okay, baby doll, fair exchange ain't never been no robbery. Let me call my boy, he has a Harley shop. I'll get him to tow yo' shit up there and check it out, I'll even foot the bill."

"Then what am I supposed to do, dude?" she said as she really looked at Jonathan for the first time. "Shit!" she said to herself, "this is one good-looking muthafucka."

"Then you can just hang out with me until you bike is fixed. What you say, little mamma?"

"Naws Papi, fuck that shit. It's my birthday today, and any nigga I kick it with tonight, gone be spending out of his asshole on me." She looked at him real good once again and asked him, "How old are you anyway?"

"I'm old enough to spend what you looking to get spent on you, and I'm also old enough to fill in for some disrespectful muthafucka that would abandon someone as beautiful as your loveliness."

With that said he just got on his phone and made the call. After doing so he told Maria to get in the Range Rover. She looked up to see the three women looking out of the living-room window, with looks on their faces that told Maria that she better not get in that truck. So she smiled at them and did just that, as she gave all three of them the finger and shut the door of the Rover. Before Jonathan got in the truck, he called Rose.

"Yeah, nigga! Just what the fuck you think you doing? And why is that bitch sitting in my truck?"

Jonathan dismissed what his mother had just said as he gave orders of his own. "Look, Rose, don't fuck with her bike, I'm going to have Tim come over here and pick it up."

"What's that wetback-ass bitch doing in my truck, Jonathan 'The Truth' Locklord!"

Jonathan just pretended not hear her and just hung up the phone. *Click!*

*****

"Oh no, the fuck, he didn't just hang up in my face?" Rose said as she and the girls looked on as Jonathan and Maria rolled out of the driveway. "Jonathan knows how Cruz feels about that bitch," Rose had spoken the words out loud even as she was only talking to herself. "I guess the drama is about to begin, God have mercy on us."

"Rose, what's really going on?" Tammy said as she looked out of the window with Rose and Shannon.

Rose looked back at Tammy with questioning eyes before she asked, "What's your real concern, girl?"

"What are you talking about, Rose?" Tammy said, still looking out the window long after Jonathan had bent the corner.

"Bitch! You know exactly what I'm talking about, your concern is not for what I'm tripping on. No! Your concern is over the nigga you selling the pussy for, so keep it real, bitch."

Tammy looked at Rose as if she were crazy, but after a short moment she looked away, as she knew that Rose was right.

"Shannon!" Rose called over her shoulder. "Tell me that this bitch is not in love with the nigga that's pimping her, please tell me that this is not the case?"

The question threw Shannon for a loop, but she shot back, "I sure as hell hope not, Rose, because I know my black ass is, and I can do without her pussy feeling the same way as mine does."

With those words, all three women burst into laughter. But the girls soon realized that Rose's laughter was mocking the situation instead of sympathizing with it when she said, "You bitches don't have a clue. Well, let me pull your ponytails to some real shit. You love a man like Jonathan by being loyal to them, know that that's the only kind of love that they understand is respect. See even when Jonathan does choose a woman, it won't be someone who's selling pussy for him. He'll be choosing her because of her loyalty to whatever he's loyal to, and right now he's loyal to the game."

Rose could see that at seventeen years old, these girls really had no idea what she was talking about. "Okay, let me give it to you live and direct. I have been a prostitute since I was ten years old cos' my mother threw me to the wolves when I was eight. I'm working for the likes of a cold-blooded muthafucka by the name of Conrad Cruz."

At the sound of Cruz's name, Tammy's eyes told Rose that she was familiar with him, and Rose could not help but wonder to what extreme.

"Do you know him, Tammy?" Rose asked.

"No, only the stories I've heard on the streets," Tammy answered. "Anyway, outside of the shit I've gone through with him, he shot Jonathan almost four years ago, and Jonathan won't let that shit go. Jonathan and I have been goin' back and forth about me leaving Cruz, but Cruz is not the type you just up and leave, you know what I mean? Jonathan has never said it to my face, but deep down I know that he does not respect the work I do, so why would he respect you for doing what he does not want his own mother doing?"

The girls looked puzzled and could not comprehend the idea that Jonathan felt that way. He never showed any clear signs that he did. In conclusion, they just thought Rose was full of shit!

"Okay, ladies, let me put it another way. As of today, I do not have a job anymore. When Jonathan rode off with that woman, he made sure of that. Ladies, it appears that we're entering into a new phase of The Truth! If you are not down fo' some real gangsta shit, now is the time to get out!"

Shannon spoke first. "I'm down fo' whatever Baby Locklord want me to be down fo', Rose!"

"And how about you, Tammy?" Rose asked.

"Jonathan's only sixteen, Rose!" Tammy barked.

"Seventeen, next month!" Rose barked back.

"Aight then, seventeen! Still, how he gon' go up against the likes of Cruz, that dude on some grown-man shit, Rose."

Rose looked at the teenage girl with contempt and exclaimed, "Bitch! I told you that from the jump, but since you can't seem to hear, I'll tell you again. The only question that remains is"—Rose gave Tammy a cold-blooded look before she continued—"are you loyal to my son?"

"Yeah, Rose, I got Baby Locklord's back."

Nevertheless, Rose did not trust Tammy but had to for now.

"So what's the plan, Rose?" Shannon said with a "let's get this shit poppin'" tone in her voice.

"First things first, we got to get the fuck out of this spot."

"Why, Rose?" Shannon asked. "This spot's fly as hell!"

"Fly or not, this is Cruz's shit. Before long, he'll be coming to blow this shit off the map."

"Who else is down with us, Rose?" Shannon asked.

Rose smiled and said, "Only Jonathan can answer that, little momma. But for now, we gone have to lie low until he puts us up on the whole get-down."

Tammy thought to herself, *How can Rose put all her trust in a teenage boy?*

She didn't understand it and having gone out with Cruz a couple of times, she could tell that he wasn't to be fucked with. Nevertheless, the question was, did she love Jonathan enough to go to war for him? Time would have to tell; until then she would have to ride for him, for the time being.

*****

"Man, you sure your boy gon' pick up my bike?" Maria said with concern.

"Don't trip, Mami, I got you," Jonathan assured her.

"You got me? Man! You don't even know me." She looked at Jonathan with sexy eyes that told him she was out of his league. Not knowing how to play her, Jonathan decided not to.

"Okay, look, Mami, you and I both know that I can't play this game with you, so this is what we gon' do. We gon' keep it real all the way across the board, feel me?"

She looked at Jonathan's face. He had baby-smooth skin, and his eyes seem to be pulling her to his very person. He looked to be at least twenty years old, but his face told another story as the youth was easy to see.

"So we gon' keep it real across the board are we, huh, hand-some? Okay! How old are you?" she asked.

"Now see, that's a question I'm going to have to refuse to answer."

"Why?"

"Well, due to the fact that you already made up your mind that I'm too young for you to waste time on, why should I answer it? You're trying hard not to give me a chance with your beautiful ass, but I'm not going to help you gun me down, so on that note: next question?"

"So I see, you gon' make up the rules to this game as you go, is that it?"

"Well, why not? After all, it is my game and what am I gon' lose by doing that? Look at you, Maria, is it?"

"Yes, it is."

"Okay, you all that and a big-ass bag of chips, shorty. And it ain't hard to see that you got niggas falling all over you. Hell! You got me trippin' and stumblin' just a little bit. But! Something ain't right, you're rollin' up and down the street like a mad woman, chasin' after a million-dollar muthafucka that don't give a ten dollars about you."

She tried to speak, but Jonathan cut her off.

"The worst part about the whole get-down is that you must not give a damn about yourself to let this happen to you."

"Nigga please! What *you* want from *me*? You don't know me from the next bitch bending a corner, so how you gon' go there with me, man?"

"You're right, beautiful, I'm totally out of line. I'm on some other shit, and I think I just took it out on you, forgive me," he said with sincerity in his eyes that seemed to melt her heart and at the same time made her wet between the legs.

"Damn, dude!" she said rocking her legs back and forth, slightly opening and closing them with each rock as if to cool herself off. "Just don't let that shit happen again. Anyway, since we gon' keep it real, tell me who that bitch Rose is to you?"

Jonathan just smiled without saying anything.

"Cat got you tongue now, huh? So that must mean you fuckin' her."

Jonathan burst out laughing.

"What's so funny?"

"Look, shorty, Rose and I are a lot of things, but I can assure you that we are not bed buddies. That's fo' sho!"

"Then what's the deal?"

"Rose is like a mother or a big sister, as she may put it, 'The Truth,'" Jonathan, answered.

"The Truth?"

Jonathan looked as if he was insulted by her not believing.

"That's right! Jonathan 'The Truth' Locklord. Is that okay with you?"

"Well, then, Mr. Truth, against all my better judgment, I'm gon' roll with you tonight, but the first time you show me other than the truth, we gon' part ways."

"That's fair enough, so let's talk about you. What do you do fo' a livin'?"

Jonathan already knew that she was one of Cruz's call girls, but he wanted to test her to see if she was going to keep it real. "Man, you really don't want to know that much about me, trust me when I tell you that."

"And why is that?"

"Because I'm a bad girl. Can I call you Jonathan?"

"No, but you can call me Baby Locklord, beautiful."

"Baby Locklord…hmmmm, I like that."

Jonathan looked deep into her hazel brown eyes and said, "I thought you were going to lie to me, thanks for not doing so."

Maria looked at him in a new light. She knew there was more to him then he was letting out, so she said it out loud. "I'm going to have to keep my eyes on you, ain't I, Baby Locklord?"

"I hope so, Maria, I hope so. So where do you want to go, Mami?"

"Anywhere that we ain't gon' bump into one of your girlfriends. I don't wanna have to kick some ass on my birthday." She said it smilingly. Before she knew it, Jonathan was up in front of Saks Fifth Avenue. *This little nigga's try'na go big*, she thought to herself. "What's up, Baby Locklord?"

"Well, if we gon' have dinner at the Bonaventure Hotel, I think we gon' have to dress to impress, don't you?"

"Yes!" she said as she smiled. "Baby Locklord, have you ever been here before?"

"No."

"So why now?"

"Well, I never had any reason worth coming to a place like this."

"And what's your reason now, Baby Locklord?"

"Don't play coy with me, my lady," he said in his best English accent. "You know you're my reason why."

Maria was flattered. "Look, Jonathan…"

"Oh, I thought we decided on Baby Locklord, my lady?"

"Whatever, handsome. In any event, you ain't got to spend this kind of money on me. You don't even know me like that, and on top of that, I want to kick it with you."

"And if you don't want to kick it with me, would it cost me then?" he said as he got out of the Range Rover before she could even answer.

But as he opened her door to let her out, she said, "So you already know what I do for a living?" She hoped that he would lie, so she could have a way out of what seemed to be a mistake about to be made.

"I thought we weren't going to talk about what you do for a living, Maria."

"Don't play with me, dude," she said angrily.

"Aight, so I've heard about you from Rose. You may think that's a bad thing, but in order for another female to talk about another, to me that's a sign of respect. Shit, isn't hating the new love? Nevertheless, all bullshit put to the side, the moment I saw you I understood two reasons why Rose was jealous of you. The first is, as beautiful as she is, it'll be hard for her to hold a nigga's attention when you walk in the room." She smiled at him before asking for reason number two.

"And the other reason would be, Jonathan?' She said his name mockingly.

"The second reason is the one I don't understand. Both of y'all are in love with a muthafucka that's not worth the love y'all willing to give. But forget all that, you gotta do what you gotta do, right?" He went on before she could cut in. "However, that don't have to stop me from digging you, does it?"

"Who are you, man?" she asked, almost dismayed at how smooth he was at a young age.

"I told you I'm The Truth, but you didn't feel that, so we decided on Baby Locklord. However, you're still calling me by my first name off and on, so I guess I'm whoever you want me to be, beautiful. Now, let's go get dressed."

He helped her out of the truck. She put her arm around his waist and slightly leaned her head onto his shoulders, thinking to herself, *Damn! I'm really feeling this young nigga.*

After he spent two grand on her fit and fifteen hundred on his own, it was off to dinner at the Bonaventure.

Shit! she thought to herself, *I'd fuck his young ass for free.*

After they ate a lobster meal fit for a king and queen, along with a conversation deeper than any she could remember having, there was nothing left to do for her but fuck his brains out.

"Jonathan, can we get a room here? I'll pay for it! I just don't want to go home tonight."

"What are you saying, Maria?"

"I'm just saying that I want this night to last a little longer, that's all."

Smiling, Jonathan took her by the hand and walked to the front desk. When she tried to pay for the room with her platinum card,

Jonathan pushed it away and paid for two nights in the penthouse suite at 1,200 dollars a night. She thought to herself, *Damn! Now, I'm really impressed.*

Once in the room, she pulled him to the bed and sat him down, then she let her dress fall to the floor, exposing all her beauty before his very eyes and simply said, "All of this is yours, do whatever you want."

Jonathan pulled her to himself and kissed her softly on the lips. causing her to drip uncontrollably from her sacred place before he spoke. "If your words are true, then let me just hold you for one night in order to appreciate your person's worth, and after I have done so, if you're still of the same mind to give your being to me, believe me, I'll go out of my way to be worthy of the gift given to me."

With that said, tears flooded Maria's eyes, but Jonathan could see that they were tears of joy. He didn't try to fix what was going on with her, instead he pulled her to the bed and closer into his person.

"Jonathan."

"Yes, Maria?"

"You're the first man ever that just wanted to hold me, thank you for that, Daddy."

"I thought I told you today that I wasn't yo' daddy," he said playingly.

"Yes, you did, baby. But if you want to be my daddy, I'll let you be just that, and I'll even show you how to be my daddy if you let me."

Jonathan just laughed, but Maria looked deep into his green eyes and said, "That's on my unborn kids, Jonathan."

He pulled her even closer and said, "You show me how, boo, and I'll be whatever you want me to be. But it's a two-way street, Mami, you got to be what I want you to be as well. But for now, let's just go to sleep."

He kissed her neck, and they both drifted off to sleep.

*****

When Cruz and the other three riders rolled up the block on the Kawasaki Ninjas, Tomcat and about four other niggas in his crew pulled their guns out—that is, until they recognized that it was Cruz and company.

"Goddamn it, Cruz! Y'all scared the shit out of us."

"That's the way to stay on yo' toes, though! Y'all muthafuckas had the big guns out." Cruz looked at both cars parked where he told Tomcat to park them. "Who did you get to help you, my nigga?" Cruz asked Tomcat.

"My girl," Tomcat said, while pulling a little honey to his side that looked as if she were only thirteen.

"Cool, this is the deal then. One of these bikes go to you and one goes to her. Now the only thing you got to figure out is, who gets the other two."

The girl almost jumped out of her outfit; Tomcat had a look on his face as if he had just hit the lotto. "Damn, big Cruz! I don't know what to say, cuzz."

"Nigga, just say that you gon' go to DMV today and get that shit off my girl's name, that's what you say."

"No doubt, my nigga!"

Cruz gave him the paperwork and a thousand bucks to cover any bullshit. He then walked up to Bandit and Bam, handed them an envelope that contained twenty thousand dollars. Pulling Bandit to the side, he handed him the keys of the Chrysler 300C and whispered in Bandit's ear. Those standing around could only wonder what all the secrecy was about. These were dangerous times, and nobody could trust anyone, even those closest to you were under suspicion. After the conversation, Cruz handed Bandit a piece of paper that Sandy had handed to him earlier with an address on it. As Bandit and Bam pulled off, Cruz told Sandy to go to the car, so he could have a word with Tomcat.

"Look, cuzz, shit gon get hot around here shortly."

"How's that, Cruz?"

"We got another war on our hands with them DTG niggas."

"The downtown gangstas? How the fuck or when the fuck did we get into it with them busta-ass muthfuckas?"

"I'll put you up on game at the meeting with the shot callers for the Hub and the Dub."

"I'm up in there like that, Cruz?"

"Just like that, but until then the hood is on high alert. Anything that don't look right coming through here, remove it off the map. Put your crew up on game cos' tomorrow night we light their asses up!"

"Cool, Cruz!"

"All right, little Loco, a.k.a in charge of the whole Eastside of Compton, I gotta roll."

Cruz got into the driver's seat of the ragtop Corvette C6, and with Ice Cube's War & Peace banging in the background as he started up the car, he threw up the set as he and Sandy smashed up off the block.

As Cruz and Sandy pushed through traffic, a lot of different thoughts swarmed though Cruz's mind. Nevertheless, all other bullshit would have to be put on hold until he spent some time with Sandy.

"Well, baby, what's on our agenda?" Cruz asked.

"You asking me, Cruz?"

"No, Sandy, I'm just talkin' to myself."

He saw the uneasiness that was written on her face, so he tried to smooth it over. "You kinda cool off this gangsta shit, aren't you, boo?"

"Cruz, you know I got yo' back, I mean, hell! This is how we grew up and came up, and it looks as if we gon' have to keep fightin' to stay up. So, baby, it is what it is. The only thing that really gets to me sometimes is, I got this college education that you paid for me to get, and yet instead of us putting it to good use, you got me fuckin' and settin' up niggas as if I was just another one of your call girls," she said with sadness in her voice.

"I understand your disposition, boo, and that's been one of my biggest concerns. Sandy, I'm going to tell you something that nobody else knows."

"What's that, Cruz?"

"I don't have anybody on my team that I can really trust. Most are down because of the fear that I have to instill constantly, others are down cos' of all the money I shell out without ceasing, and then there's you. You all I got, Sandy, you the only one that I can trust, Sandy. So if you want to put your education to good use, I'm all for that." "Fo' real, Cruz?"

"Yes, baby, shit… You the closest thing to a wifey I got. I need to do better by you."

"Cruz, I love you, and I'll always have your back, so I gotta say this. There's too many people in our business, I mean our shit's tight, but we got loose threads, baby."

"How's that, Sandy?"

"You got yo' hands in too much shit, Daddy. The bitches, the drugs, and now this plan to unite two cities. All this, with only me to trust? If that's the case, then we really need to tighten shit all the way up." Cruz knew that this was true, even if he did not want to see the real truth.

"What you thinking, Sandy?"

"You can't handle the truth!" she said in her best Jack Nicholson voice.

"I need yo' help, baby, so give it to me like it really is."

Sandy saw sincerity in his eyes for the first time in a very long time.

"Okay, Cruz, you gotta let them bitches go. I know the money is good, but if these other things go into effect, you know you won't have time to keep a real tab on your money. Shit, them bitches are already beating you out of all kinds of money now as it is. We need to start up a legitimate business that we can funnel all the dirty money in to it, we got to make it come out clean daddy, would you not agree?"

Cruz stared out the window, lost in his thoughts, but Sandy knew exactly what he was thinking of.

"Conrad, I understand your need here and there to be with young bitches, but there's other ways to get yo' R. Kelly on without having to run a call-girl service. I got you, boo," she said smilingly to take the sting off what she said, remembering what happened the last time she confronted him about his fetish.

"Sandy, I got a lot invested in them bitches, especially Rose and Maria."

"Cruz, Rose been on her way out ever since you shot her son! And Maria? Come on now, Daddy! How long you think that bitch gon' stay down? You gon' have to fuck around and kill that bitch with the way she rolls, Conrad Cruz. So that's the get-down. I know I can't say this kind of shit in front of others, but if we don't start pushing in that direction, we gon' be in a shitload of trouble before it's all over with. And that's not to mention the FBI and the DEA, boo. At some point, you gotta wash your hands and let them flunkies get their hands dirty."

"Okay, Sandy, you're in charge of this kind of shit from here on out, and let's put that business degree to use."

"What are you talking about, Conrad?"

"Forty thousand dollars is what I'm talkin' about, Sandy. Put the legitimate businesses together, seeing that we're dealing with gangs, look into putting together a record company and while you're handling all of that. See if you can find it in your heart to marry me."

"Conrad Cruz, do not play with me!"

"If you say yes, we can get on the freeway right now to Vegas!"

"Yes! Yes! Yes!"

*****

Solo reflected on the conversation he had with his mother the night before.

"Hello, Mom."

"Yes," the voice came back sleepily over the phone. "Derrick, is that you?"

Solo didn't know how to begin to tell his mother that her oldest son was dead. "Mom, I know it's late but you need to wake up."

Kathy Locklord sat straight up in the bed. "What's going on, son? I waited for you and Kenny all night, baby, is everything all right?"

"No, Mom, Kenny was killed tonight."

"Boy, it's too late for you to call here playing. Now why would you even say a thing like that about your brother?"

No answer came back. "Derrick, tell me you're playing, boy!" Still, no answer came back.

"Mom, now you know I wouldn't be playing with a matter like this," Solo said calmly.

"Where's his body, Derrick?"

Solo wondered how to break it to his mom that there's not enough of the remains to even call it a body.

"Mom, I'm on the way to your house, and I'll talk to you when I get there."

"No! You'll talk to me now!"

"He was blown up, there is no body, Mom."

"Oh my god! Derrick! How did this happen? Were you there? Do you know who did it?"

"Yes, Mom, I think I know who did it."

"Then you fix it, Derrick, you do whatever you have to do to make his mother feel the same pain I'm feeling."

All kinds of things were running through Solo's head. Deep down inside he knew he couldn't go against Cruz, and now out of the blue his mother wanted him to track down his long-lost sister. As he rolled down the street looking for the address in Westwood, he thought to himself, *What's the use? If Mom abandoned this lady like she said she did, then what's the use of sending me? Who's to say she and her family won't kick me to the curb?*

As he pulled into the driveway, he was excited and fearful at the same time. "Fuck this," he said to himself. "I should be looking for Cruz and the muthafuckas that killed my brother."

As he put the car in reverse, a pearl-white Jaguar pulled up behind him.

"Damn!" he said as the driver got out of the car, "this bitch is a dime piece and a half."

As Rose walked up to the car he was still sitting in, she stood wide legged with a look on her face as if to say, what the fuck do you want?

"What's up, Mommy?"

"Jonathan's not here, if that's who you lookin' for, and if one of them little bitches got you sitting on my driveway, all hell's gon' break loose."

"Naw, shorty, it's none of the above."

"Then if Cruz did not send you, you ain't got no reason being here!"

"Cruz? You know that muthafucka?"

"Dude, I don't know who you are, but you might wanna roll up outa this muthfucka right now."

"Bitch! I'm Derrick G. Locklord a.k.a Solo Loco, and that muthafucka killed my bother," he said while putting the car in park. As he opened the door to get out, Rose pulled out a .357 Magnum and pointed it at his face.

"Ease yo' way back in yo' bucket, dog. Don't make me have to pop yo' ass in my own driveway."

Solo did what she told him to do, and then it hit Rose, "What did you say your name was again?"

"Solo Loco!"

"Naw, nigga. The first and last name, again?"

"Derrick Locklord."

She put the gun away and said, "Who are you looking fo?"

"I'm lookin' fo' my sister Rose."

"See, now I know you're trippin'! I'm Rose and I don't have no brother."

"Well," Solo said as he got out the car again, "if you got a mother named Kathy Locklord, then you got two brothers, one who was killed yesterday by that muthafucka Cruz."

Rose looked at him good. He had them Locklord eyes. He looked dead on Kathy. But it couldn't be.

"Look, man, Kathy a crackhead that abandoned me when I was eight and—"

He cut her off. "She stopped smoking years ago, even before I was born," Solo said proudly as he showed her a picture of their mother. Rose took the picture.

"Well, I'll be damned" was all she could say. She looked back up at him and said with a smile, "She wants to see me?"

Derrick was not expecting to see happiness on her face as if this was the day she had been waiting for.

"Yeah, she wants to make things right. Look, I just found out about what happened. The way I got it was that Mom is embarrassed about it all, but she had been keeping tabs on you all these years."

"How did you get my address?"

"From the phone book."

Tears filled Rose's eyes. "Don't cry, sis. Shit gon' be cool from here on out."

"Derrick, man, you don't know what I've been through in all my life. The things I had to do in order for me to live day to day. And now I'm just supposed to forgive and forget?"

"You have to, Rose, she lost you once, now Kenny dead. You and Mom is all I got left. We Locklords! We can get past this, can't we?" he asked as if he wanted to receive a reassurance from her because he himself doubted.

"Yeah, little bro, we can get past anything. We Locklords. Come on in. We got a lot to catch up on."

As they walked to the door, she asked him to tell her about Kenny and how he died. Solo explained to her the whole situation from the very beginning. He told her about Sandy and how she set Kenny up. He told her things, which some she knew about and some she didn't. He told her about his plan to kill Cruz. It wasn't a very good plan, and that was when she told him her whole story, the things she went through with Cruz, how Cruz shot her son Jonathan who was his own son too. After they had spoken for three hours in the company of Tammy and Shannon, Rose tried to phone Jonathan, only to receive no answer.

*****

Jonathan woke up to see Maria staring at him, not knowing that five minutes prior to that she had been going through his pockets looking for some ID. He thought to himself, *My God, she's even beautiful on the wakeup.*

"Jonathan, why don't you have any ID?"

"Well, good morning to you too, Maria."

"How old are you, Jonathan?"

"Too young for you, Maria. But tell me, does that really matter to you?"

"Not right now, Papi. It's time for you to show me how worthy of this pussy you really are."

Just then, Jonathan's phone rang. But before he got to it, Maria got to it first. Throwing it to the floor, she said,

"Fuck that phone, Papi, if you want to speak to something, speak to these."

She unhooked her bra, letting her 38 double Ds spill out. After that, Jonathan did not even hear the phone ringing anymore. As she placed the fullness of his love inside her, it became apparent instantly that she would not be able to ride him the way she anticipated. So she tried to dismount him but found her attempt to be unsuccessful. Jonathan couldn't believe that not only was she trying to take the dick, but she had the nerve to try to take it all at once and even tried to hop off when she had realized that that was not about to happen. Oh hell no! He pulled her back down on at least three more inches of his dick.

"Oh my god!" Maria cried, not being able to separate the joy from the pain. Jonathan then raised her up two inches only to slam her down on his dick hard, driving four more inches up in her. Maria bit her bottom lip and just collapsed on his chest as if someone had just shot her. "Please, Jonathan, I need you to take concern with me."

He rolled her over in order to look into her eyes, and only then did he understand the fullness of her words as she said, "Please don't treat me with unconcern like all the rest."

At this Jonathan didn't know how to react; he did not know how to love a grown woman the way one was supposed to be loved. Just as he was about to say so, Maria pulled him to herself and said, "I'll show you how to be my daddy, if you just let me. I'll show you everything you need to know."

With that said, Jonathan allowed Maria to take him to school. For the rest of that morning on into the night, as well as the next day, Maria showed Jonathan sex secrets that would please any woman he would ever come in contact with. And as she did so, the two of them found something that would tie them together forever, and that something was love connected with trust. As they got dress to leave the hotel, Jonathan looked over to Maria and simply said, "When will you leave Cruz and come home?"

As easy as he asked the question, Maria answered, "I'm already gone."

"Then know this, Maria. I am not looking to turn you into a housewife."

"And you know this, Jonathan," she said while standing up real nasty, looking like a class-A hooker, "this is your pussy now, so you do with it what you will, but if I don't know nothing else, I know this—you ain't no pimp nigga. And after having all this, you ain't trying to see other muthfuckas jumping up and down in it."

Jonathan cracked a smile, letting her know that she was right, so she continued. "So you better figure a way to turn this hoe into a housewife, 'cuz this hoe is yo' hoe! While you try'na clown a bitch."

They both laughed hard before exiting the room, pushing on each other playfully like little kids.

*****

As Bandit and Bam made their way to the downtown LA area, Bam looked over at Bandit and said, "Cuzz, I'm really not cool with this shit."

"Then stay in the car, Loco, I'll handle it."

"Bandit cuzz! We go all the way back to Kelly Park Elementary, nigga, yo' mom used to take us to church! I know fuckin' well you ain't cool with doing something like this."

"Look, Bam, the way God sees it, one sin isn't no bigger than the other. We have been doing wicked shit fo' a long time now, most of which I haven't been cool with. So what the fuck do you want from me, Crip?"

The two men just looked at each other, neither one knowing what to say.

"Anyway, nigga," Bandit said, trying to lighten up the situation, "I'll keep yo' half of the money if you not going to be able to sleep tonight."

"You can keep my half of an ass-whipping if you start fuckin' with my money, nigga."

Both men laughed, even though deep down both men knew that nothing was really that funny.

As they made their way to the address Cruz had given them, Bandit stopped behind a white van in an alley around the corner from their destination. Bam could only shake his head and say, "Cruz a cold muthafucka for this one."

Bandit didn't bother to comment; he just put on the cable-man uniform, so Bam followed suit. The men exited then entered the van and drove it to the destination. With clipboard in hand, Bandit knocked on the door.

"Yes? Who is it please?"

"It's the cable man, ma'am."

"What do you want?" "Is this the Locklord residence?"

"Yes, it is."

"Well, Ms. Locklord, the cable company is recalling all the boxes in this area to replace them with new ones."

"There's nothing wrong with my box."

"That may be so, Ms. Locklord, but nevertheless we're going to need you to sign a refusal form stating that we did come by but you declined our offer."

"Hold on, please."

Kathy could not get the door open good before Bandit's .45 Magnum with silencer whispered off three shots. The first two hitting her in the chest and the last one exploding in her face, even before her body hit the ground. Without blinking, Bam pulled the door shut, and the two men retreated as if there was nobody home.

CHAPTER FOUR

When Jonathan asked Maria for her address, she didn't know what to think; nevertheless she still gave it to him. Immediately, Jonathan made a phone call and gave her address to an unknown party; at least to her they were unknown and told the person on the other line to move all her shit to a storage unit in Orange County.

"What the fuck are you doing?" was all that Maria could say.

"No matter whose name that house is in, it still belongs to Cruz," Jonathan calmly stated.

"So not if, but when he finds out that we're together, I trust that you're smart enough to know that you don't want to be there when he comes calling."

Jonathan was right, but there was a little something that bothered Maria—it was the fact that she had two hundred thousand dollars stored inside that house.

"Jonathan, I got some money put up in my house and I don't—"

"Don't worry about it, Maria, that's on my life, all of your shit will be intact."

For some apparent reason, Maria believed him and was even starting to believe in him. Within an hour to the very minute, he received a callback, letting him know that the job was done. He then told the party at the other end of the line to go to his mother's house and move her belongings to the very same storage unit Maria's things were brought to. Jonathan discerned the worried look on Maria's face so he asked the person on the phone if they found the money that was at her house. After thirty seconds he hung up the phone and told her that her safe was safe and untouched. He then called his mother, but Maria found it a little strange that it sounded as if she was up on game and sounded like she was just another member of his crew.

"You and the girls need to lie low for a few days, I'm sending someone to clear out the house. When you get to a cool spot, call me with the 411 on my voice mail in two days, and I'll call you later with the new address letting you know when to come home," Jonathan instructed Rose, but before he could get off the phone, Maria noticed that something very important was being said to Jonathan by his mother.

"What's the matter?" Maria asked, but he just waved her off. For the next four minutes, his face lost all expression, then he spoke.

"Tell him I said to lie low with you and the girls. Nobody makes any call to anybody. We need to disappear off the face of the earth until we get our shit tight. Remember, you don't know ole' boy like that, so keep yo' eyes on him. There's fifty Gs in my safe, take it out and spend what you need, the combination is 59-96-69. I love you too." Jonathan hung up.

"What was all that about, baby?" Jonathan looked Maria in the eyes, not knowing how to express what he had just heard on the phone, but after a moment he spoke. "When I was little, my mother used to tell me a story about David and how he slew a giant named Goliath. She said if you know a monster is after you, don't run away from it. Instead run at it with everything you got, as that's the only way a mere man could ever win the fight he had no chance of winning.

"Damn, Papi, is shit that deep?"

He looked at her with eyes that told her yes. "It's not too late if you want out."

Maria looked at him and said, "Your mother is a very wise woman. I feel just like she does boo, so let's go get the monster!"

For the next three days, Maria and Baby Locklord a.k.a The Truth, as they call him in the streets, handled an assortment of small business. It was not on the same scale as the business she had handled with Cruz. Nevertheless it was on a more professional level. Maria watched with close observation as Jonathan collected his money, which the young nigga did with style and grace. At times he was so smooth that Maria had to give him his props. "You a smooth mutha-fucka, Papi!" she would say. He would, in return, smile at her sexily, which made her want to just fuck him right there on the spot.

"Baby Locklord," Maria said in her sexy bedroom voice, "can we get a room, so I can sex you, boo? We been in the streets for the last three days nonstop doing you, now can we do me for about two hours that is if you can hang?" She winked at Jonathan flirtatiously. Jonathan looked at Maria as if she was crazy.

"What's that look about Jonathan?"

"Maria, we got to keep on grinding or else we going to be living in a room. Now, is that what yo' high-maintenance ass want?"

"No, Papi," she said in a tone of the little girl that did not get what she wanted on her birthday. He paid her no mind and instead slipped in an ole' school CD, "Fight the Power" by The Isley Brothers, and started dancin' in his seat. Maria could not help but laugh, and before she knew it, she too was dancing in her seat with him, as if they were both back in the days, when the song first came out. Was Maria finally falling in love, for the first time? She didn't really know as of yet, but this was as close as she had ever been.

When they pulled up in front of Crenshaw High School, Maria thought to herself, *What the fuck now?*

He simply got on his phone and said, "I'm out front."

Before long, two teenage boys came out, and each handed him a wad of cash.

"What it do, Baby Locklord?"

"What it do, Frog Dog?" Jonathan greeted back.

"I'm a little short, Baby Locklord, but I'll make it up when I give you the next payment," the other dude said.

Maria looked at Jonathan, and she could see that he was not having none of that.

"Nigga, you always short and I always let you win! But today, I need to win! So give me that shit around yo' neck, mayn and we'll call it even, playboy."

"C'mon, Baby Locklord, this shit right here cost way more than what I owe you. I ain't gonna go out like that, doggy dog," Mouse said.

"So what chu saying, my nigga? I gotta take it from out yo' ass!" Jonathan confidently said as he turned the ignition to the Range Rover off.

Mouse replied, "Get it like you live, Baby Locklord. Like I said, I ain't going out like that, cuzz."

"Fuck this!" Maria said as she got out the Range, a little bit before Jonathan did.

"I didn't sign on fo' this kind of shit," Maria said as she walked past the man with a platinum chain with a big "M" pendant hangin' from it. He smiled at her, exposing his shiny gold grill as if he was pleased with himself. Maria soon cancelled his smile by bitch-slappin' the young man on his face with a razor she had concealed between her fingers. As the blood from the gaping wound on the side of his face streamed down his neck, turning his white tee a crimson red, he could not help but stand there in shock.

"Pull the chain off, muthafucka, like my man told you to!" she demanded, as she stood with his blood dripping from one hand and her 380 clearly visible in her other hand.

"Get yo' bitch, Baby Locklord," Frog cried out as Jonathan stood behind Maria with his Desert Eagle in hand.

"Nigga, if you know like I know," Jonathan said, "you better help yo' boy get that shit from around his neck, before one of you fools end up dead out here."

Frog pulled the bloody chain off Mouse's neck without another word and tossed it to Maria.

"Get in, Papi, I'll cover you."

"Well, gentlemen, needless to say, we won't be doing business anymore, so consider our relationship terminated," Jonathan said as he got into the Range Rover.

As Maria backed into the vehicle, she said, "Maybe it's fo' the best that you put away childish things, so we can move onto some grown-man shit."

She smiled at the two young men as she shut the door.

With tires screeching, they smashed out. Jonathan looked at Maria and said, "Yo ass is insane fo' that shit girl, you know that, don't you?" She smiled at him for being pleased with her. As they rolled down Crenshaw, Jonathan pointed at the cooler in the back seat and asked Maria to rinse the blood off the chain. After doing so, she tried to hand it back to him, but Jonathan said, "No, Mami, that's clearly yo' trophy, on top of that it has a diamond-studded 'M' on it, so put that shit on and let yo' female nuts hang."

Smiling, Maria did exactly what he told her to do and asked, "How does it look on me, Papi?"

"It ain't about how it look on you, baby, it's about how you make it look, and you make that shit look good. Now turn my music back up, Mami, we got one more stop to make."

Before she knew it, they were on the 405 San Diego Freeway going south to the 55.

It's a beautiful day, Maria thought to herself as she pulled out a blunt (Peach Optimo and some purple, of course) and fired it up. She didn't know if Jonathan got high, but it didn't take long to find out he didn't. As she passed the blunt to him, he waved it off and said, "That shit's fo' losers, Mami."

"So you're calling me a loser, Jonathan?"

"Naw, baby, I'm just saying that a nigga can't win when he high all the time. Now, if you like livin' in the clouds then do you. But while you're doing you, do you think you can roll down the window, so I won't have to do you too?"

Maria wanted to blow the smoke in his face for getting smart, but deep down she respected the fact that he didn't get high, so she took a big hit and blew the smoke out the window and put the blunt out.

They got off the freeway and hit Pacific Coast Highway.

"Who do you know in Newport Beach?" she asked Jonathan, while the music played in the background.

"Nobody but us, boo." He looked at her and smiled.

She just let it go at that. She was high and didn't want to fuck her high off try'na figure out some riddle. As they pulled up into the circular driveway of a bomb ass-house that sat on a hill, which was two blocks away from the beach, she saw a metallic baby-blue Maserati GT that looked just like hers. "Jonathan! That car looks like my shit, boo!" Jonathan just smiled again and hit the horn twice. The four-car garage door opened up and she saw her Harley Davidson parked next to a pearl white Jaguar. "Jonathan, what's my shit doing here?"

"Maria, where else are you going to park yo' shit when you get home?"

"Jonathan, no! This shit ain't our shit, is it?"

"Oh we together now?" Jonathan said, half-serious, half-playing.

"Nigga, don't even play with me."

Jonathan laughed and said, "Yeah, Maria, this us but it's also my mother's, so I hope y'all can get along."

"Shit, boo, I know we will but even if we don't, big as this house is, we won't even have to see each other." She kissed his face and bounced up and down on her seat.

"Okay, boo, just remember what you said, you know how mothers can be."

"Boy, quit trippin', yo' mother and I gon' be cool!"

Jonathan laughed to himself and got out of the Range.

A man came walking out the garage with a ten-by-thirteen manila envelope in his hand, which appeared to be the paperwork for the house. *My young nigga was on his job!* Maria thought to herself as her phone rang. It was Cruz for the tenth time. As she got out of the vehicle, she took the battery off her phone and threw it and the phone in a trash can nearby.

"Goddamn! Baby Locklord, who the fuck is this?" the man said while reaching for Maria's hand, which she did not extend toward him. He looked at Jonathan, but Jonathan played it off.

"Is all the paperwork in order, Tim?"

"Hell yeah! You know I got you, my knock!"

Tim was old school. He didn't use the word *nigga* and often got on Jonathan's case about using it. So Tim would call him "my knock."

"As you can see, my boys fixed the bike. I got the key to the Maserati off the key chain to the bike. And good thing it was on there, or I would have had to pop the ignition. There's yo' mother's Jag and about the money…. I put the safe in the master's bedroom. You wouldn't want to leave something like that in a storage space, even if it is in Orange County. And last but not least, the furniture, two houses of it, is in the storage. The paperwork for the storage is in the envelope with the paperwork to the house as well as the keys to the bike and the cars."

"You a hell of a nigga, Tim!"

"What did I tell you about that word, Baby Locklord?"

"My bad, Tim. Here you go." Jonathan handed Tim a bag with an undisclosed amount of money in it, then he looked at Maria somewhat in disgust, before he made a call to his mother. Tim looked surprised to receive the money, but at the same time he was grateful.

"Hey, you!" Jonathan said over the phone.

"Hey yourself, stranger," Rose replied.

"How's things on your end, Mom?"

"Well, Jonathan, let's see. We stayin' at raggedy-ass Motel 6, we've been eating on cardboard box pizza for three day now, and we've been wearing the same shit for three days now! So how you think we doin'? Oh! And hold up, on top of all of that, I had to sic Tammy on my brother to keep him put. The nigga had his eyes fixed on Shannon, but that little bitch is too damn loyal to you. You know what she said? She said she ain't fuckin' nobody till you tell her to, especially not for free! She said she didn't care if Solo was family or not, now ain't that some shit? That little bitch is crazy, but at the same time, she cool."

Jonathan just laughed. "Well, Mom, you ready to come home?"

"Hell to the yeah, nigga! And why you keep callin' me *mom*? Is someone there with you that you can't keep it real in front of?"

Jonathan did not answer, but Rose knew what was up. "Jonathan," she said, "you know you got us in deep now, so make sure yo' dick won't get us in a trap we can't get out of, you hear me?"

"I got you, Mom."

"Okay, kid, and I got you too, no matter what the outcome is of this shit!"

"Look, Mom, I'm going to send Tim in the Range Rover to scoop y'all up. Did your brother drive?"

"Yeah: we been packing our asses in his little bucket like Mexicans. I felt it better that I didn't use my car, if you know what I mean?"

"Cool, tell him to give Tim his car and that we'll pick it up later. I want you all to ride here together."

"Why, Jonathan?"

"Why? Because if he ain't legit, I don't want our new neighbors to have to explain to Five-0 what his car was doing at our house when they start looking for his body, that's why!"

"I feel you, son, but when you see him you'll know he's a Locklord."

"Whatever, but humor me anyway, Mom. Okay?"

"Okay, son, I love you."

"I love you too."

"Tim."

"I'm already on it, Baby Locklord, but what's up with all this money?"

"No strings, my man, that's just me paying it forward. By the way, Tim, Maria and I thank you for fixin' her hog."

"Shit! If it wasn't for you and your mother, I wouldn't even have my shop. I still owe you guys! And that's why I'm trippin' about all of this money, but it ain't like I can't use it." With that being said, Tim was gone.

As Tim backed out of the driveway, Jonathan looked at Maria with a touch of discontent in his eyes.

"You know, Maria, there are women in my life that I think I can trust, my mother being the only one I know of for sure. However, there's not one man I would put my life on the line for other than the that just drove away. And we hurt his feelings tonight."

"How's that, Papi?"

"When you didn't take his hand that was some disrespectful shit! And because I backed yo' play and did not speak up on that shit, that cost me money we didn't have to just be throwing around."

"Is that what that money was for, Jonathan? You mean to tell me that you paid a nigga because his feelings was hurt?"

Jonathan looked at Maria with a look she had seen in Cruz's eyes many times before, but she was unable to make the connection between Jonathan and him.

"Maria, allow me to make you understand something once and for all. When we woke up that sleeping monster that was pimping you, there's going to be no price we'll be able to pay in order to retrieve lost loyalty. Now, is there any part of your being that don't understand what I'm preaching to you right now?"

"No, Papi, I understand completely."

"Then tell me what the fuck I'm talkin' about, Maria," he said coldly, as if ice were hanging on each of his words.

"Okay, Jonathan, Cruz is a cold-blooded white son of a bitch," she said with the same ice on her words as he had on his. "He fucks over people daily, so it's just a matter of time before somebody gives him up. He doesn't know loyalty, so loyalty don't know him," she said with her hands on her hips. "Now, I have seen you in action in the last three days, and everyone you've come in contact with loves you, boo. Well, maybe not them dudes we had to fuck over about yo' money. But you treat the few people that you fuck with: with respect, so they all loyal to The Truth, as they call you. And they stay loyal because you don't fuck them over. So if I'm not mistaken, I think you're telling me that if we stay true to the game, the game will stay true to us. Now, Papi, can I get a look at our new house, or am I on punishment?"

He handed her the keys and she ran off skipping like a little girl.

If one were to enter the estate, the first thing they would notice were the big letters on the gate that read *The Locklord Clan*. The home existed on six thousand square feet that sat on two acres of beachfront property. Security cameras were set up on the entire layout of the property, from the six thousand square feet on the inside, to the two acres on the outside of the property. Once one walks in the five-bedroom home, the first thing they would notice is the dramatic twenty-eight-foot-high ceiling. Alongside of it was a focal point where you could see the beach from either upstairs or downstairs.

No detail was spared on this dream house, even the catwalk on the upper level included high-end design touches such as the wrought-iron banisters of the balcony railing and ceramic tile floors. The log rafters overhead brought the height of the ceiling down in order to create a penthouse type cozy space, and on the third floor the master's bedroom sat all by itself.

Clear windows weren't exactly practical for the area right above the bath tub in the master's bedroom, so instead there was a stained-glass grouping designed to mimic the view of snowcapped mountains with a river running through them. The rest of the house was absolutely extraordinary, even to the deck that ran around three-fourth of the home back to the porch area.

"Oh, Jonathan!" Maria called while running back to the living room where she found him half asleep on the floor. "How in the fuck did you pull this one off, Papi?"

Jonathan looked at her as if she should have already known. "Maria, I have been pulling this off since I was thirteen, so don't think it happened overnight 'cuz a nigga ain't got it like that, boo."

She kissed him all over his face and said with a smile, "Don't worry, Papi, it's going to get greater later fo' yo' young ass!"

"Maria, look baby, I'm going to ask you something, and I need the truth. Why was it easy for you to drop Cruz and roll wit' me?"

She sat down beside him and looked at him in the eyes. Holding back the unspoken pain, she softly spoke, "Okay, Jonathan, aside of being pimped starting at the age of fourteen under the flag of a call girl, aside of Cruz using these services to lure in little girls to satisfy his fetish, oh and aside from getting my ass kicked whenever he wanted to kick it, yes aside from all this good shit, it was easy fo' me to drop him because it was you who I dropped him for! But let me see, I bet you're probably thinking that I would have done it for any baller. If that's the case, why am I taking a pay cut fuckin' with yo' young ass!" She got up, clearly pissed off, but continued anyway. "And there's this new plan he has, as if his white ass is about to take over the whole fuckin' world with the Crips and Bloods, like pinky without the muthafuckin' brain. I'm tellin' you, baby, this muthafucka's crazy! He knows that he a dead man walkin' but he bent on takin' as many as he can with him. So know this, Mr. Baby Locklord as soon as he finds out that we together, you're right the muthafucka's gon' come after you! So what now? Do you still want me? Or did I make a bad choice?"

Jonathan got to his feet as if the weight of the whole world was trying to hold him down. "Maria," he said as if he had to think hard about the statement he was about to make. "I'm sixteen, and I'll be seventeen next week."

Her face held back the look of surprise that it was supposed to express, but Jonathan still noticed it on time. "You see how that little truth damn near rocked yo' world, Maria? And it ain't like you didn't know I was young, it's just when one hears the butt-naked truth, they're often moved to some type of panic or another. So how in the hell will you be able to handle it when I force-feed you the rest of the truth?" He pulled her to his person and said, "You know fuckin' well that I want you and that I'm willing to fight for you, maybe even die for you. But if you don't feel the same way right now at this moment in time."

He reached for the brown manila envelope that contained the paperwork for the house and pulled out her set of car keys and said, "You can take these along with your show and hit the road, know what I mean?"

Before Jonathan could take another breath, Maria had slapped him. He looked as if the slap only turned him on, so she set off to hit him again, only this time he sidestepped her act of aggression and delivered a pimp slap of his own. As Maria tried to shake off the blow from where she sat on the floor, Jonathan quickly pulled her to her feet and said, "The first one was free, boo, anything else, I'm going to have to make you earn. Now, I'm a little pissed off at you, so I really don't want to chop it up with you about what just happened. But if you keep your hands to yourself, that type of shit will never happen again. I also perceive that you're a little pissed off as well, so I'm going to ask you this once, do you feel the same way I feel about you?" Their eyes both locked in heated anger. However, there was an unspoken passion that somehow overrode their anger.

"I got yo' back, Papi," Maria said as she moved in closer to Jonathan and rested her head on his chest. Unable to control her passion, she dropped to her knees and undid Jonathan's pants. Before he could even think of protesting, she was pulling him in to her mouth with a skilled touch that he had not experienced before. As she pulled and sucked him, she looked up at him and said, "You can nut in my mouth, Papi and I'll swallow it for you."

At just the sound of her words, Jonathan exploded, spilling nut all over her face but being true to her word, Maria drank the rest of it, draining it out of him until he was dry. Jonathan was in a temporary paradise. Next, he got to his knees and pulled out a black bandanna, wiping off his wasted love from her beautiful face and said, "I'm sorry for hitting you, baby."

"Don't be sorry, Papi. If you let a bitch get out of line once, she will only do it over and over again. You only did what a real man would have done."

"And my age, Maria, is that going to be a problem?"

"Well, now, Baby Locklord, a man becomes a man when he steps to the plate and starts handling grown-ass man business. In your case, age ain't nothing but a number. It seems as if you've been grown up for a very long time. My only worry is how's yo' mother gon take it when she finds out that you with an older woman?"

Jonathan looked out the window to see Rose pulling up in to the driveway and said, "We about to find out right now, Maria."

Maria ran into the bathroom to finish cleaning herself up from their escapade. She didn't want to make a bad impression on her first meeting with Jonathan's mother.

As Rose walked through the door, she could not contain her excitement. Jonathan had taken his money and pooled it with her to get them a new spot, but she had no idea that he had this kind of money. She jumped all over him along with the help of Tammy and Shannon, as Solo just stood there taking it all in. As Maria walked out the bathroom, she could hear the joy coming from the living room and was more than ready to join in. But upon entering the room, the celebration came to an abrupt end.

"Jonathan!" Maria cried out. "What the fuck is Rose doing here?"

*****

The last week with her new husband has been compounded with the stuff that dreams are made of. He didn't even call her by her first name anymore, everything was" Mrs. Cruz, do this" or "Mrs. Cruz, have you done that," and Sandy was just loving it! They had a ball in Vegas, but all good things must come to an end. As they rode on the 10 Freeway headed back to the city, Cruz turned to Sandy and said, "Okay, baby, it's time for us to separate our business from our pleasure. Now, I got some good news, and I got some bad news as well. Which of the two do you want first?"

"The good news, hubby!"

"Okay, Mrs. Cruz, it's going to take a million dollars to put a state-of-the-art recording studio together, right?"

"That sounds about right, Mr. Cruz."

"Well, then, I'm going to need about a month to put all of the money together. However, I want you to find the building and start buying the equipment, your CEO-ness."

"Okay, Daddy, so what's the bad news?"

"The bad news is that I'm going to have to keep the call-girl service for at least another year until yo' shit get off the ground."

Sandy looked at Cruz as if he had just lost his mind.

"The shit is what it is, Sandy," Cruz said. "It's not up for debate, but mark my words, it's only until you get yo' thang off the ground, aight?"

"Will I be able to hold you to your word, Conrad?"

"I gave it to you, didn't I? So that must mean you can hold me to it. Now, let's see what's up with these bitches and my money. Call Rose and Maria again."

"There's still no answer, Daddy."

Sandy had a bad feeling as they pulled up to Rose's spot. It was clear to even the untrained eye that she had taken her show on the road and had done so quickly. Cruz did not even get out of the car, as from the driveway they could see right through the house. Cruz then backed up out the driveway without a word, and almost immediately they were parked in front of a beautiful beach home in Malibu. Sandy did not even have to ask as she knew whose spot this was. Nevertheless, in her mind she was like, *Fuck them bitches, I got the ring and the last name, so they could have the beach houses.*

Cruz got out of the car without saying a word, leaving Sandy sitting inside the car mad as hell. To her surprise he came right back.

"Is everything good, Daddy?" Sandy said, knowing it wasn't.

Cruz looked at her and sadly said, "Every now and then the snake kills a mongoose. I trust that you won't let that happen to me, Sandy?"

Sandy thought, *Those bitches had crossed my man, my husband at that! And now here he is in a vulnerable state of mind for the very first time I have ever seen.* Sandy pulled Cruz to herself and said in a deadly voice, "You the only man I know that got two lives, baby, your own and the one I breathe in for you. So if a snake gon' try to kill you, they got to kill yo' snake first, so know that this snake gon' have the mongoose's back until death. Pull yo'self together, Daddy, and just remember that yo' snake seen them bitches coming the first time, and I'll see them coming the next time. Just trust me, my husband, just trust me."

He smiled so Sandy asked him, "So what's the plan, boo, and what's my role?"

"The only plan you in, Mrs. Cruz, is the one that takes care of our legitimate business. I know you got my back, but I need you to keep yo' head so that when I lose mine, you can help me find it."

"So we goin' to let them get away playin' you like that, Daddy?"

"Never that, Mrs. Cruz, by now Rose is already tangled up in my web."

"So do you think that Maria is in cahoots with Rose, Daddy?"

"Hell muthafuckin' no! Them bitches can't stand each other, so I don't know what the fuck's up with Maria."

"Well, Conrad, they were both in love with you and now they're both gone. So, dear, if you don't mind me asking, how much money did they both get away with?"

Cruz looked at Sandy with contempt. "About two hundred thousand dollars apiece," he said in a deadly tone.

"Then know this, my husband! Snakes won't bite each other as long as there's someone else for them to bite, and you've been bit, boo. And since we can't find either snake, that could only mean that both of them are in bed together, as far as this situation is concerned."

"Well Sandy, I beg to differ," Cruz said as if she did not know what the hell she was talking about. "But if in fact that is true, that only means Maria's ass is entangled in the same web of death rose is tangled up in. and if I have to, I'll chop both of them bitches up in little bitty pieces then feed them to my pit bulls. What's it to yo' ass anyway, Sandy?" he said in a playful way, trying not to show the pain that he was feeling due to what seemed to be the worst betrayal ever.

"Fuck you, Conrad, if you can't give me more credit than that. You don't think I know how you feel about them bitches especially that toy hoe of yours, Maria? Well, I do! So don't play me. All I want you to remember is one thing, tell me who is it that always had your back? Even when we were kids, I looked out for your best interest, so let me tell you what it is to me, Mr. Conrad Cruz. When somebody fucks you over from this point on, they fuckin' my ass over as well, now that's what it is to me. So you need to confide in me, boo, not a damn thang changed! You ride, I ride!"

"Okay, wifey, you sure you want to play Bonnie and Clyde?"

"Until death do us part, Mr. Cruz," she replied.

Cruz smiled at his wife as he started the Corvette and peeled out.

"Then I'm going to have to tell you the story from the get-go, Sandy. Years ago, I was hanging in the downtown area, looking to feed the monster that hides within me, if you know what I mean? Well, this crackhead bitch pushed up on me with short money. I told her to keep her money, but I hit her up with the dope anyway."

"You mean to tell me you gave something away for free, Conrad?" Sandy said, as she was trying to make light the sick shit she knew she was about to hear.

"Never that, Sandy—I was just fishing. Later that night," Cruz continued, "she came back lookin' for another hand out, so I asked her where the young lady was that I had seen her walking down the street with earlier. She was like, 'Who? You can't be talking about my eight-year-old little girl, mister!' I told her that that was exactly who I was talking about and to stop playing dumb. I told the crackhead bitch to give me the girl, and I'll keep her high for as long as she got high. She called me a sick son of a bitch and said that she wasn't going to smoke off her baby girl, but I just played it off and tossed her a bag of that good shit, you know what I mean? The boy mixed with the girl, feel me? Then I showed her a half of a kilo of Snow White, and when her eyes buckled, I knew I had her. So I told her if she knew anyone with a little girl as fine as hers, to tell them that they can have the same stuff I just gave her. You know, *that good stuff!* I had baited the hook, and all I had to do was sit and wait."

Cruz continued. "It wasn't even two hours later before she was back with the little girl. She walked up to my truck with tears in her eyes and asked me if the deal was still good. I damn near immediately felt sorry for her but decided, just as quickly, not to. So I set it up, told her where to drop the girl, I paid her and lay low until it was cool to pick the package up."

"Damn, Conrad, what's all that have to do with what we got going on?" Sandy asked.

"Everything, Sandy, see the woman's name was Kathy Locklord."

"Locklord?" Sandy cried out. "Conrad, you don't mean to tell me she was K-Loc's mother?"

"I mean to tell you that and even more, my wife. Not only was she K-Loc's mom but even before K-Loc was born, she was Rose's mother. And yes! Rose was and still is that little girl, nevertheless, in a grown woman's body."

Sandy could only look in horror as Cruz said, "So welcome to my world, my wife. And yes! It is until death do us part…"

*****

"What the fuck is she doing here, Jonathan?" Maria cried out once again, not having received an answer the first time.

Rose just looked at Maria with venom attached to her stare. It wasn't that she was surprised to see Maria, but it was her dislike for the woman that made it hard for her to see the bigger picture, if there was such a picture in this roll of film.

"Well, Jonathan." Rose said, turning the table on Jonathan. "How long are you going to keep this slow-ass bitch in the dark?"

"Please don't start, Rose," Jonathan said, sounding like her daddy.

"Well, then, you better wake this hoe up to who I really am before I set shit off up in this muthafucka, you hear?"

"You black-ass, nappy-headed bitch, why *don't* you set shit off then, what's wrong with your setter?" Maria shot back.

"Look, goddamn it!" Jonathan's voice thundered throughout the empty house. "We got too much shit to do and not enough time to do this shit. So from this day on forward, this type of bullshit will not be tolerated."

Solo folded his arms and found himself a wall to lean back on, as he enjoyed the show. Tammy and Shannon both sat Indian style with their legs crossed on the floor, both with thoughts of their own concerning the new situation at hand.

"Now, Maria, you need to understand," Jonathan said as easy as he could, "Rose is my mother."

"Rose is your WHAT?" Maria screamed.

"Look, Ria," he said with love as he shortened her name by cutting it in half. "Listen to me good and please do not interrupt. Know that it is what it is. Now you and me can go to blows about this later on, but right now"—he waved his hand to show her the others in the room before continuing—"we are not going to air our misunderstanding in front of others, okay, boo?"

Maria's mouth hung open wide as if she was trying to catch flies with it. The trip about this was that the other women were in the same disarray.

"Now I can't be letting you talk to my mother that way."

"Pull that bitch's ponytail, Jonathan The Truth Locklord, will you?" Rose almost sang.

"Mom!" Jonathan immediately cut into her song. "You will not be allowed to disrespect Maria either."

"And why might that be, Jonathan?" Rose asked with her hands on her hips.

Maria came up snuggling to her man and said, "Tell them all what time it is, Papi!"

Jonathan looked at Maria, not being able to believe the low-budget, hood-rat type of shit she was try'na pull, but everyone in the room was waiting for the words to come out of his mouth. But Jonathan would not be played, not even on the down low as he said, "Because you a part of the Locklord clan as much as everyone else is in this room, no disrespects will be tolerated."

Jonathan said this with eyes that warned her at the same time, daring her to front on him again so she would really find out what was up. "First and foremost, we a family so no one will disrespect nobody up in here."

As he looked at everyone in their eyes, he stopped at Solo and gazed at him a little longer than he did to everyone else before he spoke again, "Do I make myself clear?"

All of the women spoke up, saying yes. Rose just gave him her nod of approval, but Solo held Jonathan's gaze for a moment longer before he spoke. "Jonathan, is it?"

"Most dudes call me Baby Locklord or The Truth, but seeing that you're family, I'll let you go with that, Uncle. By the way, I didn't get yo' first name."

Solo had to laugh, thinking to himself, *The little nigga's sharp.*"

"It's Derrick, nephew."

"Okay, Uncle Derrick, it's simple enough, you're either with us or you're not. So what's it going to be, 'cuz once shit pop off, there's no turning back."

"Let me ask you this, Baby Locklord," Solo asked with hurt and hate attached to his words. "When the time comes, do you really think you can kill yo' own father?"

"I want you to understand once and for all, Rose my daddy, nigga! Cruz is just a dead walkin' muthafucka until I rock his ass to sleep, we clear?"

"Okay, nephew, I'll ride."

"Now just hold the fuck up. Am I hearing this shit right?" Maria cut in. "Cruz is yo' real father?"

Rose took Jonathan by the hand and walked him over to Maria. "Look at him, girl, you been with him for over a week now, look at him! Surely you had to have seen Cruz in his eyes by now."

Rose let go of Jonathan's hand and addressed Maria kindly this time. "Maria, I'm coming at you as a mother now. If you not really down with Jonathan, let him go, girl." She almost whispered. "It's like this, he gon' go up against Cruz with or without our help, so if you're not really down for him. Just let him go, girl, so my baby will have a chance."

"Look, Rose, and the rest of you might as well hear this!" Maria shouted. "All of this is coming at me kinda fast. Hell! It's coming at me at the speed of light, I'm try'na figure out what's goin' on, but one things for fuckin' sure and this is the truth, concerning The Truth: not for one moment do I have to figure out how I feel about my man!"

"Yo MAN?" Tammy and Shannon cried out almost with unconstrained hate.

"That's what a grown-ass woman just said!" Maria shouted back. "What, you hoes have a hard time hearing?"

Both girls were up on their feet, ready to jump on Maria, but Rose waved them off with a stern warning saying,

"Y'all don't want to go there with this hoe, she's not to be played with. Now sit yo' young asses back down, so you can see what almost happened to you."

Maria stood there calm and collected and smiled at the girls, flashing a razor blade under her tongue. As she did so, she brought one hand from behind her back, slowly exposing a barber's straight razor. "And I thought you little girls wanted to play," Maria said in a deadly tone.

"Goddamn!" Solo barked. "This bitch is insane and ready to put a hoe behind a box behind you, dog."

Jonathan walked over to Maria and whispered in her ear so that no one else could hear. "Okay, baby, you made your point."

"Well, I had to," she whispered back. "Them little bitches feelin' you, Papi, and that's cool, but they damn sure gon' know who the head bitch in charge is when yo' dick is concerned."

"Speaking of dick, did you have that razor in yo' mouth when you hit me off earlier?" Maria just smiled, and without a word her eyes told him "YES!"

Just then Solo's phone went off with the ring tone of *Scarface's Never Seen a Man Cry*. He looked at Rose and said, "What's up, sis? Can a nigga take a call yet or what?"

Rose looked at Jonathan, and he nodded his head, meaning that it was cool.

From jump street, everyone could tell that it had to be bad news, and when tears started to roll down Solo's face, it was made clear that something very wrong had gone down. As he got off his phone, Rose was the first to speak to him. "What's the matter, little daddy?" she said with love for her newfound baby brother.

His only words were, "Momma's dead."

*****

As Low Down sat in his car waiting for Solo to show up, his mind could not help but trip off the unfortunate events concerning his best friend's family. First the big homey K-Loc, and now, their mom: both dead! He thought to himself, *Anyone could see that this shit is personal. For anyone to come in to the heart of the hood and blow Momma Locklord away.*

He just shook his head, not knowing what to say. It had been two days since Momma Locklord's death, and when he couldn't get a hold of Solo, he thought the worst. But finally, his boy answered the phone.

It's getting crazy out here, he thought to himself as he fired up a blunt. *A nigga, damn near gotta sleep with his gun in order to get some rest.* Feeling the effects of the blunt, he thought he saw what looked like six of his homeboys bending the corner; they had on their basketball gear. *Yeah, that's them,* he thought to himself. So Low Down didn't pay them much attention as he hit the blunt one more time.

But what did catch his attention was the clean-ass stock '68 Chevy with four niggas in it. He put the blunt out and called out to his homeboys that were calling out to him at the same time. "Watch out, cuzz!" he cried as he pointed the .45 at the black '68 Chevy that they hadn't noticed yet. The reason why they had not noticed was because they were calling out for him to look out for the car that was fully heading his direction.

"Look out, Low Down!"

Their shouting, went unheeded as he let off one shot before he was run down by the second Chevy. As they stood there in shock, the driver of that car put it in reverse and backed over Low Down again. It was only then that one of the six young men saw the trouble that was upon them. It was Tomcat and three other members of the Compton Neighborhood Crips bailing out of the first car with guns in hand while the car ran over Low Down's corpse repeatedly. They tried to run, but Tomcat and the others chased them on foot with guns blazing, until all six men were dead as Low Down was. There was one little boy standing nearby, shaking like a leaf on a tree, while he watched in horror as his big brother and the others were getting gunned down like wild deer. Tomcat walked up to him and said, "Sorry, little man, you were just in the wrong place at the wrong time."

Tomcat pulled the trigger, killing the nine-year-old boy.

As Solo and Jonathan pulled up on the block, there was mass hysteria. Women were crying and as close as fifty DTGs were trying to figure out who had it in for them. Five-0 were everywhere, so Jonathan asked Solo what he wanted to do. "Park here and let's walk down there to see what's up."

As the two men walked closer to the scene, a woman cried out, "There his ass is! This shit is all yours and your dead brother's fault! You muthafuckas made this spot hot, and that's why the Compton niggas done killed my babies. Why, Solo, why?"

But it was as if her words were coming in one ear and out the other. A million things were running through Solo's head until it came to him. It was then he turned to Jonathan and said, "Cruz! I wasn't sure at first because I couldn't see their faces that day my brother got killed, but it had to be Cruz. Now my mother's dead. Look at this shit! Them muthafuckas killed Tiny Jack, he just a kid, dog!" He then ran toward his homeboys. "Cuzz!" he said to One Life. He says, "What the fuck happened to her?"

One life replied, "If your ass would have been in the hood instead of hiding out you would know what happened to her."

"Fuck you, cuzz! Locklords don't hide, we ride! You sorry-ass muthafucka!"

"Easy, One Life! Solo just lost his brother and mother," Solo's girl said as she walked up.

"Fuck this nigga baby, you don't have to explain shit to him."

One Life tried to swing at solo, but Solo sidestepped the punch right on time.

"So it's like that, huh, big homey?"

"Yeah, nigga! It's just like that with both of my brothers lying dead in the street."

Jonathan started pulling Solo away, as he seen that the others in the group were of the same mind.

"That's how you niggas feel?" Solo cried out in disbelief. "Then fuck y'all. Come on, Annette."

But Annette didn't move and then One Life put his arm around her and said, "This is my pussy now, so get on, nigga, before you get shitted on."

Solo looked like he wanted to cry but held it together and shot back, "Sometimes a nigga just got to let a hoe be a hoe."

Had it not been for the police, Jonathan and Solo would have not gotten out of there alive. After they viewed Momma Locklord's body, they rode back home without a word being spoken.

CHAPTER FIVE

As Cruz sat at the head of the table, he looked over the twenty-two men sitting around him. There were ten Crips and ten Bloods, all of whom were calling shots over their prospective gangs. Nevertheless, it became evident to him that, for the most part, their power only stood because of their financial status. He also informed himself that even in his success to get them on board, he had failed to convince the heavy hitters. See, the heavy hitters are those that really run the hood, those that live and die for the hood, those that do the dirty work for niggas like these sitting around this table, and they are of these that can't be controlled. However, money has always been the tool that muthafuckas like these have used, if not to control, then to somewhat contain the uncontrollable ones form their own hoods. And this was the reason that they were sitting here, if for no other reason at all Cruz told himself.

Now Tomcat, on the other hand, sat next to B. G. from the Bounty Hunters, they called Get Off.

"I invited them because they were the next generation to rule the concrete jungle, as both of their reputations preceded them. Now, Cruz has only heard about Get Off, but Tomcat on the other hand, he had no misunderstanding about this little nigga having a real fuckin' mean streak about him. He pulled the trigger on a nine-year-old kid, and when asked why he did it, he said with no emotion, 'If there are no witnesses, then there wouldn't be a case.'"

"Tomcat, Get Off, would you leave the room for a moment. I'll call you in shortly," Cruz instructed them both.

After both young men exited the room, Cruz got the meeting started. "Well, men, look around the tables, this is what we're working with. Now, the way I see it, having both cities that are willing to ride together is better than rolling with the other two halves that are at war against one another. Nevertheless! The first order of business is to unite the rest of the Hub and the Dub."

"And just how in the hell are you planning to do that?" one of the men at the table called out.

"By cutting the head of the snake, we hit them up hard and we hit them fast."

"Hit who and why?" Baby Gangbanger from Santana Block Compton Crip said, with concern in his voice.

Cruz looked around the table into each man's eyes before saying, "The muthafuckas that think they untouchable, that's who will soon find out they are not!"

Every man at the table knew who he was talking about now. The Businessmen were ex-gang members from both sides of Compton and Watts, Crips and Bloods as well. The only difference was that they prided themselves as community activists as well as businessmen. If a building was empty, they would buy it and fix it up and turn it into something that would benefit the people in the neighborhood. Cruz hated that shit, because as much as they did do, if you got in the way of one of their business ventures, you'd come up missing, and on top of that, they ain't giving Cruz a piece of the action.

"You trippin', Cruz!" Tip Toe from Tree Top Piru said with a hint of panic in his voice. "The Connected Men of Business isn't a gang, they just like us, niggas that are try'na get paid."

"If that is so, Tip Toe?" Cruz said with a hint of anger in his voice. "Then why are they not sitting at the table with us, they were also invited." Cruz looked around the room, but no one had an answer to his question. "Them muthafuckas about fifty deep and if rubbed the wrong way, they will put in more work than a hooker with a gorilla pimp. They got gangs from both sides of the Hub and the Dub backing their play, none of which are sitting at this table either. Now, you say they not a gang, Tip Toe? But I differ with you in that area, them muthafuckas are like the Black Mafia."

"So you think them muthafuckas going to come after us, Cruz?" Baby Gangbanger asked.

"Not if we get at them first," Cruz said.

"So now what, Cruz?" asked Tip Toe.

"We go to war against the Businessmen and then those that are connected to them in one way or another come after us, is that your plan?"

"Look, you simple-minded muhafucka! This is not some fuckin' game that we playing, we will no longer go to war against our ene-migos, know that this is a new day. No! Instead we move on them like a fuckin' plague, we wipe them off the face of the earth, we pull their asses up by the root so they won't grow no more, and then we plant our own seed, feel me?" Cruz spoke as if he was a politician. "We will move on them with everything we got the first time, I'm talking about all-out warfare, taking the battle right at them, hitting the at their headquarters, then whatever is left of them, we will hunt down as if they were runaway slaves. Now, we gon' handle this shit in about a week's time."

"What?" Big Daddy from Grape Street Watts shouted.

"That's right, B. D.," Cruz shouted back. "That' how we send the muthafuckin' message, and once the message is sent, the rest of the Hub and the Dub will be quick to get on board." Cruz looked at the disbelief on the men's faces but nevertheless was unmoved. "Look," he continued. "I know what you're thinking, that this is an unnecessary war. But on the contrary, this will be the war that will stop all other wars."

"Now, I'm going to need for you to find me the meanest, cold-bloodiest, youngest you can find one from each of your hoods. Not hotheads, and make sure that they can keep they mouths shut whoever they is. Tomcat and Get Off will run the twenty of them."

"Shit!" Tip Toe said in disapproval. "I thought you said no hot-heads? Them two fools are on fire!"

"That's why they in charge," Cruz shot back. "They mad dogs! Evil rubs on easy! In the end I want their evil to rub on the rest of their crew."

They all looked at Cruz with uncertainty: those that knew him knew that he never displays his whole plan. Nevertheless, none sitting at the table were willing to take the task at hand, so if Cruz had some grand plan, they were willing to let it play out for now.

Cruz knew that if he were going to pull both cities together, he would have to get rid of the Connected Men of Business a.k.a the Businessmen. But money had made the men sitting at the table with him soft, and just the sight of them was starting to make him sick. He needed lions, not lambs, to get this job done, and that was where the B.G.s came in.

"Last but not least, I'm going to need a lot of you to put up two grand, this in order for us to get the necessary equipment to get the job done. Now, if there's a reason you don't want to come out of pocket in order to support the cause, it will be noted and I'll then come out of my own pocket to cover you. However, you will not partake in the spoils once this job pays off."

"40-Gs, huh?" Tip Toe said with suspicion in the tone used.

But Cruz looked at the man as if he were looking right through him, and without breaking his gaze, he hit the button on his phone.

"Yes, Daddy?" Sandy's voice came over the phone, sounding really sexy.

"How's my sexy-ass wife doing?" he asked, even though she was sitting in the next room.

"I'm just sitting here babysittin' these little mannish gangstas you sent in here."

"Well, take a break then, baby. And bring me some sugar along with my wallet, would you?'

"I'm already there, Daddy."

As she walked through the door all eyes were on her. On a scale of one to ten, she was only a seven, but for whatever she lost in looks, she made up for it with style and grace. She was so down, in fact, that everyone in the room were aware that she had and would again kill for her man at his request. And that became all the more clear at the sight of her shoulder holster, which contained a .45 automatic inside of it.

This bitch is most definitely wifey material, Baby Gangbanger thought to himself.

Sandy walked in real seductively, and more than one dick in the room got hard as some of the men shifted their position in their seats. She walked up to Cruz and planted a wet but very sweet kiss on his lips. As she bent over to do so, her skirt rose slightly, exposing her thick Hershey-colored thighs. If some did not get hard when she first walked in, for sure they were now. When she finished giving her husband the sugar he had asked for, she slammed the briefcase she had been holding on to the table and said, "Here's your wallet, Daddy." And with that, she walked out with the same class she had walked in with.

"Sandy," Cruz called after her, "send the little homeys back in."

"That's a done deal, Daddy," she said without breaking her stride.

Cruz looked back at Tip Toe as he opened the briefcase, exposing more money than the man had ever seen in his whole entire life and said, "If in fact you're having money problems, Piru, I'd be happy to hit you off at 15 percent a month, that is until your train comes back in. Now, as you can see, my wallet is full, so I really ain't got a problem lookin' out. But muthafucka, don't you ever look at me as if I'm some stick-up kid in need of a forty-grand lick. Now! Do you need for me to put you in or what?"

Tip Toe did not answer. Instead, he pulled the two grand out of his inside coat pocket, which made him the first of the twenty to lie in on the table.

As Tomcat and Get Off walked into the room, Cruz smiled like a proud father. "For those of you that didn't know and don't understand why I picked these two other than the reasons I already gave you, here's one more—they're half brothers! Now, if there is no other business at hand, you gentlemen can be on your way and I'll be in touch shortly."

As the men filed out of Cruz's office, he told Tomcat and Get Off to stay.

"Look, I'm depending on you two, this is the dawn of a new day, the start of a new empire. An empire where you two will reign as lords and be respected like kings. I need to know that you're not only willing to work together, but also willing to do whatever it takes in order to fulfill our new destinies. Now, can I depend on you or what?"

Both young men looked at each other and back to Cruz and almost at the same time said, "We got this."

"Good," Cruz said. "Now what do you say we hit the clubs tonight?"

"Us, with you?" Get Off said in shock as he looked at his half brother.

"Yeah, man, if I had sons, I would want them to be just like you two, we gonna do a lot of kickin' it." Cruz was playing with the young men's emotions, knowing that their father died when they were too young to remember him. This gave him the opportunity to fill them shoes so to speak, in order to have them do his bidding. He then hit them both off with two grand apiece and told them to go get fresh.

"I'll pick you both up at nine thirty."

"Cool, Big Homie," Tomcat said as the two brothers rolled out.

As he sat in his office alone, Sandy walked in and could once again see that her man needed her support. "What's the get-down, Daddy?"

Cruz looked at her from afar, as if he were there but not really there at the same time—before speaking. "If I'm going to get this done, boo, I can't put the starting lineup in."

"Okay, Daddy, then play with your rookies."

Cruz looked at her and smiled as she mixed words with him in code.

"What the fuck you know, Sandy?" He said as if he really wanted her to know something.

"Well, Daddy, I know you're running the point, so it really don't matter what team you got in the game. Besides, when the fourth quarter comes, it's Cruz time, game over, muthafuckas!"

Cruz looked at her again, but this time with that I-want-to-sex-you look, and no words were needed, as Sandy very well knew that look. So without being told to she removed her panties and mounted him right there on his office chair.

"See, Daddy, who can make it better if Momma can't?" she said this over and over again as she bounced up and down even faster, causing both of them to cum together in lustful love.

*****

It's been two months now, Shannon thought to herself, *and the Locklord Clan is still laying low.*

The women were at each other's throat, and Solo was starting to question Jonathan's leadership abilities. Though he did not say it out loud, anyone could see what he was thinking. On top of that, Jonathan was disappearing for long hours on in to the night, and Tammy was sneaking off as well, from time to time. As she sat on the couch, she couldn't help but ask Rose, who was sitting beside her, "Rose, what the hell's going on around here?"

Rose was feeling Shannon and knew exactly where the young lady was coming from but still played it off as if everything was cool.

"The shit's under control, Shannon, damn! Yo' ass be on some paranoid shit."

"Is that right, Rose? Shannon stood to her feet with her hands on her hips.

"Yeah, bitch, that's right," Rose shot back.

"Is it cool for Tammy to creep up out of here on the late-night tip?" Shannon said, almost whispering with a hiss so that no one else would hear. Now she got Rose's attention.

"How many times?" Rose also whispered.

"At least three times. Somebody in a black 300C has been scooping her ass up."

"What, bitch? Why you just now speaking up on this bullshit?"

"I didn't think it was a big deal until I asked her what was up then the bitch went off on me."

"This is not good," Rose said softly. "Have you told Jonathan yet?"

"Hell no, Rose, he would kill her ass."

"Shannon, this is some real shit. Our every move must be one that won't cost us, and that little bitch is up to something that could cost us everything."

"I'm sorry, just start being about Locklord business and handle that shit accordingly, Shannon."

"What the fuck y'all whispering about?" Solo said as he walked into the room.

"Female shit, why?" Rose asked.

"You feeling like a little girl talk, baby bro?"

"No, but I do feel like getting the fuck out this prison Baby Locklord got us held hostage in!"

Just then the front of Jonathan's truck hit the living-room window.

"Speaking of the goddamn king…," Solo said with a hint of hostility in his voice.

And at that same moment, Maria come running down the stairs like a little girl that was happy 'cuz daddy was finally home. So Solo continued, "And all hail the muthafuckin' queen!"

Before Jonathan could fully enter the front door, Maria jumped up on him, wrapping both legs around him.

"Papi, I can't stand it no more! I gotta get the fuck out of this house! These muthafuckas are driving me loco!" And with that the whole clan joined in with her complaint.

"Okay, okay, I got some good news, people! We gon' celebrate tonight! Name the spot, and the Locklords will be in the hizzouse!"

The whole house went crazy, and even Solo had to smile. At that very moment an unfamiliar voice asked, "Do any of you even care what we are celebrating tonight?"

No one paid him much attention, no one other than Rose.

"Oh my muthafuckin' god! Is that who I think it is?" Rose cried out. "I know damn well that's not who I hope it is."

"I *said*, does anyone care to know what we're going to celebrate tonight?"

This time the room got quiet at the thundering of his deep voice, but only Rose's voice could be heard now. "I would like to know, Mr. Stanton," Rose said like a schoolgirl. Everybody in the room looked at her after that statement and then back to the unknown man, and it was clear to them that there was some type of connection between the two.

"Well, my beautiful black queen, if I may refer to you as such?"

"You may, my good sir," Rose said.

Shannon looked at her, thinking to herself, *Who the fuck this bitch think she is, Scarlett O'Hara?*

"Well then, my Lady Locklord, behold your son the high school graduate!"

Rose looked at the certificate Mr. Stanton was holding up, and tears flooded her eyes.

"How did you do it, Jonathan? When did you find the time, baby?" she said as she walked up to Mr. Stanton and removed the GED certificate from his hand.

"Well, to answer your first question, Mother, I'm a Locklord, that's how I did it. And where I found the time, well, I'll let Mr. Stanton tell you how that went down."

Rose looked in to the man's eyes and softly said, "What part did you play in this?"

"Jonathan came into my office about two months ago and simply told me that he made you a promise that he was going to graduate from high school and asked me to help him keep it. At the same time, he said that he needed to drop out. After going back and forth with him unsuccessfully, I finally asked him that if I helped him get his GED, what I would get in return."

"And?" Rose asked curiously.

"And our little man tried to pay me off. But, Ms. Locklord, some things money can't buy, and I believe that education and love are two of those things," Mr. Stanton said while looking deep into Rose's eyes.

"Oh, so exactly how much did this piece of paper cost my son?" she asked while waving the certificate in his face.

"Oh, stop beating around the bush, you two!" Jonathan was tired of the little cat-and-mouse game. "He blackmailed me, Mom. He told me that the only way that he'd help me is if I asked you to go on a date with him. So let's get this shit over with, give him a yes or no, so we can get this party started!"

"Well, Mr. Stanton, are you going to ask me or not?"

All eyes were on him now. "Ms. Locklord, each hour I spent with your son, five days a week, for the last two months, I was already asking you out! And when I walked through this door and called you my beautiful black queen, I was once again, asking you out. So I'm just going to wait for your answer."

Rose wanted to shout, hell yeahhhhh! But she didn't know how Jonathan would feel about it. She looked over at her son and Jonathan said, "Don't be looking at me, Rose. That shit's on you."

"We got a lot of shit going on right now, Mr.—"

Cutting Rose off, the principal said, "Call me Donald, Rose, if I may?"

"You may," she said as she blushed. "Like I said, we got a lot going on right now, and I should really say no, but for no other reason that you helping my son keep his promise to me, I am going to say yes. Come on, girls!" Rose called out. "Will somebody please wake Tammy's lazy ass up 'cuz we gotta go get our party on! Haaaaayy!"

As Maria and Shannon ran up the stairs to go get dressed, Rose pulled Jonathan and Solo into the kitchen. "We got a situation with Tammy. I wasn't going to say nothing until I was sure—"

Jonathan cut her off. "I'm aware of the shit she try'na pull. I got cameras set up around this muthafucka. Don't worry about that bitch, let's just go and have a good time."

"Do we need to get heated, Jonathan?" Rose asked.

"Yeah, Rose, I think it would be wise if we all stay strapped from here on out. Now go get dressed and let's go have some fun," he told his mom as he kissed her on her forehead.

"I love you and I'm very proud of you, son."

"I love you too, Mom."

As Rose walked away, Jonathan looked at Solo and said, "You ready to dance with the devil, nigga?"

Not knowing what Jonathan was talking about, Solo just looked at him.

"You family, Solo. That hoe-ass shit you been spilling out yo mouth when I'm not around, I'm gon' let it slide this time. But starting from now on, if you think you ready to run this shit"—Jonathan took one step closer to Solo—"then step up, homey, and take this shit from me."

The two men looked at each other in the eyes, but Solo didn't cross the invisible line. At that very moment, Mr. Stanton walked in and noticed that the tension in the room was thick, so he walked right back out.

"Jonathan," Solo said in love. "You and Rose is all I got left in this world, man. True, I don't like the way this shit is going, but I'm not trying to step to you."

"Cool, big dog, then let's go get fresh and go have a good time."

As they pulled out, Jonathan, Maria, and Shannon rode in Maria's Maserati GT and Rose, Solo, Tammy, and Donald Stanton rode in Rose's Jaguar.

On the way to the club, Jonathan spoke to Maria and Shannon. "Look, here's the get-down, that bitch Tammy's fuckin' sleeping with the enemy."

"What?" Maria cried out. But Jonathan paid her no mind. Instead, he lit into Shannon.

"Shannon, I should kill yo' ass, you knew the bitch was creepin' out, the only reason I'm going to let you live is because I don't believe you knew with who she was creeping with."

"Who she been creepin' with, Papi?"

"Shut the fuck up, Maria! Yo' ass should have been on top of this shit. Now, is everybody strapped?"

Both women nodded their heads to say yes.

"Well, can I at least ask where we're going, Papi?"

Jonathan looked at her and simply said, "We're going to dance with the devil tonight, that's where we're going."

Rose had a bad feeling, so when she gave Tammy her gun, she made sure it wasn't loaded. And when Jonathan and Maria's car came to a stop in front of a club that Cruz had part ownership of, that said it all. As they exited their cars, Rose walked up to Jonathan and said, "I take it that you know where we're at, Jonathan."

"Yeah, Rose, it's time for us to show our faces."

"So be it," Rose said as she turned around and addressed the rest of the Locklord clan.

"Okay, the shit is about to hit the fan, ladies and gentlemen. We about to dance with the devil himself, but fuck him. We walk up in this bitch like we own it. If you're scared, now is the time to kick rocks, but if you down, then stay down to the fullest. Now we ain't gon' trip until they push the envelope. Understood, Solo?"

Solo was looking like a man that was ready to go all out. Having had lost both his mother and brother, he was ready to get down right about now. Jonathan had seen the look on his face and said, "Uncle Derrick, we can't let these muthafuckas see our pain. We got to throw them off, feel me?"

Solo didn't say a word, so Jonathan continued, "We got the upper hand right now, big dog, because they can't see us coming. If you wake them up to what we know, we still might get Cruz, but one thing's fo' sho, we ain't getting out of there alive, and I like living. Just follow my lead, and we will all get what we want, Cruz's head on a platter. Now, do y'all feel me?"

Solo just nodded his head in agreement. "Then, let's do this shit!" Jonathan exclaimed.

Rose turned to Donald Stanton and handed him her car keys.

"Donald," she said, like a little girl who had just gotten into trouble, "I'm sorry, but I can't explain to you right now what's going on. Please take my keys and go, Donald, I'll pick it up when I can."

"Rose I can't do that, at least not without you. I just got you back, and I'm not going to lose you over some bullshit."

"Then go back to my place and wait on me there, but you can't stay here.""

Okay then, but I'll be waiting on you at your place no matter how long it takes."

Rose ran up to him and kissed him hard on the lips before walking away.

*****

Sandy could not believe her eyes when the Locklords walked through the door as if they owned the spot. Without hesitation, she called Cruz, who was already on his way to the club. When they sat at one of the VIP tables, she told the waitress that was going to serve them that she would handle this one. As she walked in their direction, she could see Maria sitting up under some fine-ass, light-skinned nigga, with Rose on the other side of him. Two other females sat on each side of this handsome, dark-skinned dude, which looked as if he could be related to Rose. And just as fast as that thought popped in to her mind, K-Loc appeared in her thoughts, and she remembered when and where she had seen this man before. She almost stopped in her tracks as she recalled the day of K-Loc's death and remembered how this young man tried saving him. Only later did she find out that this was K-Loc's baby brother; at that moment she could only wonder if they knew. The closer she got to their table, the more fear gripped her very soul, but one would never realize that this was what she was feeling, for she hid it real good. Getting even closer, her focus was once again on the light-skinned young man. There was something very familiar about him, but she could not make the connection as she got to the table.

"Rose, Maria," Sandy said as she nodded to the rest of them. "What can I get for you this evening?"

"Three bottles, of your finest, whatever that may be," Jonathan said with a sexy smile on his face.

"So, Sandy," Maria said kind of flippantly, "I see you got a new career. What's up? This' the best you can do with a bachelor's degree."

"Well, what's wrong with running your husband's business for him in his absence?" Sandy replied as she flashed the pink diamond in their faces.

"You mean to tell me that you and Cruz got married?" Rose almost shouted.

"That's right. We would have sent you both invitations," she said, pointing at Rose and Maria, "but it seems that you have both been in hiding for the last three months."

"Well, bitch! We in the house now!" Maria shot back. But Jonathan cut her off before she could get a full head of steam going.

"Well now, beautiful lady, if you're married to Cruz that that makes us family. As a muthafuckin' matter of fact, that would make you my stepmother," he said with that sexy Cruz smile on his face, and that was when it hit Sandy like a ton of bricks. Eighteen years ago, Cruz moved Rose in to her own spot knocked up by some trick, which did not make any sense, because Cruz always preached about using condoms. He would have killed any girl that did not use them. Examining Jonathan real thoroughly this time, she could see that it was truly Cruz who had been the trick that knocked Rose up. She looked at Rose with bitterness in her heart, and as Cruz and his boys walked through the door, the sight of him for the very first time made her sick in the stomach.

Cruz walked in with Gangster Bam, The Outlaw Bandit Loc, Get Off, and Tomcat. When Tammy saw Cruz, having had already made up her mind, she planned on leaving with him tonight. Cruz waved his boys off to a nearby table, and he made his way to the table where the Locklord Clan was sitting.

"What's up, Mommy?" he said to his wife before addressing the rest.

"You tell me, Daddy, and we'll both know."

"Well, from the looks of things, we have some old friends here, as well as some new ones!" he said as he looked at Tammy with a smile.

"But what about the rest of you? Would you be friend or a foe?" he said, this time looking at Solo and Jonathan.

"Well, Cruz," Jonathan said, "there's nothing but family here. For the most part, you know my mother Rose, the one you pimped from the age of twelve up until not too long ago. And Maria here, I know muthafuckin' well, you been missing this good-ass pussy." He put his hand between Maria's legs and started massaging her pussy. "This over here is my mother's brother, Derrick Locklord a.k.a Solo Loco, which makes him my uncle. This over here is Shannon, the bitch down by law but more so then that she loyal, and loyalty is very important to me. Me, well, I'm the son you didn't have a need to claim, and I can live with that. But what I can't live with is disloyalty.

So tell me, Cruz, what would you do to a disloyal muthafucka, you know, the one that's try'na cross you?"

Cruz looked at his son, wondering where this was going. At the same time, he admired the kid for having balls to even come to his spot like this. "I think you already know what I would do, Baby Locklord."

"Oh, I almost forgot, this here is Tammy but she ain't family, she's just dead."

With that being said, Jonathan pulled out his 9 mm and blew her brains out from across the table. In shock, Cruz tried to go for his gun, but Shannon was already on her feet with gun in hand.

"Just say the word, Baby Locklord, and I'll make you a bastard child!" she shouted with her weapon damn near in Cruz's mouth. Rose had her gun pointed at Sandy, as Maria along with Solo were trying to keep the men that came with Cruz in check.

"Papi! These niggas with the business. I can see that it's about to get ugly up in this bitch."

"Don't try it, Gangsta Bam," she cried out.

"If I don't get no one else, yo' ass won't live to know about it."

"Fuck this bitch!" Get Off said. "They can't get us all, fan out!"

As the men got ready to make their move, a voice thundered from the front door. "The next muthafucka that moves can cancel Christmas!" Donald Stanton stood there with six other men, all holding AK-47s. Cruz let out an eerie laugh that sent chills down Shannon's spine, so she slapped Cruz across the face with her gun and at the same time fired off a shot right by his ear. Stumbling to the bar, Cruz grasped at his face in a panic, thinking he had just been shot.

"Muthafucka, can you hear me now? If you can, shut the fuck up because I didn't hear anyone tell no jokes," Shannon said.

"You muthafuckas are walking dead men. Don Juan, you backin' these muthafuckas up?" Cruz asked in anger. "Nigga, I thought you was out of the game, what the fuck's up with this shit? How you gon' just, run up in my spot with AKs and shit?"

"Cruz, just because I am not in the game no more, that doesn't mean I stopped being a Businessman. It's never personal with the

Connected Men of Business, it's just all business, Cruz, you should know that by now."

"And what business you got in my spot, nigga?" Cruz shot back.

"Rose is the business I got up in this muthafucka, and the next time you call me a 'nigga,' I'm killing you my damn self," Donald said in a calm, cool and collected voice. "Rose, are you okay?"

"I'm fine, Donald."

"Okay, let's get out of here before Five-0 gets here. Jonathan!" Donald called as he pointed at Tammy's corpse.

"Is that your mess?"

"Yeah, that's me," Jonathan confessed.

Donald Stanton waved at two of the men with him, and they rolled the body up in a nearby rug and moved it to the van that was waiting, as the other men collected the guns from Cruz's men.

"So this is how it's going to end huh, Maria? Huh, Rose? After all we've been through?"

Before any of them could get a word out of their mouth, Solo hit Cruz in his mouth so hard, with his gun, the force of the blow sending three of his teeth flying out.

"Get yo' papers in order, you sick muthafucka, 'cuz next time you meet the Locklord Clan, trust me, that will be the day you walk through death's door."

With that said, the Locklords and the Businessmen backed out of the building.

CHAPTER SIX

Back at the house, they all sat in the living room, reflecting on the night's events. It turned out that there was more to Mr. Stanton than what met the eyes, and Jonathan planned to find out. Right when Jonathan had an opportunity to get at Mr. Stanton, all of a sudden, Shannon had a burning desire to speak to him. After what she had done earlier that night, he wasn't about to put her on hold. She said, "Baby Locklord, can I holla at you alone?"

"Hell yeah, shorty!"

As they walked into the den, Jonathan fired up a blunt and hit it once and passed it to Shannon. He really didn't get high, but 'cuz Maria was smokin' around him so much, he started liking the smell of it, or at least that's the excuse he told himself.

"What's up, Momma?"

"Baby Locklord, you know I love you and would do anything you ask me to do for you, right?"

"Yeah, boo, I know you got me."

"Well, Baby Locklord, you stuck on Maria and I can't have you as long as that's the case, can't I?"

"Shannon, I love you too and that's on some real shit, but I'm trying to be true to Maria just like I would be to you if we were together."

"I know, Baby Locklord, and that's one of the things I love about you the most. But this time it ain't about me wanting you."

"Then what is it about, Little Momma?"

"Well, tonight I saw Solo in a different light."

"Hold the fuck up! You mean to tell me that you want to give Solo some pussy? Is that what this is all about, Shannon?"

"Is that okay, Baby Locklord?" she said with sadness in her voice. "I wasn't trying to make you mad."

"No, I ain't tripping, boo, I'm just a little shocked. Shit! I've known yo' ass to chase me since the fifth grade, that's all. My feelings a little hurt, but if you feelin' my family like that, then I guess in time I have to get over it."

"Baby Locklord, all you have to do is say the word, and I'm in yo' bed no matter who I'm with."

"Get the fuck out of here before I take you up on yo' offer. By the way, Solo up in the camera room, go surprise his ass with a shot of that stank-stank."

"Thanks for understanding, Baby Locklord!"

As they walked back into the living room, Maria's face was twisted up as if to ask, "What the fuck you up to?" So to put her jealous ass mind to rest.

Jonathan kissed her on the lips and whispered in her ear, "I'll put you on game later, baby."

"So, Mr. Stanton—"

"Why don't you call me Donald instead," Mr. Stanton cut Jonathan off.

"Why don't I just call you Don Juan?" he asked sarcastically, but Donald didn't bite into it.

"Aight then, why don't I just call you Baby Locklord or The Truth then? Is there some type of problem? Have I offended you in some type of way that I don't know about?"

"Have you? I mean you show yourself as one thing, but you end up being something different altogether. I thought you was a teacher, but no! You, my man, got more gangster in you than a teacher should have, from what I saw tonight. Hell, you don't have to tell me nothing, but on the other hand, you seem to be feeling my mother! Plus, you're sitting up in my spot. You're probably going to get lucky with my mother after tonight's events. So hell muthafuckin' yeah you should tell us a little more about yo'self!"

Donald looked over at Rose to see if she was going to put her son in check, but her face also showed that she was more interested in finding out who he really was.

"All right, all right, I used to be from Kelly Park Compton Crips. I grew up with Cruz, but at the age of sixteen, I grew out of that senseless shit that Cruz and a whole lot of others are still participating in. I took what money I had and started the Connected Men of Business. As you may already know, we do a lot of good. But sometimes, shit happens! And that's when we have to get into some gangster shit, as you saw tonight."

"Jonathan," Rose broke in, "I think that's enough."

"I ain't trying to rain on your parade, Rose, so I am only going to ask Batman here one more question. What made you come back?"

"I don't understand where you're coming from, Jonathan."

"Then let me put it in another way, what made you put yo' ass on the line for the Locklords, Mr. Don Juan? And not only your ass but also the lives and the so-called upstanding reputation of the Connected Men of Business, or should I say Businessmen?"

Donald once again looked at Rose and then back at Jonathan and simply said, "Since we're keeping it one hundred, Baby Locklord, my desires for your mother made me do it. Now what?"

Jonathan looked at his schoolteacher transform before his very eyes to the founder of what some were now calling "The Black Mafia" in Los Angeles. And as he looked at him, he saw how Rose looked at him. She didn't look at him with the eyes that wanted to beat Donald out of everything he was worth. No, this look was attached to a different kind of hunger. The man he saw in her eyes was a man that she was falling for.

"You got to be fuckin' kidding me. Rose!" he called to his mother, breaking her trance. "Are you falling for this shit? Because from here yo' ass look like a lovesick little girl, not a paper-chasin', money-getting Locklord."

"Hold the fuck up, child of mine! I've never pulled your card concerning the pussy that got yo' dick standing at attention, now have I?" she said as she looked at Maria. "No less frontin' you off in the presence of those who aren't Locklords. But Jonathan The Truth

Locklord, we connected in a deep way, so I feel what you're saying and I also feel what you're not saying. If you want me to kill what I'm feeling for the first time of my much-fucked-up life, I'll do it. But you best believe, I wouldn't do it for no one else but you. Now, what's it going to be, child of mine?"

The two of them looked at one another as many unspoken words passed through their eyes. Jonathan was aware of the loneliness Rose must have felt for years, and now that that happiness was within her grasp, she would have given up the opportunity at her son's request without questioning why. However, it was a request that he could not make and still keep the peace in the Locklord house.

"You're right, Rose, and I'm out of line. I want to apologize to you, Donald, it's just that there's a lot of shit goin' on right now, and Rose is much more than just a mother to me. She is the reason why I want to be! So if you're digging her like she seems to be digging you, then let that be the reason I kick the fuck back. But in any event, everyone in this room knows that we got a real problem on our hands where Cruz is concerned, so let's not let our hormones lose sight of the danger that just might be hidden in the shadows, feel me?"

This time everybody nodded in agreement. With that, Jonathan pulled Maria up off the sofa, and they started on their way to their bedroom when Rose called after them. "Look, you two," she said as she walked them to the top of the steps, "I know what's at stake here, and trust that I know how to separate my personal life from the business we got to take care of."

Maria spoke first. "Girl! Fuck what's goin' on for tonight, Jonathan and Derrick can handle this shit. Look at him! Donald's fine, plus he paid! And he is feelin' the fuck out of you. So for tonight forget about everything, and let that fine-ass muthafucka clean out the cobwebs in that dusty-ass cave of yours!"

The two women burst out laughing, but Jonathan just shook his head and peered in to the night as he gazed out of the window. "You know that I love you, Jonathan," Rose said as she caressed his handsome face and pulled it into her own in order to kiss his cheek softly before saying, "How long was I supposed to stay lonely, Baby Locklord?"

"I understand Rose," he said as he tried to force a smile on his face.

"Maria told you right, so go do you, but keep your wits about you."

"What else you got to say, Jonathan?" his mother was smiling as she said this.

"Damn, Rose! You already know that I love you, why you gotta make me say it all the damn time!"

She just looked at him as if he had just lost his mind.

"Okay, I love you too, Rose."

She jumped on her son and kissed him all over his face. "See, this is the shit I'm talking about, Rose. You on some soft bullshit, now get off me."

She gave him one last kiss and said, "He wants me to go home with him tonight, is it cool, Daddy?" She asked as if she really needed his permission.

"Again, go do you, Rose. But make sure you got yo' heater with you just in case you run into some type of trouble."

"Yes, Daddy, will do."

With that, Rose ran off to pack an overnight bag.

*****

Shannon walked into the camera room with a full-length leather coat on and asked, "What you doing, Solo?"

"What the fuck does it look like I'm doing, Shannon? I'm monitoring the cameras, making sure that don't nobody creep up on us."

"Fuck them cameras! Let the German Shepherds do that shit! You should be about monitoring this!" She dropped her coat to the ground, and to Solo's surprise, Shannon had nothing on under it.

"Damn, girl, that's how you feeling?"

"Solo, you have no idea how I'm feeling, but after I get threw with you, you gon' have a clue."

"Hold up, Shannon, what brought all this on?"

She put her hand between her legs and said, "Do you want to play twenty-one questions, or do you want to play with this pussy?"

With that, no more words were said. Solo took her right there on the spot. However, little did Solo know, tonight he would find out what a "wild thing" really meant. Shannon was into violent sex; the art of lovemaking was lost on her. If it wasn't rough, it wasn't going down with her! Recognizing that Solo played the game to the fullest, at the end of their escapade, one would have thought that they were both involved in a domestic dispute, instead of a lovemaking session.

*****

After Cruz's run in with the Locklords and the Businessmen, he went to the dentist that very next day and got an all-platinum and gold grill put in to replace his four front teeth. And soon after that, he got medieval. The first to feel his wrath were the DTGs. He rained hell on them to the point that the LAPD would only send the SWAT team when calls related to gang warfare in the downtown area were made. Within two weeks, the Hub & the Dub had complete control over the downtown area. Even though he knew where the Locklord Clan lay their heads, it was almost impossible for him to hit due to all the cameras that were installed and the heavy security deployed around the perimeter, which were on patrol 24-7. Even the Businessmen had beefed up their so-called staff, with about twenty more armed killers. The same heavy hitters he was unable to get on his team were now working for the Businessmen. It was as if somebody had tipped them off. So he put one of his girls by the name Candy Cane on the job, as he suspected the leak was an inside job. Come to find out that Tip Toe was related to Don Juan and had been playing both sides against the middle. See, Candy Cane was what Cruz called "The Great Equalizer." She was a fine-ass Filipino broad mixed with black, and it had been said that the pussy was to kill for if it didn't kill you first. See, she was a carrier of the AIDS virus, and Tip Toe had been barebacking her for a week and a half. Cruz took pleasure in bringing the bad news to the man at a get-together yesterday. He saw Tip Toe getting at this fine little honey, and as easy as this Cruz just said, "This nigga's been fuckin' a bitch with full-blown AIDS, trust me. You don't want any of that dick."

As the little cutie walked away, Tip Toe asked Cruz what the fuck was he talking about, and Cruz plainly spoke, "I'm talking about you trying to cross me with your punk-ass cousin. I'm talking about you being a walking dead man, and I'm talking about my bitch Candy Cane, a.k.a yo' death wish, nigga! That's what I'm talking about! Now get the fuck on and go die in peace before I just kill yo' ass right here on the spot."

Cruz knew that he had made more than just a foe on this day, but nothing really mattered to him the way it used to. When he found out that Maria was fuckin' his son, that hurt but it almost killed him when he found out that Rose was with Donald Stanton, a.k.a. Don Juan. He still loved Rose, and he couldn't stand knowing that another man loved her aside from a trick, and the worst part of it all was that she was loving him back. As Cruz sat in his undercover bucket at the end of the block, he couldn't help wonder how things had gotten so out of control. "How did it come to this?" he spoke the words out loud, not caring that Tomcat was seated on the passenger seat witnessing him somewhat falling apart. Not understanding this new side that Cruz was showing, Tomcat decided not to comment one way or the other. Just then, a car at the other end of the block flashed its lights. It was Bandit and Bam. Seeing what they were warning him of, he flashed his lights back at them in order to tell the men to continue as planned. With that, Bandit and Bam exited the stolen car with pistols in hand. Cruz looked at Tomcat and said, "If I can't have the bitch than the bitch need not to exist."

*****

"I really enjoyed myself this last week, Donald."

"Well, if that's the truth, Rose, why don't you show a brother how much by moving in with him."

"Donald, I still think it's too soon, but that won't stop me from being your bed buddy until such a time," she said with a smile as she wrapped her arms around his neck. Just then, she noticed the flashing lights of a car at the end of the block. "Donald, I thought you told me that it was just us tonight."

Without turning around to look in the direction that Rose was talking about, Donald Stanton said, "Keep your head about you, stay focused, and get your heater ready. It might be something, and then again it might not, however it's better that we're prepared."

Rose made as if she dropped her purse, only to pull out the .380 she had strapped to her inner thigh.

*****

"They took the bait," Cruz almost said as if he were sorry that they had. Seeing his lights flash, Rose and Donald Stanton started walking in the other direction, not aware that Bandit and Bam were waiting to ambush them. The night almost moved in slow motion from that point on. Rose noticed a street hooker being reprimanded by her man, or pimp, a hundred feet away.

"Where's the rest of my money, bitch?" the man asked the woman angrily.

"That's all I got, Daddy, please don't hit me again!"

Somewhere in the night, a baby was crying, and in that moment Rose wondered about having another baby, but this time with a real man who would truly love her and the baby. She wondered if the bum laying in the gutter up ahead ever had known true love. The gun she had in her hand, all of a sudden, didn't fit as it had in times past. Nevertheless, even in the face of unseen danger, she felt safe with the likes of Donald Stanton. As they made their way past the hooker that was getting her ass kicked by her man, Rose wanted to dump on him and take him out of the game for whoopin' on a defenseless woman that way but let it go as in this city you were better off minding your own business.

"Don Juan!" the pimp called out all of a sudden. As we, once again looked in their direction, it became crystal clear that Rose should have shot the pimp dead after all.

*****

Bam and Candy Cane were putting on an Academy Award performance when they flipped the script to some gangsta shit, Cruz thought to himself. As from where he sat, ready to play his part in the drama, he could see the fire jumping from Bam's .357 Magnum, sending Don Juan airborne. But much to his surprise, he also saw fire jumping from Rose's fingertips, sending Bam into a tailspin. Candy Cane tried to run away, but it's hard to run with a hole in your head.

"Hey! What's going on?" the bum said as he stumbled out of the gutter. At first, there was no real threat coming from him; that is, until he raised his hands as if to question, "What is going on?" Then the threat was revealed at the sight of the twin 9 mm Glocks he had hidden underneath the blanket that was wrapped around his shoulders. The bum was the Bandit, and he wasn't going to give her a chance to raise her gun in his direction.

*****

As he stumbled over, through the disguise, Rose could now finally see that it was The Outlaw Bandit Loco. Now, this was a man that was very close to Cruz, but at the same time this was a man who had two sides to him. He would talk about the things of God as if he were a preacher, and then he could kill a man with his very next breath.

"Rose," she could almost hear the very faint voice cry out. "Rose." Rose looked down to see Donald more dead than alive as he seemed to be breathing out of the three holes in his chest. As the air from his lungs pushed the blood out of his body, somehow he found the strength to get off two shots in Rose's direction. At first, she thought that he was shooting at her, but when she turned around, she realized that Bam tried to make one last attempt at glory. Nevertheless, he failed at his effort as his body once again dropped but dead this time.

Donald really did love me! Rose thought to herself as the world again started to move in slow motion. She turned back in Donald's direction only to see that one of the two guns that Bandit had pointed in her direction was now pointed at Donald.

This is my chance to live. Maybe I can even save the life of my one true love to be. Could I get my gun up in time? Why was the world moving in slow motion? Why is my hand taking forever to get the gun pointed in Bandit's direction? Here we go, I'm almost there. Come on, Rose, pull the trigger! My brain was commanding my hand to dump on Bandit, but fire was already flying out of his gun in the direction of my true love.

"Noooooo!" Rose cried out in vain, as her true love's face was no longer beautiful with a new hole in it. Now, her finger was more than ready to follow her brain's command and pull the trigger, but for some reason her brain was focusing on a new matter at hand.

She thought to herself, *Why am I lying on the ground? More importantly, how did I get here? Did Bandit get me before I got him?*

The world was no longer moving slow. In fact, it was now moving too damn fast.

"I got to get on my feet," Rose told herself, but it was as if she forgot how.

The next thing she saw was Cruz's face. Rose thought to herself, *Cruz will help me get up, he helped me when my mother threw me away at eight years old.*

"Cruz, help me get up from here, I can't seem to move for some reason."

Cruz placed the sawed-off shotgun that he had just shot Rose with on the ground and then he pulled her into his arms. "I'm right here, Rose baby, I'm not going anywhere. I'm right here."

Now tears flooded his eyes and stormed down his face as he pulled out his handgun.

"Cruz, am I going to make it? Will I be all right? Please tell me the truth, am I going to make it?"

As they sat in a pool of Rose's blood, Cruz simply said, "It doesn't really matter anymore, Rose. Nothing matters anymore. But know that I would never let you suffer."

And these were the last words Rose heard before Cruz pumped two bullets in to the back of her head, executioner style.

*****

"So what do you make of this situation, rookie?"

"Well, Lieutenant, we got three bodies here, two females and two males. We also got three handguns near the three of the dead bodies. I'm thinking a love triangle gone bad."

"Well, rookie, I wish it were that simple. If it were we would be home by dinnertime, but that's not the case in this matter. First of all, this fifty-cent-piece-sized hole in this one's back shows that there was another shooter with a bigger gun. And the two holes in the back of her head lets me know that this was more than just some kind of love triangle. No, the shit that happened here tonight was personal, rookie."

"Personally, I think it was a fuckin' waste of ass, Lieutenant. Look at her, she's a looker!"

"Yes, kid, but it is what it is. Did any of them have IDs?"

"Just these two, sir, Donald Stanton and Rose Locklord."

"Locklord? Hmmmm, Locklord… Wasn't that woman in the unsolved shooting downtown named Locklord?"

"That's right, Lieutenant, and get this, the dental work came back on the man that was blown up in Long Beach."

"So?"

"So his last name was Locklord, Kenneth Locklord."

"No shit, rookie?

"No shit, Lieutenant."

"Okay, rookie, you got two weeks. If you can tie this shit together, I'll see that you make detective without you having to jump through the hoops. Now let the next of kin know that this black beauty won't be making it home for dinner."

"I'm on it, Lieutenant."

Shit! I'm so fucking sick of this city that I don't know what to do, Phillip Sunset thought to himself. Deep down he just wanted to write it up as just another gang-related homicide, knowing that in a week or two it wouldn't matter one way or the other to anyone but their loved ones. It's funny, but in the ghetto they don't have the money to put up a fuss and for the most part, even their loved ones know that deep down, this kind of shit is a way of life in the concrete jungle. However, if the three Locklords are related and all have been murdered in the same year, somebody should have been putting up some kind of fuss. It was not that he truly gave a fuck, it was more of a need to satisfy his own sense of wonder.

"What kind of son of a bitch would be trying to delete a whole family?" he asked himself. And at that very moment, he got that funny feeling again. It had been many years since he had a true desire to really do some detective work. "Okay, little lady, we are going to go to bat for you and the rest of the dead Locklords," Phillip Sunset said as he made a call to an old friend.

*****

As Cruz walked through the doors to his and Sandy's Chino Hills home, he was a bloody mess from head to toe.

"Cruz! Oh my god, baby! What happened, are you all right?" Sandy shouted as she pulled his clothes, looking for bullet holes or some kind of cuts.

"It's not my blood, baby, it's Rose's."

"Oh? What happened tonight, baby?"

Before he could explain, a little eleven-year-old girl walked in, pulling her little brother of who was about six.

"Momma, what happened to Cruz?" It was clear that both kids bore a strong resemblance to Cruz, but he never claimed them as his own. This is why Sandy was surprised when Cruz told her that she could start bringing the kids over on the weekends. Up until now, her mother had been raising the kids, and to keep it real, that was cool with Sandy because they both got on her nerves. But Cruz was diggin' kickin' it with the kids, and that made Sandy really happy. And as long as she was happy, it made it a little easier to tolerate their little bad asses.

"Come here, Shay Shay," Cruz called the little girl.

"Yes, Cruz?" the little girl answered as she moved slowly toward his direction.

"How would you like to start calling me Daddy, Shay Shay?"

Sandy looked as if she was about to pass out. After all these years, this white muthafucka was ready to start playing daddy. but what the little girl said next took the cake. "If we start calling you Daddy, will both y'all start treating us like we y'all real kids? Will we see you and Momma more? Will you both stop gangbanging so we can be a real family?"

"Where did you get that shit from, Shay Shay? Yo' stupid-ass Auntie been runnin' her mouth, or did you get that from yo' wicked-ass grandmother?"

"Well, Cruz, they know too but I mostly get it from the kids at school."

"Bring yo' smart ass here, Shay Shay," her mother called out.

"Look, take your brother upstairs and run him some bath water, and don't make it too hot either."

"Okay, come on, boss," Shay Shay took her bother by the hand.

"She didn't mean anything by that, Daddy, she just a kid, what the hell she know?"

"She's smart, Sandy."

"I know, Daddy, too damn smart, if you ask me. So Rose is really dead, Daddy?" she said as she pulled his bloody shirt off him.

"Her, Don Juan, Candy Cane, and Gangsta Bam."

"Shit! Cruz, how they get Bam?"

"There was no they, Rose got him and Candy Cane before I got her."

"You mean to tell me, you're the one who pulled the trigger on Rose?" she asked in disbelief.

"What the fuck do you think, Sandy? If one of my dogs got sick, I ain't taking him to the vet so they can put him to sleep, I'll put him out of his misery my damn self."

She could see the hurt in his eyes despite the tough words he used. So she asked him if he wanted to talk about it. He looked at her and said, "What do you want me to say, Sandy?"

"I want you to tell me the truth about how you're feeling where this situation is concerned."

"Okay, Sandy, this is what I'm feeling. I'm feeling that I should have never let my mother drive a wedge between Rose and I, that's what I'm thinking, Sandy."

Sandy did not have to ask him what he was talking about, as he was more than ready to tell the story now.

"When Rose got pregnant, I knew it was mine. Hell! I was happy with the possibility of being a new father. To make a long story short, I was out of town when she went into labor. She was shopping on the other side of town when her water broke, and she ended up at the same hospital where my mother was the administrator over. The stupid little bitch named her son Conrad J. Cruz Jr., and when the paperwork hit my mother's desk, she looked at Rose's age and flipped her wig. The staff was trained to contact the police when the mother was underage. My mother was angry and ashamed of me. She told me to fix it or our relationship would never be the same again. I love my mother, so I fixed it the only way I knew how, I went down to that hospital and told Rose if she named that boy after me that I would kill her. So I'm feeling like I lost a part of me, Sandy, and now I'm going to lose another part of me because I have to kill my firstborn son."

"What about our kids, Conrad?" she said, still being jealous of Rose, even though she was a dead woman. Cruz looked up the steps to where the kids' room was then turned his sight back on Sandy and said, "If our kids are to survive, baby, then their older brother has to die after what happen tonight. So are you with me?"

Sandy knew she had to be concerned about how easy it was for Cruz to kill his firstborn son's mother, and that was the last flag that needed to be raised for her. She had been seeing someone else on the side that wanted her to leave Cruz. It wasn't an option at first, but now she had to think about the lives of her kids as well as her own. When he said that the kids' brother had to die in order for the two little ones to live, that was the very first time Cruz had ever referred to them as *his* kids, which was music to Sandy's muthafuckin' ears. Oh, how Sandy longed to be a family and now as soon as the danger was over, it looked as if her dreams could come true. But deep down she knew that if she stayed with Cruz, there would all ways be some kind of danger. Nevertheless, she had to play it off.

"Yes, my love! I'm with you until the wheels fall off this muthafucka!"

*****

As Tim was wrapping up one of his biggest sales he had ever made since he opened up the shop, his mind could not help but flash back to Rose and Jonathan. They had helped him when no one else would take a chance on his idea, and for that, he would forever be in debt. As he watched the six Harleys roll off his showroom floor, he thought back to the first time he met Jonathan. The boy had his arm in a sling but yet had enough heart to sell dope in a hood he did not belong to. When the older boys from that hood hit him up, Tim foresaw the trouble but wasn't sure if the little brother seen it coming himself. They had him backed into a corner when Tim stepped out on to his front porch, but the preteen was fearless and refused to back down. Little did Tim know that the kid had a loaded gun inside his sling when he said, "My momma got to eat too, dog. There's enough money out here for all of us to get paid, so let me get mine."

"We can see that you don't know any better, little nigga," one of the teens said. "So we gone give you a pass if you raise the fuck up out of here right now"

"Look, I don't gangbang, dog, and I really don't want no trouble. Feel me? But my mother is a hooker, and I got to get paid, so she won't have to hoe no more. So I'm not going to be takin' yo' pass, but at the same time, I'm not gon' be takin' no shorts either." Jonathan addressed the young men.

"What, muthafucka?" the older boy that had been doing all the talking cried out.

It was about to go down, so Tim stepped in. "You still need that ride, little man?"

"You know this nigga, Tim?"

"Yeah, he's family. Why, what's up?"

"He's trying to get paid on our block, that's what's up!"

"Well, shit!" Tim said, "I've been living here since 1975, so don't that make this my block too? Give me my money, little man."

Jonathan just looked at Tim at first, not knowing what he was up to, but Tim winked at him so Jonathan played along, hoping not to have to kill one of these muthafuckas about his money.

"Here you go, folks, it's all there, you can count it."

"Bet yo' ass I'm gon' count it."

The older boys just looked at Tim with suspicion, but before long they just walked away, puzzled to whether he was telling the truth or not.

"Get in the truck, little man."

As Tim drove him home, he asked Jonathan about the sling his arm was in. Jonathan told Tim that it was his mother's pimp that had shot him.

"What?" Tim exclaimed. "Did your mother call the police on him?"

"No."

"Why?"

"Because we gon' kill that muthafucka, that's why. Now can I get my money back?"

That's when Tim noticed the handgun that was in Jonathan's sling. His eyes showed the truth, and Tim sensed that Jonathan meant what he had said. It wasn't until much later that Tim found out that the pimp was Conrad Cruz, one of the most cold-bloodiest muthafuckas in Los Angeles, and on top of that, he was the boy's father. Life was really a bitch and then some on the mean streets of South Central Los Angeles. It was truly a dog eat-dog-kind of city. Now here it was, four years later, and the word on the streets was that Cruz was on the warpath; some new clique ran up in his spot with the Businessmen of all crews and roughed him up.

They should have killed him if they knew like I know, because now the streets are about to run red with blood, he thought to himself. He hoped that his young "knock" Jonathan wasn't tied up in this new bullshit, but deep down in his heart, he knew Jonathan was somehow involved. And just then…Tim's phone rang.

"Tim here."

"What's up hometown?"

"Sunset, this you, muthafucka?"

"Who else, Tim?"

"What you want, man? A brotha don't hear from you unless you want something."

"Come on, Tim, we go all the way back to high school. Can't I call an old friend just because?"

"Muthafucka, cut the bullshit, what do you really want?"

"Okay, you got me man, I'm investigating a new case."

"So what's that got to do with the price of tea in China?"

"Well, you know how the streets talk, Tim. I was hoping you could share some of that street gossip with me, my man."

"So who are you, Sunset? Are you Starsky or would you be Hutch? You gotta be one of them muthafuckas because evidently, you think I'm Huggy Bear or some kind of TV antic."

"Nah, my man, it's not like that at all. It's just that I got this case that's really starting to get to me. See, I got three unsolved murders."

"And what's so unusual about that in this city, Sunset?"

"That's the part that's getting me, Tim. Three different murders at three different times in three different cities within the county of LA. And well, they all have the same last names…Locklord."

"Locklord? Did you just say Locklord, Sunset?"

"Yeah, you know anything about it, my man?"

Before Investigator Phillip Sunset got the words out of his mouth, the phone line went dead.

*****

Almost simultaneously, Jonathan's phone rang as the buzzer at the gate sounded off.

"I'll get the gate, Papi," Maria said as Jonathan answered the phone.

"The Truth here."

"Jonathan! Shit, you all right, man?"

"Who the fuck is this?"

"This is Tim, my knock."

"Ahh, what's up, Tim? Why wouldn't I be all right, Big Daddy?"

"Jonathan, it's the police!" Maria cried out.

"What? Man, what the fuck is the police doing at my spot?"

"Jonathan!" Tim said loudly.

"Look, big dog, I got to get back at you, the police is at my spot."

"Do you want me to buzz them in, Jonathan?"

"Yeah! But make sure ain't no guns or other shit laying around that's not supposed to be laying around."

"Jonathan, is Rose there with you?"

"No, Tim, look I got to go."

"Look, I'm on my way over there—"

But the phone went dead before Tim could get the rest of his statement out.

"Damn it!"

*****

"Yes? How may I help you, Officer?" Maria said.

"Hi, I'm Officer Higgins, is this the Locklord residence? Does a Rose Locklord reside here?"

"Yeah, man, what's the fuckin' problem?" Jonathan cut in.

"Well, sir, she was murdered tonight. I'm sorry to have to be the one to deliver the bad news to you. Here's the address, we need someone to come down and identify the body."

Jonathan did not hear another word. It was as if his whole life was flashing before his very eyes. He tried to speak, but no words would come out. He tried to walk, but his knees only buckled. He tried to cry, but no tears would come out. He himself wanted to die, but death would not come at this very moment. As his body slumped to the floor, there was no life in his eyes even as he was clearly alive.

"Jonathan, baby, are you all right?"

He did not answer. Instead, Officer Higgins spoke for him.

"I don't think he is, ma'am. I've seen this before, you might want to call an ambulance, because he's going into shock."

CHAPTER SEVEN

*I*t's been three weeks since Rose's death, but it seems like a lifetime as Jonathan is still in meltdown mode, Maria thought to herself. Jonathan did not even make it to his mother's funeral. This was because he was still in the hospital when Rose was buried. Because Jonathan was still a minor, the doctor needed additional information concerning his medical history, so Maria had to go back to the house to attain it. As she was going through Rose's shit looking for the paperwork the doctors needed on Jonathan, she found her stash.

The bitch had 350,000 dollars put up, shit! she thought to herself. *With the 250,000 dollars I clipped Cruz for, I could just get lost somewhere, a place where nobody could ever find me.* Jonathan had been footing the bill for the whole Locklord clan, so Maria didn't think he had a lot put up, but when she had opened his safe, there was another 100,000 dollars in there. And 700,000 dollars was a lot of money! A lot of fuckin' money. *Then why is it so hard for me to roll out with it?* was the question she kept asking herself. *Solo and Shannon seemed to be lost without Jonathan's leadership. And me, I was just lost without Jonathan.*

He had been home from the hospital for almost a week now, and as Maria sat by his bedside just looking at his beautiful face, she was glad that he was asleep. As when he awoke, he just looked at the ceiling with lifeless eyes.

"Oh, Jonathan! You just got to pull up out of this!" Maria cried out to his lifeless body. "I can't handle this shit by myself," she cried as she buried her face in his chest. "Come on, nigga!" Maria cried real tears for the first time in a long time. "You said you had me! I got you, boo, was you words." Maria shook him in anger and fear of the unknown. "Why you make me fall in love with you if you was just gon' abandon me like this! Why did you lie to me? You said you had me! Why did you lie to me, Jonathan!"

"I do got you, Mami," a weak voice answered back.

Maria thought she was hearing things. She was afraid to pick her head up and look to see if it was real, only to be disappointed if it wasn't. However, she did and it was. Was her man back? She didn't know what to do, so she fired him up. He was so weak he could barely ward off the blows she rained down on him.

"You sorry muthafucka! How could you leave me like that?"

"I didn't want to, Mami, it's just that I didn't know how to be strong with the death of my mother. Tell me, how does one stand up under a situation like this, Maria?"

She had no answer for him. She did not know how to make him man up at the age of seventeen; that was something he would have to figure out on his own.

"Anyway," he continued, "I'm sorry." He reached up to pull Maria toward him and said, "But it's all going to be all right now, get the funeral plans together and let's go view the body."

Maria looked at Jonathan if he had come back with some kind of sick sense of humor, but his face had never been more serious.

"Oh Jonathan, baby." She could not find the words to say what needed to be said.

"What, Maria? Spit it out!"

"Jonathan, you damn near been in a coma for almost a month now. I buried Rose three weeks ago."

"What the fuck you talking about, Maria?"

"I had to bury her, Jonathan, that's what I'm talking about, baby."

"Bitch! Who told you that you could plant my mother without me being there?"

His hands were around her throat now, and instinctively, Maria's straight razor jumped into her hand.

"Jonathan!" she said through clenched teeth. "Yo' ass been all but dead fo' a month now, yo' momma's body was starting to stink, nigga. Cruz got muthafuckas watching our spot, and today I spotted someone tailing me until I lost them. I've been so scared lately that I was going to leave yo' ass here fo' the wolves to get you like your so-called family did, Solo and Shannon are gone Jonathan. But against all odds a bitch is still here, so get yo' fuckin' hands from around my neck before I cut that pretty face of yours."

With ice in her every word, only then did he see the razor, so he obeyed her command.

"I'm not going to hold this shit against you, Papi, because I know you're hurting right now, but you got to pull yo'self together or we some dead muthafuckas, boo. These muthafuckas are all over us. just go look at yo' cameras, damn it, you'll see what the hell I'm talking about."

He looked at Maria with eyes that had a lot of pain in them, but they seemed to understand at the same time. Maria could only wonder if he was about to slip away from her again, as his sea-green eyes told her that he could go either way, then he spoke, "Give me ten minutes alone, Maria, to mourn my mother's, death and I'll be right with you."

Maria displayed an unsure look on her face and Jonathan must have perceived it for what it was, because he said, "I promise you, Mami."

No sooner than Maria walked out the room, she heard the door lock, and then the next sound she heard was all-out chaos. "Jonathan!" she banged on the door, but he wouldn't open it. This went on for ten minutes as it sounded like he was knocking down the walls with a wrecking ball, and then the noise just stopped as suddenly as it had started. Maria continued to bang on the door, but another five minutes passed before he came out. But when the nigga did come out, he was fly as hell in his new Sean John fit, with brand-new Nike Air Force Ones on. His wavy shoulder-length hair was now pulled back into a ponytail, and with his Desert Eagle in hand he had that look in his eyes again.

My man is most definitely back.

"Where is the rest of the family, Maria?" was all he said.

"Daddy, they held up in a motel in Paramount."

"Well, let's get them!"

"Fuck them, Papi. Solo was scared to hold it down for you when he saw them muthafuckas watching the spot, and that little bitch that you think is so down for you. Where she at? You see, she didn't let no grass grow up under her feet trying to get the fuck out of here either. So fuck them! The only one that stayed down for you is myself and yo' boy Tim."

"Tim?"

"Yeah, Tim! He's the reason why the Businessmen are still providing us with some type of security. They were out here day and night at first, but they shit's falling apart now that Don Juan's dead."

"Don Juan's dead too?"

"Yes, Jonathan, he was with your mother when she was killed. If it's any consolation, boo, the word on the streets is that Rose got two of them before they popped her."

His face had half of a smile on it, so she told him of the kills. "She killed that slimy bitch, Candy Cane. And get this, she also killed Gangsta Bam! Jonathan nodded his head as if to say that one there is a good kill."

"Okay, boo, let's go get the rest of the Locklords."

"Papi!"

"Look, Maria, you were scared too, but you stayed down. That's why we have to go get them. Look, it's been said if you kill the head, the body will die. Well, we got to show the rest of the family that the head is still alive, back from the dead so to speak. Look, you got to understand that everybody not as gangster as you. Now let's go get them, okay?"

"Yes, Papi, but I ain't got to like it, do I?"

"Yeah, Mami, you got to like and love it!" he said as he picked her up off her feet and kissed her softly on her forehead. Then he put her down and said, "Thank you for staying ten toes down for me, baby, you know you're all I got left in this world. Right, boo?"

"Don't worry about me, Jonathan. You're stuck with me. I couldn't leave you even if I wanted to."

"And why is that, Maria?"

"Because I'm head over heels in love with you!"

"Is that right?"

"Yes, Jonathan, that's right," she said seriously.

She walked away, and when she came back, she handed him the whole 650,000 dollars and said, "This is how much I love you, and a million times more. Now, do you love me, Jonathan? And if so, how much?"

"Again, Mami, you all I got left in this world. Do I really got to say them three words to confirm what I'm feeling for you? Please, Maria, let me love you in truth within my own time. Don't back me into a corner just so you can hear what you want to hear. Okay, baby?"

She looked at him long and hard this time before she said, "Take your time then, Papi. But I want you to know this. Love can only live when it's being loved in return, so don't take forever."

With that, she led him to the camera room. "See that car, Papi?" She zoomed the camera in onto the car getting a close up of the two men sitting in it. "Those niggas don't have any business in this neighborhood, now do they?"

"No, boo, they don't."

"So let's ride on these muthafuckas and dump them out of the game, Papi."

Jonathan looked at her with love and said, "You don't like living here anymore, Maria, is that it?"

"Yes, I like living here, what type of question is that, Jonathan?"

He didn't answer her. Instead, he picked up his cell phone.

"Nine one-one, what's your emergency?"

"Yes, I was on my way back from the county club when I spotted two black males with handguns entering a car."

"Where are they now, sir?"

"Strangely enough, they're still sitting in their car on Beach Front Avenue and Ocean Street."

"And what's your address, sir?"

"Look, I don't want any trouble," Jonathan said, using his best white man's voice. "I don't want them to come after me. What if they find out my address somehow? No. No, forget I even called."

Click!

Maria was cracking up in the background.

"Now what, Jonathan?"

"Now, we just watch the cameras until Five-O gets here."

"You got game, baby! I would have never thought of that."

"Yeah, well, go get some of your shit together because we ain't gon' be able to stay at the house for a while."

"Papi, do you really think we gon' make it through this shit?"

Before he could answer, she continued, "I just want you to know that I would never think less of you if we just took the money and got on a plane to go somewhere, Jonathan."

He pulled her close to himself, kissed her long and softly on her full lips, and said, "The funny thing is, boo, that if you condone such an act by a nigga you with, it'll be me that would think less of you. Now, are you saying that yo' man should run off and hide?"

"No, Daddy."

"Then get yo' shit, so we can ride."

As they pulled out the driveway in the Range Rover, the police had two men in cuffs. Jonathan rode by slowly, looking right at the men. No words were needed, as they both knew that he was the one that called the police. And he wanted them to know.

"Rose was wrong, Maria," Jonathan said as they pulled into traffic.

"How's that, Papi?"

"We can't go head to head with Goliath, he's too damn strong for us right now, and he has too many soldiers coming at us."

"So what we gon' do, Jonathan?"

"Guerilla warfare is what we're going to do. We gotta get down like he's getting down."

"How's that, Papi?"

"He's try'na get us out in the open so he can finish the rest of the Locklords off. But we gon' lie low and get down like he got down, and when he shows his face, we gon' chop his muthafuckin' head off!"

"Well, Papi," Maria said, not knowing how he'd fell about her next statement; nevertheless she said it anyway. "I know where Cruz's mother lives. Oh and Sandy's mom too."

Jonathan looked at her without blinking an eye and said, "Then there's no reason why they should both be alive by the end of the week. Right, Maria?"

Before she could answer, he told her to get Tim on the phone.

"Thank you for calling Harley World, this Tim speaking. How may I help you?"

"Tim! This is Baby Locklord."

"Son of a bitch! They were counting you out, Baby Locklord! But of course, I said that you'd snap out of it, and you did! That's my boy!"

"Look, Tim, I don't want to talk over this phone if you know what I mean, so can you meet me in Paramount?"

"Hell yeah! There's some shit that I need to put you up on anyway, kid."

"Okay, here's the address, Ready?"

"Yeah."

"Okay, it's 2334 West State Street. Oh and, Tim, come alone."

"Will do, Big J. By the way, I'm sorry about Rose. I got your back on whatever, all right?"

"Cool. I really need you man, peace out."

After Tim got off the phone, he thought to himself, *Well, it's time to pay my debt. God have mercy on us. I got a feeling this shit's about to hit the fan.*

*****

Tim pulled into the motel about one minute after Jonathan and Maria arrived. They all embraced one another then walked to the room together.

Knock, knock, knock!

"Who the fuck is it?" Solo shouted at the door with his 9 mm in his hand, paranoid as fuck.

"It's Baby Locklord. Open the muthafuckin' door, nigga!"

"Baby Locklord!" Shannon screamed, jumping off the bed as she ran to open the door. "Baby Locklord, please don't be mad, we didn't know what else to do."

Shannon was all over him as if Maria weren't even there.

"Don't trip, shorty. A bitch is only going to be as strong as her man is. Wouldn't that be right, Solo?"

"Look, Jonathan—"

"No, nigga! It's The Truth to you. Now address me as such!"

Solo just looked at Jonathan. He still had his gun on his lap, but Jonathan did not seem to care. Solo looked at Maria, who had a 9 mm of her own in hand, and her eyes seemed to almost be daring Solo to go for his gun. "Nigga, say my muthafuckin name!" Jonathan said, this time rushing up on Solo.

"The Truth, man. The Truth! Why you trippin', cuzz?"

"Muthafucka! Are you fo' real?"

He looked at Maria and said, "Boo, tell me this nigga's plyin' with me!"

"I don't know if he even got enough heart to play with you, Daddy," Maria said, trying to pump Solo up.

"I'm trippin' 'cuz my mother, that would be yo' sister, is dead! I'm trippin' 'cuz yo' mother and brother are dead! And if that ain't enough, muthafucka, I'm trippin' 'cuz you a Locklord, but you hiding like some fuckin' coward!"

Solo just hung his head, but Jonathan lifted his face up and looked directly into his eyes before saying, "You got to man the fuck up, dog! I need you because I can't do this shit by myself. We blood, Solo." He put his mouth to Solo's ear and said, "Locklords don't hide, we ride. Wasn't that what you told your homeboys?"

Solo just nodded. "So you with me or what?" "Yeah, I'm with you, Truth."

"Until the death, my nigga?"

"Until the death, dog."

Jonathan then pulled Solo's face into his and kissed him on the lips mafia style before saying, "I'm going to hold you to it this time, family. Trust that I'm going to hold you to those words. Now that the family is cool again"—he looked at each person in the room—"let's get this meeting started. You got the floor, Tim."

"Well, J. I got this old friend that I went to school with that's a cop. He's on the Locklord case, so it won't be long before he finds out that all three of them that were murdered are all related."

"Can we use him, Tim?"

"Not this one, Jonathan. He's a hard-ass, but he on the up-and-up. I don't think he can be bought."

"Does he know about me and Solo?"

"Well, he doesn't know you as Jonathan, but he got your birth name of Baby Locklord."

Shannon broke in, "I didn't know that was your real name, Baby Locklord."

But Jonathan ignored her, so Tim continued. "And I don't know that much about Solo, but if his name is Derrick G. Locklord, then Detective Sunset is up on him too, J."

"Shit! Who is this fool?" Solo screamed. "And how'd he get all this information?"

"Kick back, Solo, everybody in this room family."

"Don't trip, youngblood," Tim said. "All he got is a name. Other than that, he's just fishing. The trip part about it is, I really think he's trying to help, I mean, he's really trying to solve this case. And in the end, that can only benefit the Locklord clan."

"Anything else, Tim?" Jonathan asked.

"Well kid, there is one other thing. The connected Men of Business and/or the Businessmen as they're known, well their shit's raggedy right now, Jonathan."

"And? What the fuck's that gotta do with us, Tim?"

"Everything, son, everything! Rose is dead right now because the leader of that organization failed to protect her. Now, I'm just an old cat, but if I were a young man about your age, I would feel as if the organization was my inheritance. Feel me?"

Tim looked around the room at each person before speaking again. "Look, Jay, I don't really know none of these other folks in this room but you do. So can I keep it real in front of them?"

"Again, Tim, we all family in this room."

"Yeah okay, well, here's the get-down Jay, you not going to take Cruz down with just this lot, no matter how down you think you are. But with the help of an organization behind you, the world is yours."

"How, Tim?"

"Heart, Jay, with heart. That's all I got, kid, but in closing, if you don't make your play, your father will and then his plan will be complete."

Maria nodded her head, being knowledgeable of what Cruz's plan is.

"Let's do it, Papi."

Jonathan looked at everybody in the room to see if they were in agreement. All nodded in approval.

"Okay, that will be the first order of business. So where do you stand where all of this is concerned, Tim?" Jonathan asked.

"I got ten guys at the shop I can depend on, and I got another five, whom I had guarding your house."

"I was under the impression that the men that were guarding my house were members of the Businessmen."

"No, Jay, those are some cats that I served with in Vietnam, personal friends of mine."

Jonathan just stared at Tim. He trusted Tim and knew that Tim had his back, but taking over the Businessmen was a golden opportunity and since Tim already had connections inside. Jonathan could only wonder why Tim wasn't taking control of the reins himself.

"Why me, Tim, and not yo' damn self?"

"Well, Jay, it's like this. You're the heir to the throne, kid. You father is the evil king right now, and even if the streets aren't talking about it, they know he killed your mother and so do we. You're the fuckin' Truth. The goddamn prince of LA, only the street don't know that shit yet, but we do!" Tim looked around at the rest in the room. "Somebody's bound to kill Cruz, it's just a matter of time. But tell me, who has more right to do that than you? It's your destiny, kid!

See, I'm an old playa, but I'm the one that knows if you stay true to the game, the game will stay true to you. You and your mom played fair with me, now I'm just paying my debt back. And to answer your question, Big J, I stand with The Truth. It's like you said, we all family in this room, right?" The room let out a resounding "HELL YES!" as they were inspired by Tim's short speech.

"Okay then, get yo' shit, Solo, we need to find you and Shannon a better spot that this."

"Why can't we just stay with you and Maria, Baby Locklord?" Shannon cried out."

"Because that's not gonna happen after the shit you pulled, bitch!" Maria shouted back.

"You made yo' bed with Solo, now lay in it, hoe!"

"Look, Shannon!" Jonathan said, to smooth Maria's words over. "All of us don't need to be in one spot together, at least not until this shit comes to pass. Now get yo' shit together so we can roll."

Shannon started packing her things with tears in her eyes. She really loved Jonathan, and in his heart he loved her as well. It had been seven to eight months since he had hit her off, and he knew that he might have to do it again in order to keep her ten toes down for him. He wondered how Maria would feel about a threesome. After they found her and Solo a spot in Cover City, he and Maria hit his and Rose's hideaway in Venice Beach. Maria was impressed that Jonathan had a plan. However, he didn't tell her that it was his and his mother's spot. He just said, "Nobody knows about this hideout but you and me now. And I'd like to keep it that way for our own safety."

She did not say a word, but she understood. "Can I show you in another way how much I truly love you, Jonathan The Truth Locklord?" she said in her I-need-it-right-now voice.

"You think you up for it, shorty?"

She just nodded her head up and down as she undressed. Her body was so tight that just the sight of it was always enough to erect Jonathan's manhood. She had taught him every trick she had known in order to get a woman off, and tonight she hoped he was up to using each and every one of them. He picked her naked body up and folded her up in his arms as if she were a sleeping child. And as he entered the bedroom, he asked her how she wanted it. To this her reply was, "I want it any way you want to give it to me, Daddy."

As he sat her down on the bed, she removed his clothes, and as they both stood there like they came into this world, his next statement damn near made her cum all over herself.

"If I love you back, Maria, the way you say you love me, will I someday regret having done so?"

Tears formed in Maria's eyes as she spoke. "I'll never let you regret loving me, Jonathan. Just give me a chance, baby, that's on my life! You'll never regret it. Now fuck me as if you'll never have this pussy ever again."

With that said, she backed onto the bed with Jonathan in hot pursuit of her. Snatching her by one of her legs before she could get away, he pulled her already moist volcano in to the danger zone that would be his tongue. With his hands under her thick ass cheeks now, he buried the center of all that her love was into his face. With her clit in between his tongue and upper front teeth, he sucked her gently until she sang like Anita Baker. Maria's pleasure was so intense that she almost fought to escape what could only be described as pure ecstasy, but Jonathan's strength would not allow her to be victorious. Instead, he pulled her up underneath him and took her with long and deep strokes.

"Oh my god!" Maria screamed as Jonathan put her legs on his shoulders. With every stroke, he took everything she had to offer, until there was no part of her insides that wasn't consumed with the meaty nine inches of magic he stuffed up in her.

"Ohhh! Baby Locklord! Fuck this pussy! Fuck it, Daddy! Fuck it good for Mommy!" she cried out in unexplained joy.

After they had exchanged one position after another, after time had gotten away from them to the tune of three hours, after both had cried out in unashamed love for the other to show mercy at times, they then rested in sheets that told the stories where words couldn't be used. The kind of story that could only be explain how sex, love-making, and plain old "ghetto hood" fucking had a lingo all of its own, the stories in between the sheets.

"Maria," Jonathan whispered after he caught his breath.

"Yes, Papi?"

"I want you to start going a little easier on Solo."

She looked at him to see if he was playing before she spoke, and when she did speak, her voice showed no respect for Solo.

"Baby Locklord, I know that's yo' folks, but that nigga's on the weak side."

"Maria, that nigga's seventeen."

"And so, Papi? You seventeen too! What that got to do with it?"

Jonathan grabbed the remote control for the stereo system and played Jill Scott before he answered her. With the song "How It Make You Feel" banging in the background, Jonathan simply said, "Yes, but you and I both know that I'm a different kind of seventeen year old. Now don't we, Ria?"

"Damn! It makes me so fuckin' hot when you call me Ria, Papi!" she said as she tried to go down on him, but he pulled her back up so as to look in her eyes.

"Look, Maria, we all he got. And him, Tim, and Shannon is all we got. This shit's super real right now, so our every move is going to depend on the loyalty of one another. So we! That is, you and I are going to have to build the people up we deal with instead of tearing them down. So tell me you understand, beautiful?"

Maria did not say a word. Instead she reached over Jonathan and grabbed the phone. "Shannon, may I speak to Solo? Solo, it's Maria."

"Yeah, what's good, Maria?"

"Look, boo, I've been on some other shit lately, and I've been coming at you kinda wrong. So I want you to forgive me for being a bitch, know what I mean?"

"Damn!" Solo said, being surprised at Maria's new attitude. But he played it off as if he hadn't really been tripping of it. "It's cool, Maria, we family. I know how y'all get when it's that time of the month."

"Yeah whatever, nigga! Oh um, by the way, can Shannon come kick it with me tomorrow night? Jonathan got some shit to take care of, and I don't want to be in this new spot all by myself."

She looked at Jonathan, who had a puzzled look on his face.

"Maria, me and Shannon just fuckin'. I dig her, but she's Jonathan's girl, and that's the only nigga she answer to."

With that, Solo handed Shannon the phone.

"What's up, Maria?"

"What's up with you, bitch?"

"Nothing, just sitting here bored out of my fuckin' mind, and on top of that I am really missing Rose."

"Yeah, we didn't get along that much," Maria said, looking at Jonathan. "But deep down I miss her too. Anyway, a bitch gon' scoop you up tomorrow night and show you one hell of a good time. You down?"

"Hell yeah! That's if it's cool with Baby Locklord."

Maria couldn't believe Shannon. "Hoe! Don't worry about all that shit, just be ready at 8:00 p.m."

Click!

"That bitch crazy about you, Papi."

Jonathan did not say a word, instead he looked at Maria with eyes that asked her what she was up to.

"Papi, do you trust me? I mean really trust me?"

He looked at her and said, "With my every other breath until you can show me that I can breathe without you."

"And how might that happen, Big Daddy?"

He looked at her with sleepy eyes and said, "By some act of disloyalty."

"Well, that will never happen, so you gon' have to get used to breathing with my help," she said with somewhat of an attitude. "Anyway, Mr. Jonathan," she said, clearly mad. "I got you, so don't ask me any questions about that phone conversation, just trust me. That is if you can!" She said this and then turned her back to him. But that was cool with him. He fired up the half of blunt she was saving for her wake-up high, and that really got her attention. "Now you're trippin', nigga! You know yo' ass don't even smoke that shit, so why you playin' with me?"

But Jonathan didn't say a word. He just took the remote and turned up Jill Scott's "Hate On Me." Maria looked at him with disgust, turned over, and went to sleep mad as hell.

*****

When Maria woke up, Jonathan was already dressed and on the phone with Tim. She looked over at the clock, and it was only seven thirty in the morning. She looked back at this nigga, and he was suited and booted looking fly as a muthafucka.

Maria tried to act like she was mad still because she didn't have her wake-up high, but from the chair he was sitting in, he was looking all high class and proper. He tossed Maria an ounce of that sticky icky without even looking in her direction. The nigga had on a two-piece double-breasted royal-blue pinstriped suit with the businessman suspenders on like he was some kind of CEO. Maria could only wonder where he got the fit from, because his ass did not know how to dress like that. As he talked business on the phone, Maria rolled herself up a fat one, and yes, she did blow that shit before she brushed her teeth. When she looked back over at him, Maria noticed that Jonathan's hair was down this morning, with one of them Al Capone brim hats sitting on the knee he had crossed over his lap.

Damn, I wanna fuck him right here on the spot, Maria thought to herself. The scent of his cologne—Cool Water—did not help the situation either. At that moment, Jonathan turned into a man right before her very eyes, and she had never wanted him as much as she did at that very instant. He got off the phone and gave her that sexy-ass look he gave her the first time they met and every time he was feelin' himself.

"When you finish blowing yo' brains out, get dressed because we got a meeting with the Businessmen this morning."

Maria hit her blunt one more time before she even looked his way.

"Well, Mr. Locklord, a bitch not going anywhere with you until she gets as fresh as you."

"So get yo' fine ass up and get dressed."

"Don't even try it, nigga, you know I got to hit the stores in order to get that fresh!"

"You got to be fuckin' playing with me, Maria, you dragged three suitcases full of shit from the house."

She just looked at him with that I'm-ready-to-fight look with her hands on both hips. "Damn it! I can't believe you, Maria."

"Believe it, Baby Locklord!" She said his name with stank attached to it. Knowing he wasn't going to win this one, he just smiled to keep from getting mad.

"Then get yo' high-class ass up so we can get started."

As she got out of the bed butt-ass naked, she put on her sluttish walk to the bathroom in order to get him hard, and it worked.

They had to hit four stores in order to put one fuckin' outfit together for Maria. Jonathan could only wonder why women couldn't get all their shit at one spot like men could when every minute counted. Nevertheless, when she came out of the last dressing room, she looked like a million bucks. Now, if Jonathan didn't have the hottest bitch in California, he was inclined to believe she had to be the hottest one in LA.

"Damn, Mami! If I haven't told you before, know that I am telling you now, you are the finest bitch in the world!"

That was the very first time Maria had ever heard the word *bitch* come out of Jonathan's mouth in reference to her, but for some reason in the way he used it, she took it as a compliment.

"Thank you, Daddy. I think," she said with her mouth twisted up.

"Where we going to, Jonathan?"

"We got that meeting with the Businessmen this morning, but before that I got to make a stop. Is that cool with, you Ms. Thang?"

She did not even answer him. She instead fired up the rest of her blunt. She passed it to him, but he declined, which was also cool with her. Before she knew it, they were pulling into this dealership, and the first person Maria saw was Tim dressed to impress as usual and leaning up against a nice-ass Mercedes. Tim was fly for an older dude, and if Maria wasn't so in love with Jonathan, she could see herself giving him some ass. As they pulled to a stop, her eyes focused back on the Benz. It was a 2007 S550 sitting on Torino Machined Centers 22" rims, prison bar gray and fully loaded with the deep tint on the windows and a sunroof.

"Get all yo' shit out of the Range Rover, boo, and go put it inside your new ride."

"What? Jonathan, don't be playing with me."

"Too many people up on what you rollin' in and that shit in Cruz's name anyway, so I'm going to trade yo' car in and downgrade you a little bit. But at least this ride will be yours and in your name."

Maria screamed before she straddled him on the driver side of the Range and then kissed him all over his face.

"I love you, Papi. I love you! I love you so much!" she cried as she hopped out of the Range on his side and almost ran to the car. Tim tossed her the keys, and she snatched them out of the air without breaking her stride. Maria jumped around in her new car as the two men embraced and then Tim helped Jonathan gather his and Maria's things out of the Range.

"The rest of the shit that was in Maria's Maserati," Tim said, "I'm going to put in the truck of the Benz with the rest of these bags, J."

"Cool, I'll be right with you after I get me and Maria's hardware."

"Look, J, we are going to a meeting, not a shoot-out, kid."

"So if I shake you down right now, Tim, will I find you heat-free?"

"Shit, youngblood, I take a bath with my heater."

Both men laughed out loud.

"So how much we have left over, Tim?"

"Well, baby boy, with the trade-in you made off like a bandit. After all, it was a Maserati you traded in." Tim said, as he handed Jonathan the seventy-five Gs that was left over. He was also impressed with the knot he had pulled out, Tim got a little jealous.

"Let me put you up on some game, J. Never pay it in full, baby."

"Why?"

"Because they have to report all cash money purchased, so you should always pay on it for a year or two in order to keep the IRS off your ass. So I only paid it halfway off, that way Maria can make payments on it. And that will also teach the bitch a little responsibility, you feel me?"

"Cool, good looking, Tim."

"That's what I'm here for, Little Daddy, that's what I'm here for. By the way youngblood, you're too good to that bitch!"

"That's only because she too good to me as well, Big Daddy. Cruz really never done nothing for my mother or any of his broads. Everything that he's given them has always been his shit anyway. It's about time she gets something of her own, big dog!"

"Yeah I can see that, but a 2007 S550? Shit! No bitch is worth that much of a car," he said as he walked off to handle the rest of the business on the car. "All I can see them in is a bucket. But it's big pimpin' on mine!"

When Tim came back, Jonathan got out of the car and told him to follow them in the Range Rover to Solo's spot.

"By the way, I'm also going to give him and Shannon one hundred grand of this money to split. Sometime tomorrow, we will go out and get her a nice little get around to roll in."

"What the fuck, Jonathan?"

"Hold up, Ria. Before you even get started, this is they last ride, boo. They're not going to be eating off us anymore. And in any event, I got to see how Solo handles his money before I even have him oversee any part of ours."

"What do you mean by overseeing our money, Jonathan? Why would he have to oversee any money that has anything to do with us."

"Look, Maria, I'm going to say this one time and then I'm going to leave it alone. We about to walk off in to an unestablished business and take that shit over. Now what part of your mind thinks that me and you can do this on our own?"

Maria didn't say a word. She just kept her eyes on the road because she knew that he was right. "I know that I'm young in your eyes, Maria, and I know that deep down you wonder about some of the calls I make. But if we gone to pull this shit off, you have got to stop second guessing me, and I mean from this day forth! Now, do you understand where I'm coming from, Maria?"

"Yes, daddy," she said with a little attitude attached to it.

"I hope you do, Mami, because the next time we fall out in this manner, I can assure you that a little bit of shit is going to hit the fan, aight?"

Maria looked at Jonathan to see if she was really going to get at her like that. Over the six months that they had been together, he had grown another inch. He was now six foot one, close to six two. He had filled out a little more as well, now at 230 pounds. He had the build of a football player, my God, but did he look good. Even with that five o'clock shadow on his face that he was all proud of, even if he didn't say it, she loved him. So she was ready to submit all control to him, not only now but forevermore.

"Damn, Daddy! Yo bitch knows who's in control. You don't have to beat me to get me in line," she said, to lighten up the mood a little bit. "Put something on, Daddy, would you please?"

Next thing she know, DMX was bangin' hard and loud on the stereo system. "Y'all gon' make me lose my mind…up in here, up in here! Y'all gon' make me lose control…up in here, up in here! Y'all gon' make me act a fool…up in here, up in here!"

Jonathan was feelin' himself, and Maria liked that 'cuz the last thing she wanted was a weak nigga. No more words were exchanged on the way to Solo's spot. They just bounced their heads to the head bangin' sounds of DMX.

They pulled up slowly on Solo as he was washing his bucket. The nigga almost went for his gun until Maria rolled down her window, showing him that there was no danger at all.

"That's how you going to get at a bitch by shooting up her new ride?" Maria shouted as she flossed the Benz on Solo.

"Damn! That's how the new queen bee rolling now?"

"Hell no, nigga! This is how the Locklords roll from here on out!" Jonathan screamed out the sunroof as Tim pulled in to the driveway and tossed Solo the keys to the 2006 Range Rover.

"Nigga, don't play stupid! Didn't I say this is how the Locklords roll starting from here on out?

"That's what I heard, Papi!" Maria shouted from the driver side of the car.

"Is that a tear in yo' eye, my nigga? Shit! Daddy!" Maria popped. "I know this soft ass nigga not going to shed a tear?"

"You need to check yo' sawed-off bitch Baby Locklord, before I call INS and have her ass deported back to that shitty little rock she floated over here from."

"Whatever, nigga!" Maria shot back. "But I'm not surprised that you on some we-tip shit. Tell Baby Locklord who you going to tell on after you tell on me."

"That's enough, you two." Jonathan stepped in. "You mother-fuckas fight like y'all sister and brother or some shit like that."

But he could tell that they both were happy to have new rides. Nevertheless, Shannon look was not the same as all of theirs until Jonathan told her that he was going to buy her a car tomorrow. And before you know it, all three of them were dancing in the middle of the street to DMX, but Tim ever sticking to the plan had to rain on the parade.

"All right, that's enough of this shit. Come on, J, we got shit bigger than who gon' get a car and what not to do. Let's roll."

"Where we off to, Baby Locklord?" Solo said, ready to roll out.

But Tim gave Jonathan a look that said it wasn't cool.

"Not this time, dog, I got to take care of this business alone. But I want you to hear me well. Big shit's about to happen for all of us," Jonathan said as he handed Solo the envelope with the hundred grand in it. By now Tim was in the back seat of the car. Jonathan could hear him and Maria disagreeing over the music that was playing. All of a sudden, "Jaheim" started bumpin' the smooth sounds of "If you think you're lonely now, wait until tonight, girl." Jonathan looked around to see Maria with her mouth twisted up like a girl whose daddy wouldn't let her go out and play. When Jonathan looked back at Solo and Shannon, they both had real tears in their eyes.

"Look, you two, I want you both to split that, fifty Gs apiece. We ain't gon get all soft about this shit, seeing that I'm only giving this to you both to see if y'all can make this money work for you, as there will be no more free rides, feel me?

"I'll get back at y'all later."

"What we owe you, Baby Locklord?" Solo called after him.

"Loyalty is the only thing attached to that, family! Just stay loyal to The Truth."

As Jonathan walked to the car, Maria got out to let him drive, but he got in the back seat with Tim and said, "This yo' shit, we just here for the ride, boo, now let's push."

"Be ready tonight when I come get you, Shannon!" Maria shouted as she pulled off in her brand-new Benz. As they pushed down the road en route to their new destiny, Maria handed Jonathan the little black bag that contained their guns. If he had a plan, Jonathan left it unannounced from both Tim and Maria, but as she looked at him through the rearview mirror, his eyes told her not to worry. So Maria smiled at him as he handed her her gun. When she stopped for the light, she loaded her own weapon and placed it in her purse. When they pulled up to the Connected Men of Business Office Building, Jonathan went into a mode she hadn't seen him in before. He got out of the car and placed his gun in the waistline of his Stacy Adams suit. He buttoned up his coat and then put his Al Capone godfather-type brim hat with the blue feather and cocked it slightly to the side. The nigga was all gangster now, Maria was now the eyes on the back of his head.

"Where the hell did he get that suit?" Maria said loud enough for Tim to hear.

Tim looked at Maria then popped his collar before saying, "Your man is like a son to me, Maria. On top of that, he's The Truth, so it's my duty to make sure he dresses the part. Now, let's go do this shit."

At that, they both got out of the car. Tim took the lead, and they entered the building as if they had owned it from the very beginning. The two men at the door were clearly well-dressed gang members, but Tim walked past them as if they were not even there. Nevertheless, Jonathan never forgot a face. He looked at them, and they nodded to him, but he didn't nod back. They pushed up in to the conference room, and Tim spoke directly to the man at the head of the table.

"This is the young man I spoke to you about, Tip Toe! Baby muthafuckin' Locklord, a.k.a. The Prince of Los Angeles, a.k.a Conrad Cruz's firstborn son, a.k.a. The Truth, muthafuckas! So let it be told!" Tim said, as he looked around the table. "Now, let me say this before I sit my ass down. Y'all can deal with The Truth, or y'all can deal with his father, but one thing's for damn sure, you will deal with one or the other." And with that, Tim sat at the table with the rest of the men.

"Look at me!" the skinny half-dead-looking man thundered across the table. "I've already dealt with his father! His father already killed me, I don't have shit else to lose. I'm a walking dead man."

His voice lost some of its sting, only to regain it again when he said, "So why shouldn't I kill this muthafucka, him being Cruz's firstborn son and all?"

There was a seat open at the end of the table, so Jonathan pulled the chair out for Maria. He then took his hat off as well as his coat, clearly exposing his 9 mm to all twenty men at the table. After he looked into the eyes of each man at the table, he removed his hair tie and ran his fingers through his hair and made his way to the end of the table where Tip Toe was sitting. Without saying a word for the first ten seconds, he just looked into the eyes of a man that really did not have long to live. Nevertheless, Jonathan's eyes showed no compassion for the dying man. he pulled out his gun slammed it on the table and said, "Do yo' best, slick! But I want you to know this, nobody in here that's with you will get out of here alive. See, you may be dying, but me I came here to die, so let's get on with the business of doing so."

Jonathan was playing his ace in the hole from the jump, hoping that the five men Tim had told him that was with them were sitting at the table. Not knowing what was going on, Maria had her hand inside her handbag, wrapped around her gun.

"What the fuck you talkin' about, nigga?" Tip Toe screamed.

"This is what he's talkin' about, you sucked-up muthafucka!" Maria shot back as she stood and jacked off her 9mm.

Tip Toe let out an evil laugh before he said, "Is that all you got, Baby Cruz?"

"It's Baby Locklord, nigga!" Tim said as he stood up with his gun in his hand. He snapped his finger, and almost immediately, five other men stood up with pistols in their hands. "So show the New

Prince of LA the respect due to him, or the first muthafucka to die in this room will be you."

"You niggas done lost yo' ever-loving minds." Before Tip Toe could say another word, the phone on the table rang.

"Who is it? I told you to hold all my calls."

"It's not for you," the voice on the speakerphone said. "It's for Tim, but I think you're going to want to take this call," the woman at the desk said as she sat with a pistol to her head.

"Then put it through!"

"Tim, we up in this bitch and we got all exits covered. Tell Baby Locklord, on his word we'll set it off on this hoe."

Jonathan looked around the table and said, "I don't have any beef with anyone at this table. Just to show you where I'm coming from, anyone that wants to get one can just walk out the door, and you got my word on that. But those that want to stay on with this organization can do so with a 20 percent raise in pay. However, and in any event, the bitch is under new management. So what's it going to be, gentlemen?"

Only two men got up and got on.

"What's up with these two niggas, Baby Locklord?"

The voice came over the speakerphone. "Let them go, I gave them my word."

Jonathan now spoke to the men at the table. "So I take it that the rest of you are staying on?"

One by one the men nodded their heads yes. Jonathan picked up his gun and placed it back in his waistband and spoke to Tip Toe again. "Look, man, I really don't mean to be rude, but you need to be about getting your ass out of my seat. If you're staying on, have a seat at the table with the rest of the men. If not, then you know where the door is."

Tip Toe looked like a boy who had just got his ass kicked and his brand-new bike taken from him, but he got up and took a seat at the table with the rest of the men.

Sitting down in the head chair, Jonathan told those with pistols still in hand to put them away and have a seat.

"For those that don't know me, I'm The Truth. That there at the end of the table is my wife, the lovely Lady Maria."

His wife, hmmm, I like how that sound, Maria thought to herself.

"But don't let the word *lady* fool you, she'd cut your throat at the blink of my eye."

With that, Maria flashed the razor she kept under her tongue at all times.

"Now, I ain't no gang member, and I don't have anything against any of you that used to be gang members. But we cannot have active gang members working here like them two at the door. Why? Because who knows where their loyalty lays. Cruz got a fuckin' army out there now. That's a lot of ears. We don't need no double agent running their mouths about our business, feel me? It will be business as always. Everybody does their same job. If for some reason you feel that you should be in another position and/or that you should be making more money, get at Tim, and he'll get at me and we'll fix what's broken. Is that cool with everyone?"

Once again everyone nodded their heads yes.

As Maria passed out the money, Jonathan looked at each man to see what he could see on their faces.

"Are there any questions?"

"Yeah, I got one," Let Loose said across the table. "My name's Let Loose, I used to be from your father's set. Anyway, we're the thing that's stopping him from entirely taking over the Hub and the Dub, so if we kick the ones that are still bangin' to the curb, how much easier would it be for him to fulfill his plan?"

"I feel where you're coming from, Let Loose, but I'm looking down the road. See, this is a business, and nothing will bring it down faster than Five-0 finding out that there's gang activities involved in it. However, your concern is noted, so I'm putting you in charge of finding out who's for us and who's against us. Is everybody cool with that?"

Nobody said a word, so Jonathan continued. "But them two brothas at the door from Rolling '60s got their own agenda, and I feel that it may cost us in the long run."

"I told these muthafuckas that shit about a month ago!" a cat named Tenguns cried out.

"Them LA niggas is trouble, shit! The sixties got beef with Compton that go all the way back to 1988 in the Crip Muldrow on the 4800 floor."

Jonathan did not know what he was talking about but decided to roll with Tenguns.

"Then that's it, we pay everyone from LA off and send them on their way."

One of the men at the table hopped up and said, "Hell! I'm from LA, so what's up with that shit?"

"What's up with it is that you're already paid, it's not personal, but you can be on your way now," Jonathan said, very business-like. "You niggas gon let this half-white muthafucka get away with this type of shit? I've been with the Businessmen one and a half years now, and this nigga just walk up in this muthafucka from the streets and fire me? I'm not even from the Rolling '60s. What's up with this shit, Tim?"

Tim knew that Jonathan called this one wrongly but rolled with him on it anyway. After all, Tim thought to himself, once the full plan is played out the whole house would be cleaned out anyway.

"It is what it is, Bo Pete."

"Well, I'll tell you what, Tim, fuck you and this nigga! I should be running this shit anyway!" he said, going for his gun at the same time. But this would be the last time he would ever make a play for it, as Maria got off five shots, slumping Bo Pete over the table.

"Damn!" one man cried out as he sounded like a scared woman. "She killed Bo Pete!"

"That's right, nigga, Bo Pete's dead! Now anyone else think that they should run this shit other than The Truth?" Maria violently asked.

Nobody said a word. Most just stood there, with a look of disbelief on their faces.

"Yeah! That's what a bitch thought," Maria added.

"Gentlemen, please—please have a seat," Jonathan said as the phone once again rang.

"This The Truth, but this really ain't a good time."

"Is everything OK with the home team, Baby Locklord?"

"We are all one team now, baby boy. However, we short a player now, so could you send in a cleanup crew?"

"I'll bring the van to the back door," the voice said over the speakerphone.

"Cool."

"Well, gentlemen, it seems that this meeting has ran its course a little earlier than I planned," he said, looking at Maria. "But I will see everyone here at 8 a.m. in the morning, won't I?"

Still in shock, the men nodded their heads yes. After everyone got on, Maria looked at Jonathan and said, "He was going for his gun, Daddy, I had to rock his ass to sleep. It was either you or him."

Jonathan just smiled. "Tim, what kind of new trouble is this going to cost us?"

"Not much, J, but we should get at his folks so the shit won't get misconstrued, with that 'he say, she say' bullshit."

"Cool, set that shit up. Also put some guards on payroll to watch the building and, of course, yo' spot and my spot in Newport. You got a way home?"

"Yeah. I'll get rid of the body myself then take the van to the shop and clean it up so that shit will be done right."

"Aight, me and Maria's outa here. I'll see you in the morning."

"J! You know that you the man now, don't you?"

"Yeah, I know. That's why Tip Toe can't see the light of a new day. Can you get someone on that, Tim?"

"I think that's something we should take care on our own. You feel me, J?" Tim said.

Jonathan did not bother to answer. Instead he looked at Maria and said, "Well, Mami, it looks like I really do have some business to take care of tonight. So you go and have some fun with Shannon tonight, okay?"

Maria looked over at the corpse, and with a bit of worry on her face she said, "Papi, I'm not leaving you here with these muthafuckas. We don't know who might make a play on you next. Hell no! I am not going, fuck that!"

"Did we not have this conversation earlier in the car, Maria? Tell me you're not second-guessing me again, Mami?"

"No, Daddy, I'm not. I'm just scared for you, cuz', we don't know these niggas! Some of them the real deal, Jonathan. Don't nobody got yo' back like I do."

He just smiled that Baby Locklord smile and said, "For the last time, boo, just do what I told you to do. Now let me walk you to your new car."

That surely put a half smile on her face.

"Please be safe, Jonathan, and come home in one piece."

Before he and Maria walked out of the building, they stopped at the front desk where the two dudes from the Rolling '60s were being held at gunpoint.

"I'm sorry, gentlemen, for this misunderstanding," Jonathan said. "We had a breach in our security and had to gain control of the situation fast."

"Man, who the fuck are you, cuzz?"

"I'm the new boss of this establishment."

"Don't I know you from somewhere, homey?" the men asked him.

Jonathan knew that they were the two that hit him up at World on Wheels a few months back, but he chose not to put them up on game. Instead he just handed them an envelope and said, "Here's two Gs apiece, that should more than make up for this misunderstanding. By the way, don't bother coming back to work tomorrow, this spot is under new management."

"Just like that, dog?" one of them called after him.

Without turning around, he said, "Just like that, gentlemen, this kind of shit happens every day, so please don't take it personal, it's just business."

After Jonathan put Maria in the car, he kissed her on the lips and said, "You the downiest muthafucka I've met, Maria. I really didn't see that shit coming back there. I was too busy feeling myself. And yes, I know nobody ain't got my back like you do, but I got to command respect from you in the presence of others, do you understand?"

"Yes, Jonathan, it's a man thing. But that male pride will get you killed."

"No, it won't, not as long as I have you backing my play, Mami," he said, which made her smile.

"So, Ria, what can I do to say thank you, boo?"

She looked at him with real love in her eyes and said, "You can start by changing my last name from Sanchez to Mrs. Locklord."

He had never thought about marriage before. Could he really marry an ex-hooker? She had caught him off guard with this question, but he knew he had to answer her quick, so he said, "As far as I'm concerned, you're already a Locklord as well as my wife, baby. But if you think you need a ring to make it official, we can talk about it in detail when I get home, okay?" He handed her ten grand.

"Okay, Daddy. What time, do you plan on coming home tonight?"

"About nine o'clock if that's cool with you, boo?"

"Can you make it ten, Daddy? I need time to get my surprise ready for you."

He smiled and said, "Okay, ten o'clock it is then, now get going."

She kissed him long and soft before pulling off. As the two men sat in their car looking at Jonathan and Maria, all of a sudden, it hit the driver. "That's it! Now I remember where I seen that yellow-ass nigga before! That's that young pimp nigga that calls himself The Truth! The one that had them fine young bitches putting in work at World on Wheels a couple of month back."

"Well," the other man said, "it don't matter who that nigga is, when Cruz find out that he's short-stopping his money, his ass is gon' be 'Truthfully' dead."

*****

Maria didn't want to go in, so she phoned Shannon before arriving there to make sure that she was ready to go by the time she got there. Sure enough, she was standing outside when Maria pulled up. Shannon almost ran to the car when she saw that it was Maria pulling up.

"What's up, girl?"

"You're what's up in this tight-ass Benz!"

"Yeah, it's cool." Maria was playing it off as if it were just another car.

"Where's Solo?" Maria asked, not seeing his Range Rover parked in the driveway.

"Girl, now get this, I haven't been feelin' that nigga as of lately, so he met some little bitch in the building next door. The hoe came over here, jockin' the Range rover and all that, the next thing I know, they roll up outa this muthafucka together! I started to show my ass, not that I care, but that shit's disrespectful. Know what I'm sayin'? Anyway," Shannon said kinda sadly, "I don't dig him that much to be living with him and all that, feel me?"

Maria understood fully but was determined not to feel sorry for her, so she put it out there.

"Look, bitch, I ain't gon' be playing no games. I'm not Rose, so don't be looking at me like some type of mother figure because I'm not. I only got yo' back because Jonathan go it, as I usually don't put up, roll, or even kick it with bitches. See, bitches in the end only want to fuck your man just like you want to fuck my man."

Shannon had a surprised look on her face.

"What?" Maria went on. "You thought I didn't know that you wanted to fuck my man? Well, I do know! So I'm going to let it happen, but that shit's only going to happen according to my rules. I call the shots over that dick!"

"What are you talkin' about, Maria?"

"I'm talking about you, me, and Jonathan pulling an all-night thing with some hot, sweaty, steamy sex. That's what I'm talkin' about!"

Shannon placed her hand over her mouth; her face was turning red with shame.

"Bitch! Don't tell me you're shy? What? Now you don't want to fuck, Baby Locklord?"

"That's not it, Maria, everybody knows I love Baby Locklord and that I would live and die for him. It's just that I've never been with a woman before." She said it with a giggle as if she had told a dirty little secret. Maria seen at that very moment what Rose loved about Shannon; it was that childlike innocence about the girl.

"Well, bitch, if you ever plan on fuckin' Jonathan, you may as well plan on fuckin' and getting fucked by me too. So it's time to grow up!" Shannon just laughed out loud at this point.

After they had gone to Victoria's Secret to get some sexy lingerie, it was back to the house. Maria really did have fun with Shannon and was starting to feel her. As they talked, she found out that the girl never knew her mother or father. Their stories were the same; both having been foster kids gave them an understanding for each other. That would be the bond that would hold them together from this point on. Once in the house, they put on the lingerie and started modeling for one another. Maria had been with a woman before, but this would be her first time breaking one in and turning one out, if you will and the thought of that, turned her all the way on. Shannon's body seemed so brand-new, she thought to herself. Everything was in place, nothing too big nor was anything too small. From head to toe she was just right in Maria's eyes.

"Come here, Shannon," Maria said in a husky voice. Shannon walked to Maria slowly until they were face-to-face. Maria took the last step, closing the gap, and then kissed her on the mouth. Shannon giggled at first, but to Maria's surprise she kissed her back. Maria pulled the girl to the bedroom and told her to lie down on the bed. Shannon did as she was told. Maria climbed on to the bed and parted Shannon's legs. Before Shannon knew it, Maria was eating her out.

God, it feels so good, Shannon thought to herself, but she did not know how to or if she should, express her appreciation to another woman. However, she could not help herself as she started pulling Maria's hair and softly moaning her name,

"OH GOD! MARIA, UHHH, MARIA, YOU'RE, YOU'RE, YOU'RE GOING TO MAKE ME CUM! OH MY GOD, I CAN'T TAKE IT NO MORE! OH SHIT, HERE IT COMES! UHHHH! HERE IT COMES! OH GOD, OH GOD! OHHHHH GODDDDDD!"

*****

As Jonathan walked through the door, the smell of sex strongly lingered in the air and the sounds of the "Oh my gods."

The first thing he did was pull his gun out. If it was what he thought it was, both Maria and the nigga she was fuckin' was going to die, if for no other reason than having the balls to fuck up in his spot. As he made his way to the bedroom door, the door was wide open.

Well, it's about to go down, he thought as he peeked around the door. *What the fuck?* he almost spoke the words out loud. Maria had her face buried in some bitch's pussy. Oh shit! It was Shannon! He just stood in the doorway at that point. He wanted to be mad, but just as fast as he wanted to be glad. He had always known that Maria was out of his fuckin' league, and now it was official. He looked at his Rolex, and it was 10:00 p.m. on the dot. So this was the surprise! He wondered how he was supposed to feel about it, trying to see the bigger picture, his brain telling him of the storms that could come with having such a relationship with two women, but as he felt his dick starting to wiggle inside his boxers, that same brain said, "Fuck the muthafuckin' storms, nigga! You The Truth! I know damn well you can stand the rain!"

He decided not to interrupt them. Instead he got undressed and started hitting Maria from behind. She was startled when he first entered her, but realizing it was her man, Maria matched his stokes as she continued to eat Shannon's pussy.

"Don't cum yet, Daddy! I want you to save it for Shannon."

This was the first time Shannon had realized that Jonathan was in the room. Maria pulled away from his dick and softly said, "Put it in Shannon, Daddy!"

Jonathan looked at Maria as if to ask, *Are you sure about all this?*

"Fuck this bitch for me, Daddy!" Maria said as she played with her own breasts.

"Fuck her brains out, but just don't cum in her, Papi!"

No more words were needed. Jonathan entered Shannon gently at first, but soon after that started fucking her like some street whore. Maria was shocked at the change in his sexual behavior with Shannon, versus the way he made love to her. Jonathan looked up at

Maria and said, "That's right, Mami, this is how the little bitch likes it. She likes it rough."

They were like two animals. Maria didn't like it rough, but watching them made her hotter than she had ever been in her life. "Fuck her then, Jonathan!" she cried as she played with her own pussy. "Fuck her brains out!"

"Oh my lord! Oh god, I miss this dick! I'll do anything for you, Baby Locklord, ANYTHING! Just say you won't take this dick away from me again, oh shit, I'm about to cum too!"

Jonathan blurted out in the heat of passion: "Oh shit, Shannon!"

"Pull it out of her, Papi, so I can drink it!" Maria demanded in a begging voice.

Maria lay down on the bed next to where he had been fucking Shannon, so Jonathan pulled out of Shannon and shot his load in Maria's mouth until it ran down the side of her face. As he lay between the two of them, they both snuggled up against him, and Maria spoke first, "Can we keep her, Daddy?"

"Please, Baby Locklord, can I stay?" cried Shannon. "I'll stay in my place, I know Maria come first, I won't be any trouble."

"Well, Papi, can she?"

He looked at both of them and said, "The first time one of you bitches trip, I'm going to kill both of you."

"Now, why would you kill us, Papi?" Maria asked.

"Because I'm not going to be able to see someone else receive the loving I'm getting from you two."

"So can she stay, Papi?"

"Yeah, Maria, she can stay."

CHAPTER EIGHT

"In other news today, known gang leader Tony Thompson, a.k.a. Tip Toe, was found dead with his tongue cut out and two bullet wounds to the head. And if that wasn't gruesome enough, the note pinned to his shirt further baffled the investigators. We have Detective Sunset here with us live on the scene. Detective, can you tell us anything about this murder and the strange note pinned to the victim's body?"

"Well, the murder is being investigated as we speak, so there's not much I can tell you at the moment. However, the note reads, 'Next time, do the job right, Father. With no love for you whatsoever, your son, the Bastard Child. PS. When, was the last time you saw your mother?'"

"And what do you make out of that Detective?"

"Lady, I don't know what to make of that. Nevertheless, that's all I have for you right now," the detective said and walked away.

"Well, Jim, there you have it, back to you for now."

"Thank you, Katy. Now in sports, the Lakers are on their way to the big dance…"

As Cruz sat watching the news, he tried to ignore the "whys" and "what fors." Nevertheless, he was unable to put two and two together.

Maybe it's some kid getting even for his mother of whom Tip Toe fucked over in one way or another. Anyway, fuck it! he thought to himself as his phone rang.

Ring! Ring!

"What it do?"

"You have a collect call from Tomcat, who is an inmate in the Orange County Sub Station Jail. To accept the call, please press 5. To reject the call, please press the pound key or hang up."

Beep!

"Your call is now being connected. Thank you and have a nice day."

"Why the fuck is you calling me collect, dude?"

"Because Get Off and I are locked up, man! That's why I'm calling collect, homey!"

"Newport Beach, let me tell you what happened, Cruz—"

"You done lost yo' mind or something, my nigga?" Cruz cut in. "Don't tell me shit over this phone, cuzz! Just sit tight, and someone will pick you up in an hour."

Click!

Fuck! These niggas makin' my shit look raggedy as a muthafucka, Cruz thought to himself as he called Bandit on the phone.

"What's up?"

"Is this Bandit?"

"This me."

"What the fuck is that I hear in the background?"

"That's a choir, muthafucka, what does it sound like?"

"Aww snap! Don't tell me yo' black ass is at church?"

"I go with my mother once a month, you know that, Cruz."

"Yeah! But that was when we were kids. You mean to tell me you're still keeping up that façade?"

"Whatever, muthafucka! Is there anything I can help you with before I get off the phone?"

"Yeah, when you finish giving the father seven Hail Marys, get one of them ex-crackhead bitches you fuckin with to go down to the Newport Beach Sub Station and bail Tomcat and Get Off out."

"Cool, I'm sure I can find one that's not *retarded* to the point where she can't handle business. Man, I told you them little niggas wasn't ready for a job that big. You ass never listen to me, so will there be anything else?"

Cruz wanted to tell his friend just how much he appreciated him for staying down with him through it all but didn't want to sound soft. So instead he kept it gangsta and disguised his appreciation for the man in another way.

"Let's do Vegas for about a week when this madness blows over, cuzz! Just me and you, Bandit. I'll pay for the whole trip."

"Yeah, Cruz, I'm down for that but you and I both know that the kind of life we live never blows over. I got love for you too! So fuck Vegas, my nigga, just buy me a beer and send me on the next mission, now do you feel me?"

"Yeah, cuzz, I feel you."

"Then tell me this, Cruz, do you still believe in God like you did when we was little, nigga?"

The question caught Cruz off guard. Nevertheless, Cruz didn't waste time in answering it.

"You know, Bandit, I really did believe in God. That is, until I realized I was possessed by the muthafuckin' devil. So no disrespect for what you believe, Loco, but fuck a god. The way I see it, I'm a god until a muthafucka prove me otherwise."

The next sound Bandit heard was a dial tone.

As Cruz sat staring off into space, he could only wonder how the game had changed and, without warning, gotten so much bigger than him. Yes, he was in control, but he knew at the same time that the streets were not going to let him maintain this kind of control for long. He had fucked over a boatload of gangsters on his way up, along with some of the old ones he had pushed overboard. There was a new and more vicious breed now helping to pull on the side of his boat. He wasn't foolish; even in his greed and lust for power, he understood that the longer he stayed in the game, it would be just a matter of time before his boat capsized. So now more so than ever, he was really ready to go legit.

The recording studio Sandy had started was doing okay, but he needed to repair his reputation within the community. His plan to unite two cities was working in part but in order for it to be a complete success, he had to get the rest of both cities on board. This was why it was mandatory that he gained control of the Connected Men of Business Inc. However, a couple of second-rate Crip gangs in South Central, Los Angeles, got word that the Hub and the Dub had took over the Downtown District, and now they wanted their piece of the pie. So in order to maintain control, Cruz had to insert one of LA's finest, the West Side Rich Rolling, Neighborhood Rolling '60s Crip gang, and this as he had to leave out the Grape Street Watts car. Cruz could not see them with half of the downtown drug trade action, but it was either that or another war, and that could quite possibly bring in the rest of the LA neighborhoods, this in order to back the sixties play. Now this was a war neither side wanted, but it was every other set in LA, and he had crossed the line. They didn't give a damn about the DTGs.

This shit is a clear case of blackmail that would cost the Rolling '60s dearly when the time is right, he thought to himself.

Yes, the game was surely trying to outgrow him. It was as if he had stepped into some quicksand, and struggling would only cause him to sink faster. So for now, all he could do was be still and let this shit play itself out. Just then, his phone went off. It was Cee Rag from the '60s. This nigga and his road dog S-Roc were the silver lining that would be in a dark cloud. They went to the highest bidder, played for the team with the longest money if you will, and they were the two Cruz had placed in the Businessmen's organization.

"Tell me that it's good news, hoodsta," Cruz said as he answered the phone.

"Shit! I hope yo' ass is sitting down, Cruz. 'Cuz if you ain't, this news might knock you down," Cee Rag said.

"C'mon, what's up, cuzz?"

"Well, a crew of well-armed, well-organized, and well-dressed muthafuckas pushed up in the Businessmen's spot yesterday and took that shit over."

"What?"

"That's right, Cruz, and get this, they taking orders from a young nigga I happen to know ain't a day older than sixteen or seventeen years old."

Cruz thought to himself, *It can't be,* and asked, "Did you happen to get this walking dead man's name?"

"Yeah, man, we met him about a month ago. I thought the young nigga was a small-time pimp, but he bigger than I—"

"Did you get his muthafuckin' name, damn it?" Cruz rudely cut in.

"Yeah, man, Truth! The Truth is what he calls himself."

At the sound of the name, Cruz hung up the phone. And then the detective's voice from the news program earlier popped into his head. The note simply stated, "Next time do the job right father. With no love for you whatsoever, your son The Bastard Child. P.S. When was the last time you saw your mother?"

"No, muthafucka, noooooo!" Cruz cried as he fumbled with his phone to call his mother's house.

*****

"You can have my money. I'll even take you to the bank and give you more, just please don't hurt me," the fifty-five-year-old lady begged for what life she had left to live. Although her two assailants still did not say a word.

"Is it sex you want? Because if it is, let's just do it and get it over with. I promise I won't put up a struggle," she said as she started to undress. The two men looked at each other, one shook his head no, but the other nodded his head yes, so his partner shrugged his shoulders as if to say, "That's on you." They had been held up in the lady's house for a day and a half now with one of the men fucking her off and on when the phone rang. As one of the assailants walked to the phone, the caller ID let him know that this was the call they had been waiting on. The man by the phone pulled off his ski mask and spoke for the first time.

"This is the call we been waiting on, so if you going to fuck that old bitch again, make sure she enjoys it because my father is going to be listening."

The woman did not know what was going on; maybe this was just some sick fetish that their whole family took part in. Well, it didn't matter, on top of that she hadn't been fucked like this in years, she thought to herself. If this meant she would stay alive, she was going to fuck his brains out, and if he wanted her to enjoy it, then that wouldn't be hard either in order to live and see another day.

Jonathan picked up the cordless phone as Solo took his dick out and shoved it into the woman's mouth.

"Hello."

"Who the fuck is this?" Cruz's voice thundered over the phone.

"Now come on, Dad. You know muthafuckin' well who this is, this is your bastard son! The Truth, you white muthafucka!"

"Jonathan! You don't want to do this, man."

"See, that's where you're wrong, Dad. I'm already doing it."

"Look, little nigga, take a minute and think about what you're about to do. She's yo' grandmother, you stupid muthafucka!"

"No! You look!" Jonathan thundered back. "How the fuck is you, of all people, going to try and reason with me? You the stupid muthafucka for forgetting I got the blood of a madman running through my veins. Nevertheless, this is what I'm gon' do fo' you, *Dad*! I'm gon' let you hear yo' mother enjoying the last bit of dick she'll ever have."

"That's your grandmother, Jonathan! You can't do that!" Cruz tried to protest, but Jonathan cut him off.

"You're right, Cruz, I can't."

Cruz sighed with relief at Jonathan's words.

Jonathan continued, "And I won't, but the ironic thing is that my uncle can, has, and is more than willing to continue to do so. You remember him, don't you? You should, you killed his mother, his brother, and his sister, and now at this very moment as a matter of fact he's up in our mother right now, long-dicking her right in front of me, now is life a bitch or what?"

"Don't do this, Jonathan," Cruz almost begged as he grabbed his car keys and headed to his mother's house.

"Not only am I going to do this, I'm going to let you hear how much she's enjoying it."

"I'm going to kill you muthafuckas!" Cruz screamed wildly over the phone.

"Oh, I'm sure that you're going to try, Cruz," Jonathan said in a deadly tone. "I'm sure you're going to try."

With that said, Jonathan put the phone next to the woman's mouth as Solo was hitting her off doggy style from behind.

Thinking this was the next phase in her assailant's sick fetish, the woman played along putting on the performance of a lifetime. One would have thought she was really enjoying it as she was backing her ass back up on Solo's dick. "That's right!" she yelled into the phone. "Fuck this hot pussy, you young motherfucker! Fuck it good for mama! Ohh shit! It's been a long time since it's been fucked like this, Big Daddy! Yes! Yes! YES!"

"Mom!" Cruz cried out over the phone. But his voice was muffled by Jonathan's hand over the ear part of the phone, so she never heard her son. Instead she found herself about to cum as Solo spanked her roughly on the ass.

"Ohhhhhhh Shhhhiittt! I'm about to cumm! Harder! Harderrrrr! Hit my ass harder, you fucker!"

"I'm going to kill you muthafuckas!" Cruz yelled once again as he made his way through traffic.

"I'm cumming!" she yelled again as her pussy juices painted the base of Solo's dick.

At that, Jonathan gave Solo the eye, and he pulled out of the woman and wiped his dick off on the back of her skirt.

"Please don't stop!" she begged, wanting more, that is until she saw Jonathan with the gun in his hand. "Please, mister! Don't kill me. I did everything you asked of me, please don't kill me!"

"Lady, this is not even about you, it's about you son."

"Who? Conrad? What's he got to do with all of this?"

"Why don't you ask him, he's on the phone."

"The phone?" the lady cried out. "But you said that your father was on the phone?"

"Look at me good, bitch!" Jonathan roared as he pulled her naked body to his person. "You mean to tell me that you don't see your son in me?"

She looked at the young man real good this time. "OH MY GOD!" she cried as her mind took her back to the day Jonathan was born, and now she could see clearly the little black girl that bore her son's baby on that day, the same girl that wanted to name the child after Conrad. As her mind took her back, she could remember her plot and the part she played in making sure Cruz would have no part of the baby nor the girl. *So it's come to this?* she thought to herself as she looked Jonathan in the eyes. It became crystal clear to her that she wasn't getting out of this alive. "You're Baby Locklord, you're my grandson, OH MY GOD! What have you done to me?"

Jonathan looked at her with nothing but hate in his eyes, until she sadly said, "And what have we done to you?"

"Ask your son, bitch!"

She put the phone to her ear and simply said, "Well, son, our sins have finally found us out."

"Don't worry, Mom!" Cruz shouted. "I'm on my way."

"Well, son, I believe that to be the truth, but I also believe that it's going to be too late. Just know that I have always loved you no matter what evil things you have done."

Cruz was now crying over the phone. "Don't worry, Mom, I'm almost there!"

She looked at Jonathan, who raised his gun to her head by this time, and she smiled with love for the grandson she would never get the chance to know. When she spoke again, her last words were "You know something, Conrad? This one: more so than any of your other kids, looks just like you."

The next sound Cruz heard was "*Click, click… BOOM!*"

"Noooooo!" Cruz's voice cried over the phone until the line went dead.

*****

As Jonathan pulled up to the gate of his Newport Beach estate in the S550 Benz, with Solo following him in the Range Rover, a man walked down the driveway and unlocked the chain on the gate.

"What it do, Cannibal?"

"It's all good, youngblood. I wasn't expecting you, though."

"So what you saying, Cannibal? I gotta call before I come home?"

"Hell no, youngblood, how do I say this?"

"Just spit the shit out, Cannibal!"

"Well, I've been looking out for the house for a month now, and I got a little lonely."

"So what you saying?"

"I got a young tender in there, Truth."

Jonathan just laughed and said, "Does she think this is yo' shit, as well?"

"No, man, I didn't get down like that."

Jonathan laughed out loud because he knew that the old man was lying, but he wasn't mad when he said, "Then who we supposed to be, O. G.? You sayin', we can be ourselves? We ain't gotta play if off like we someone else, do we?"

"Well, if you could just be my grandchildren just for the night, that would be doing me a big favor."

Jonathan just pulled up into the driveway, laughing even harder than before.

"It's so fuckin' good to be back home, Papi," Maria said with joy in her voice. Jonathan even had a smile on his face as he was glad to be back as well. He hit the button to open the garage, and there was Maria's Harley Davidson sitting next to rose's pearl-white Jaguar.

"There's my baby!" Maria bounced up and down in her seat, all excited. "I'm jumping on that shit tonight and rolling out, can I, Papi?" she asked before she had seen the sadness in her man's eyes as he stared at his mother's car. "Jonathan, are you all right?"

"I'm cool, baby. Just trippin' on the last time I seen my mother. That shit still hurt a nigga, just to keep it real.

"It's going to be all right, Papi, I'm not you mother, but Mommy can make it better if you let me," she said with her hand on his dick, which got hard instantly.

"It's good to know that I can still make it get up, Daddy," she said with a little girl's sad face.

"And what's that supposed to mean with yo' sexy ass?" Jonathan shot back.

"Well, you tell me, Papi. When's the last a bitch got some dick on the Solo tip? I mean, it's been two weeks since the last time Shannon or I had any. I'm tired of sucking pussy, shit! I need some of this dick up in me," she said as she was still holding on to it.

"You right, boo, I've been so tied up with the business at hand that I haven't been looking out for you, please forgive me. This is what we gon' do. You gon' give Shannon yo' hog and—"

"The hell I am!" she cut him off.

"Okay cool, I'll just buy her a new one."

"My bad, Daddy. I'm trippin', you can give her the old one. Does that mean I'm going to get a new one?"

"That's the plan, boo! Because there's no way I'm letting you roll out on yo' own! So start teaching her how to ride."

"Damn! Every time I bounce she gotta come with me?"

"Do I have to answer that stupid-ass question, Maria?"

"No," she said as she looked at him with a sad face.

"Now don't make me spank that ass."

"Nigga, don't promise me a good time and not deliver it, bad as a bitch need spanking right now, spank this wide ass if you got the heart!" she said as she raised her ass up in the seat, and both of them started laughing hard.

"Jonathan."

"Yes, baby?"

"Are you in love with me?"

"You know I am, Ria."

"Then you need to do right by me, Jonathan The Truth Locklord. I shouldn't have to say the 'M' word, Papi. You said you was gon' get at me about it the last time I said the word. But in truth, I feel like you try'na play yo' boo. Now, I'm a big girl, if you not feeling me that way, just say it and I'll freeze on that shit."

Just then, Solo knocked on the window of the Benz. "Y'all coming up out of there or what?" Shannon said, feeling a little left out of the loop as she stood next to Solo.

"Yes, bitch," Maria said. "Just keep yo' thong on. Well, let's get out, baby."

"Maria, you right, don't worry. I'm going to do right by you."

She gave him a kiss on the mouth and said, "We will see, Papi, we'll see."

Once they got into the house, Maria's whole disposition changed when she saw what looked like a street hooker sitting on her brand-new sofa.

"Oh hell no!" she said right before Jonathan put his hand over her mouth.

"Hello, miss. We the grandkids. We just gon' go up to bed now, you and Grandpa have a nice time."

Solo and Shannon burst out in laughter, but Maria was bitchin' all the way up the steps.

They all went in to the camera room to spy on the hooker and her sugar daddy.

"Turn that shit on, J!" Solo cried out as if it were the latest porn DVD.

"Hold the fuck up, dog, you know I don't know how to work that shit that good, this yo' department, nigga!"

"Then get yo' ass out the way and let me do it, J."

Jonathan stepped aside, and Solo went to work. Before they knew it, he had it zoomed in on the living room where Cannibal had just walked through the door.

"Watch this, and know that Big Brother is in the house, mutha-fuckss!" Solo then flipped a switch and tuned up the sound clear like their favorite radio station.

"Ain't that a bitch!" Jonathan said. "Why you didn't tell me this shit pick up sound, Solo?"

"Shit! You the one who paid fo' Big Brother! I just assumed you knew."

Jonathan wondered how often Solo had used this little bit of entertainment for his own pleasure, then said to himself, *Fuck it! If that's the way the nigga gets his kicks, so be it.*

"Turn that shit up a little bit," Maria said.

"I don't think your grandbabies are feeling you having me here this evening, Big Daddy," the lady said.

"Well, let them feel whatever they feel, little momma. Right now, all I care about feeling is you sitting on this big black dick," Cannibal said as he whipped it out.

"What? Oh hell muthafuckin' no!" Maria screamed at the top of her voice. "Jonathan! I know you not gon' let that old-ass niigga fuck that two-dollar-ass hoe, on my muthafuckin' brand-new sofa?" She tried to go for the door, but Jonathan snatched her off her feet before she reached her destination.

"Slow yo' ass down, Ria, it's just a couch."

"Yeah, how you just gon' stop a nigga before he get his nuts off, Maria?" Solo said, almost drooling over what was about to take place.

"You muthafuckas on some freak shit," Shannon said even as her pussy needed some dick to bounce on.

"Damn, Big Daddy," the hooker said as she slipped Cannibal's dick inside her already moist pussy.

"That old muthafucka is hung like a bull!" Shannon said.

"Yeah, but look at this bitch," Maria added. "Her nasty-ass pussy's like the black hole. The stank bitch done swallowed the whole shit up already."

They all broke out in laughter as Solo zoomed the camera in even closer. Jonathan had the top-of-the line camera equipment installed in and outside the house. The picture was so clear that they can almost see her love juices as they painted his nine- to ten-inch pole.

"Yes! You big-dick muthafucka! Yes!"

The sound came clear over the camera-room sound system.

"I don't care what y'all say about this bitch," Jonathan said. "This bitch can ride a dick."

"Oh shit!" Cannibal cried out. "Ooooh shit! You freak-ass bitch! Come on then, make a nigga cum then!" Her ass was jumping up and down like a jackhammer. "That's it, you freak bitch! That's it! I'm cumming. Here it comes… AHHHH AWWWW SHHITT!"

The house was quiet, and the only sound that could be heard in the camera room was the sound of Cannibal's heavy breathing. And then without warning, the silence was broken when the hooker said, "You gon' let me spend the night, Daddy?"

Cannibal smiled at the hooker and handed her what looked like forty bucks and said, "Nah, bitch, that's not going to happen, but if you got a card, I'll take that, and we can do this again someday soon."

"Damn!" The camera room erupted as one. "This shit like some kind of hood-rat soap opera," Solo said laughingly.

"So that's how you feel? Can I at least get a ride home?"

"Well, you see that my grandkids are here now, the best I can do for you is call you a cab."

"Damn! You gon' at least pay the cab fair?"

"Now I can do that." Cannibal handed her another 20 bucks and showed her where the phone was.

"Abidi-abidi-abidi-that's all folks!" Jonathan said as he used his best Porky Pig voice before turning off the living-room camera.

"Well, Solo Loco and ladies, we gon' call it a night. And that means all of us. The streets too muthafuckin' hot right now for any-one to be riding Solo. Now, I know that after what we had just seen, everybody's a little horny."

Jonathan looked into the eyes of everyone in the room and he saw that they all knew what he was talking about.

"So this is what we gon do. Shannon?"

"Yes, Baby Locklord?"

"I know that you're in love with me, but I need to know if you love me enough to do anything I ask you to do!"

"Anything, Baby Locklord."

"Then I'm going to need you to give my uncle some of that sweet-ass pussy of yours. I don't want no one creeping out this muthafucka. Now, you ain't gotta do it, I'll respect you one way or the other. So what's it going to be, little mamma?"

Shannon looked at Jonathan for a long moment before saying, "Jonathan, I'd jump in front of a bullet for you, kill ten men for you, so if you want me to fuck this nigga for you, consider it a done deal. All I have is one request. I'm not going to do any kissing or sucking, and we must use a rubber. Is that cool with you, Baby Locklord?" she said with somewhat of a hurt in her voice.

Jonathan walked up to her and ran his hands through her hair, looked her in the eyes, and said, "You have always been loyal to me, Shannon, know that a part of me dies every time your loyalty to me costs you something because of a request made by me."

He then pulled her close and kissed her with the most passionate kiss he ever gave her. After it was over, she looked at him lovingly then took Solo by the hand to do what she had been asked.

"Hey, you two! We meet at 8:30 a.m. to go over how we gon' get at Cruz."

As Jonathan pulled Maria to their room, she stopped him once they had got in the room.

"How the hell did you get so smooth, Jonathan?"

"Boo, what you need to be asking or telling me is how do you want it."

"Daddy, after your performance, my pussy wants it like you would give it to Shannon if you was fuckin' that bitch tonight."

"Do you think you can play ball on that street, Maria? I got to warn you, baby, that's a very rough block."

Maria slapped Jonathan hard on the face and said in a fearful voice, "What are you doing in my room? And why do you have my husband tied up in that chair?" She slapped him even harder this time, causing blood to flow from his lip. Jonathan licked the blood from his lip and then turned to walk away, but before Maria knew it he had turned back on her and slapped her so hard that she went airborne and landed on the king-size bed. The rough role-playing was underway.

"Bitch! If you must know, yo' husband owes me mo' money than he can pay me. Now that's where you come in."

Maria was clearly dazed; nevertheless, Jonathan had no mercy on her. She wanted to play, and in doing so she had to pay. He pulled her by her hair back to her feet and pulled her to the dresser. Once he got there, he removed a pair of handcuffs.

"Take yo' clolthing off, bitch!"

Before she could say a word, Jonathan kicked her feet from under her, sweeping her off the floor. As Maria landed on the floor hard, Jonathan pulled the buck knife off the dresser and cut off what she was wearing and pulled her back up by the hair and flung her back on the bed. She tried to fight him off, but he smacked her three more times in the face and said, "Bitch! Do you think this is a game?"

He flipped her on her stomach and pulled her up to the head-board, cuffing her to it. "I told you that yo' nigga owed me money."

With that said he rubbed some KY jelly all over his dick and inserted it in Maria's asshole. She screamed bloody murder, and still Jonathan showed no mercy. However, as he pulled it out and thrust it back in, she began to move with his motion as she got used to the pain.

"Why didn't you pay him his money? Now look what's happening to me." Her words made Jonathan nut, so he shot it all over her back then pushed his dick back in her, this time inside her pussy. As he hit it like a jackrabbit, he asked her to tell her husband how good the dick was.

"Tell him, bitch! Tell him!"

"Oh god, this muthafucka got me ready to explode! Please take the cuffs off me and let me ride it, mister."

Jonathan took them off and remembered what he said about the hooker and the way she could ride a dick. Maria hopped on his dick backward facing the opposite way and with every time she dropped her pussy on his dick, she would butterfly her knees just so he could get all the pussy. Even as with every time she did so, it felt like his dick was going to bust through her insides, she still gave him her all. She wanted to show him that Shannon nor any hooker couldn't outfuck her. From here on out he could get this pussy anyway he wanted it.

"Oh god, you're killing me, Papi!"

"You haven't seen shit yet!"

He pushed her off and put her upper body on the bed, with her legs hanging off. He parted them and rammed his dick in once again. This time he had complete control of the pussy.

"Damn it, baby, you're hurting me! Ohh shit, you fucker! Please! Damn you!"

But before long, she started to get into it.

"Oh yes! Yes, right there, Jonathan! I'm feeling this shit now. Oh god, oh god, Papi! A bitch about to cum now! Ohhhh Lord! I'm cumming! OH SHIT! You fucker! Here it COMES!" she hollered as she came hard, causing Jonathan to nut as well. Jonathan looked at

Maria with love as she pulled his dick out of her and wiped it clean with a rag, only to start sucking it until he was hard again. Only this time she let him nut and explode inside her mouth. His body jumped out of control with a jerking sensation as she sucked every last drop of the nut out of him.

As they laid in the bed, Jonathan was quick to speak.

"Maria?"

"Yes, daddy?"

"There's a lot of shit on our plate, boo. I mean I've been looking for a way out in my mind, but for the life of me, I can't find it."

Maria just looked at him. She didn't try to fix the situation as she knew he needed to unload this heavy-ass shit on someone, and that someone was her.

"I can't just let that muthafucka get away with what he did to Rose, and then there's you and Solo and the shit he did to y'all. I've hit him with my best, and he just keeps coming. The muthafucka just keeps coming, boo!"

Maria took her weed box from under the bed, twisted a blunt, fired it up, and passed it to Jonathan who waved it off.

"Are you starting to doubt yourself again, Jonathan?" she said softly.

"No, baby. It's just that I can see the outcome of this shit. Can't you, Maria? Because if you can't, then we in deeper shit than I thought."

"Papi, I see a lot of shit," she said as she blew out the smoke from the blunt. "A house with kids running in the yard. A husband coming home from work that I cook and clean for. That everyday average-Joe blow shit, Jonathan. But I've been on my own for as long as I can remember and hooking just as long. So what do I really know about any of the bullshit I just put out there to you Jonathan?"

He didn't say a word.

"The one thing I do know, Papi, is this. I do not want to lose you! You the only *real* thing I got in my life. Not one time have you asked me to sell my body, not one time have you treated me like the whole I really am, that is unless I ask you to do so," she said, thinking about the hardcore sex they just had. "You never even ask me for money nor have you taken money away from me. You don't beat me up but instead you treat me like a queen, you do the opposite of all the shit I'm used to being done to me. Anything good I know, Jonathan, I've learned from you. So if there's a way out of this shit, baby, you gotta show Momma the way because all I know is what we do, but I'll do whatever you want me to do if you show me the way."

He kissed her softly on the lips and asked her, "Do you love Shannon, Maria?"

She looked at him for a long time before answering him, "I love her because you do, Jonathan, and I love her because she would die for you."

"Well, you better start loving her for reasons of your own, because I'm going to marry you both."

"What?" Maria cried at him as if to let him know he was losing his mind."

"If I marry you, Maria, I'm going to have to be faithful to you, and I can't do that if I'm cheating on you with Shannon."

"Are you for real, Jonathan?" she said as if he were playing. "I do believe that shit is against the law just in case you didn't know that."

"Fuck the laws of this land. The only ones that will know about it is us, and we not going to tell on ourselves, are we?"

"Baby! You for real?" she said with excitement in her voice.

"Yes, I'm for real, Maria."

"Then when, Jonathan?"

"Let's roll out to Vegas tonight and make that shit happen on the fast track."

Maria jumped up and down in the bed so high that she almost hit her head on the roof of their bedroom.

"Get up, Jonathan! Let's go tell Shannon!"

As they burst into Shannon's room, she was riding Solo's dick into the sunset.

"Bitch!" Maria shouted. "Get off that pony. Daddy's taking all of us to Vegas!"

"Well, Solo?" Shannon said. "I hope you got yours, 'cuz when Daddy calls, a bitch gotta roll."

"You too, Solo, let's go! Let's spend some money and have a good time."

Solo looked at Jonathan as if he were trippin'.

"Nigga, are you fo' real? We gotta go to Vegas to gamble? We can spend some money right her in town!"

"I need you to be my best man, Solo."

"Yo' best man? Nigga, what you talkin' about?"

"I'm going to get married!"

Shannon's face dropped to the ground when she heard the "M" word. "Now that's the shit I'm talkin' about, dog!" Solo was happy for him.

"So you not feelin' the good news, Shannon?" Jonathan asked.

"What do you want me to say, Baby Locklord?"

"Bitch! I want you to say 'I do' when we get to Vegas!"

She looked at him with tears in her eyes. "Don't play with me like that, Baby Locklord, don't do me like this."

Maria walked up to her and said, "Don't cry, girl, he not playing, he gon' marry the both of us!"

"But how, Maria? How can that happen?"

"Bitch, don't worry about all that. Let's just go get married."

Maria dragged her out of the room, so they could go get cleaned up.

Solo looked at Jonathan and said, "Damn! I guess that sweet-ass pussy is off the table from here on out, huh, J?"

"Yeah Solo. I won't be able to ask her to do shit like that no more."

"Look here J, can I just keep it real, nephew?"

"Do you, dog," Jonathan said, giving him the green light.

"Them two bitches the downest bitches I've ever known. But they hoes, J! Nigga, you can do better than that."

"That may be so, Solo but the truth of the matter is, I don't want to do better than that. So you with me family or what?"

Solo smiled at his nephew and said, "We Locklords, my nigga! You The Truth! So let that be told! When it's all said and done, we all we got!'

"Thank you, dog, that shit really means a lot to me."

*****

As Bandit pulled away from Cruz's house, all kinds of shit ran through his mind. His nigga Bam was dead, the only nigga he could really talk to. After Bam's death, he started going to church with his mother more often. Life is funny like that. He had always taken his mother to church, but now all of a sudden the shit the preacher was saying started to get to him. As he pulled into his mother's driveway, some of the little kids in the hood ran up on his car.

"Bandit! Bandit! Bandit, can we wash your car today?"

"Look at my shit, little niggas, so it look like it need washing?"

"No," they said sadly.

"I'll tell y'all what, there's some badass gangsters after me, I just need y'all to keep a look out for anything that don't look right."

"Okay, Bandit, we got your back!"

They knew that they was going to at least get a dub apiece, so they would have took an ass whipping trying to warn me of coming danger if in fact there was any coming, Bandit thought to himself.

"How's my favorite girl doing?" he said to his mother that had been standing in the doorway.

"Hey yourself, Mr. Late," she said as she punched him in the arm.

"Now, what was that for, Mom?" he said like a little boy that had just gotten in trouble.

"Them kids look up to you, and that's your way of leading them in the right direction?"

"Come on, Mom, now just what would you have me say to their little badasses, you boys stay in school, don't do drugs, and keep hope alive?"

"Yes, Tyrone, something like that. Now come on, let's go, we're already late."

As they were rolling down the road, his mother spoke again. "Tyrone baby, I had a dream about you last night."

"Don't start up, Mom"

"No! you need to hear this, boy! God spoke to me concerning you. He told me that he was going to give you a way out of this sinful life that you've been living, but if you do not take it, baby, your end will be at hand," she said with conviction. Bandit did not say a word, for he knew deep down that God had been talking to him as well.

"Baby, he also showed me that girl you used to bring to church with us three or four years back, what was her name?"

"You talking about Rose, Mom?"

"Yes, baby that was her name."

"Momma, what made you bring her up?"

"I keep seeing her and that handsome little boy she had in my dreams. That boy look so much like Conrad."

"What do you think them dreams mean, Momma?"

"I don't know, son, it's almost like she was trying to tell me something. And whatever it is, it's got something to do with you. So if you don't already know what it is, Tyrone, maybe it is you that needs to ask God about what my dreams mean concerning you. Oh, son, let me out right here in front of the church, so I can give Sister Betty a little bit of that street money of ours," she said as she held out her hand. Bandit gave her a c-note, but his mother put fifty of that in her bosom. "Her gas is off, baby, but we not trying to pay the whole bill. Now don't you be telling nobody her business, boy, you hear?"

"Mom! What am I, five years old or something?"

"Just let me out, boy."

After church, Bandit dropped his mother off and had a lot of time to think about some of the things she said. And to add to her dreams, the preacher was stepping all over his toes this morning.

Shit! If I didn't know any better, I would have put money on it that Mother put my business out there. Shit, I don't know. I will say this, though. God, if in fact you are talking to me, please make it clear to me what your trying to say because I can't keep living like this. If I don't know nothing else, deep down I know that to be the truth. But what if I did get out of the game, would Sandy get out with me? No! the only way I could really have her is if Cruz was no longer among the living. Well, God, can you fix that for me? Bandit thought to himself as he acted as if he were really listening for an answer. And when he did not get

171

one, he said to himself, "I didn't think so. Some shit a man just gotta fix for himself…"

*****

"Girl, I'm telling you, I hit that nigga off so good last night, that when I woke up this morning, he was standing over the bed with breakfast in hand. I didn't even have to ask him for no money, the nigga just kicked it out of his ass as if he was a ready teller."

The younger lady enjoyed a hard laugh with her beautician.

"Well, baby," the older lady said in a tone that told the younger lady that there was a lesson attached to it. "Just remember, he's not likely to buy the cow if he's getting the milk for free."

"I don't understand. What do you mean? I'm getting paid, girl! He be spending all kinds of money on me."

"No, baby, it's not always about the money, do you love him?"

"Well, yeah." The younger lady blushed.

"Have you been to his house yet?"

"Yes! Well, it's his and his homeboys' spot, but we gon' get our own place real soon."

"How old are you, baby?"

"I'm seventeen."

"And how old is he, if you don't mind me asking?"

"He's twenty-five."

"Twenty-five is he now?" the older asked with concern in her tone. "Anyway, you told me that him and his friend stays together, but I bet it's only a one-bedroom apartment with a mattress on the floor in the room."

The young lady looked at the older woman in shock. "How you know that shit, girl?"

The older woman knew that the cat was likely married and was just using the young lady in order to get his rocks off with a young booty call here and there, but she didn't have the time to school her as it was closing time. So she ignored the girl by handing her the mirror.

"How does that look, baby?"

"Damn! You hooked me up this time, Ms. Betty!" Shannon said, still playing her roll.

"Okay, let's get it together, baby, I got to close up early tonight. My daughter is asking me out on the town tonight."

"Didn't you tell me that she was a record producer?"

"That's right, baby," the woman said as she picked up a picture of Sandy and Cruz. "It was touch and go with her there for a while, but all that's changed. Now her and her husband are upstanding citizens of the community."

"Ms. Betty, I can tell that you're very proud of her. Well, let me call my dude and tell him I'm ready. Hey, man, I'm ready to go... What do you mean it's going to take you an hour, you only five minutes away? I can't walk at this time of night in this neighborhood, Frog! But they about to close up shop, man! You make me sick!"

Click!

Betty did not want to get involved, but Shannon had been coming to her shop for a month now, and she was starting to like the girl. As she looked at the young lady collecting her things with tears in her eyes, she went against one of her number-one rules: *never help a stranger!*

"Look, baby, you don't have to walk. Ms. Betty will give you a ride. But I'm going to say this, I believe you can do better than a bum like that. Now, let's go."

When the two women got into the car, Shannon looked at Ms. Betty with tears rolling down the side of her face and said, "I'm so very sorry, Ms. Betty, now that I know you, I wish you didn't have to get caught up in this bullshit. Please forgive me." Shannon reached over to hug the woman.

"That's okay, baby. It's not your fault that you're in love with a dog."

Shannon's hug was starting to get tighter and tighter.

"That's enough, baby, you're going to hug me to death" were the last words that Ms. Betty would get out clearly. Her mind quickly abandoned Shannon's bear hug as she grasped for the metal wire that was now around her neck. As the woman kicked her legs wildly at the floor and dashboard of the car, Shannon struggled to hold the woman down on the front seat, nevertheless, squeezing as tight as she could and saying that she was sorry the whole time life was slipping away from the woman. In an attempt to free herself, the woman grabbed at Maria's hair, but Maria pulled on the wire so hard, that she almost pulled Shannon along with the woman into the back seat. When the woman's attempt to stop the choker failed, she began to beat Shannon on the back with deadly force for what seemed like forever. But before long, her punches became weaker and weaker, and the kicks that were so deadly at first lost all their sting. Now there were only faint attempts to collect air that could be heard—Maria's heavy breathing from the struggle and Shannon's not-so-quiet weeping for a woman that had to die because of the sins of another…

CHAPTER NINE

When Bandit, Tomcat, and Get Off pulled in to the Gunz Blazing Recording Studio parking lot, it was clear to see that something was a mist. The parking lot was much fuller than it should have been for this time of day. But more so than that, Baby Gangbanger's car was parked in Bandit's parking spot, and that shit made him hot right off the back.

As the three men walked into the building, there was no music playing, nor were there any hustling and bustling coming about. The look of everyone's face spoke of death without using the actual words. Sandy had made Bandit the vice president of the recording company. The two of them were becoming very close as of lately. When Bandit walked through the door, some put a little more pep in their step, but others—mostly women—were crying. Bandit did not bother saying anything to any of them. Instead he just walked into the conference room with Tomcat and Get Off, hot on his heels.

When they walked into the room, the first person Bandit noticed was Cruz, who was turning up a bottle of Dom Pérignon. Sandy sat in a corner of the room looking as if she was somewhat in a daze, as her kids ran around clearly high from contact with all the blunts being smoked in the room. At least twenty niggas and bitches from the Hub & the Dub sat around the big table, each looking as if they were high off the drink or drug of their choice. Cruz didn't drink much, but when he did, he became very unstable. So playing it cool until he could feel Cruz out, Bandit simply said, "Who do I need to kill to set this shit straight, Cruz?"

Cruz looked up from the bottle of Dom Pérignon he was drinking into the eyes of his best friend, and it was clear to Bandit that at some point in the day Cruz himself had been crying.

"What the fuck happened, Cruz?" Bandit said with more concern in his voice this time.

"That muthafucka raped my mother, Bandit! Cuzz, they raped her and killed her as I listened on the phone, and there wasn't a damn thing I could do about it."

Bandit looked at Cruz and could not believe his ears. That is, until he'd seen the tears rolling down Cruz's face. As he sat down next to Cruz he could only ask, "Who?"

"The same muthafucka that killed my mother!" Sandy cried from the other side of the room.

Bandit just sat there wondering who could do some low-down shit like that, and then it hit him like a truck. Before he could turn his thoughts into words, the phone rang, cutting him off.

"What the fuck is it?" Cruz cried out into the phone.

"Detective who? How the fuck did Five-0 get up in this bitch? Never mind!

Click!

"Five-0 up in the house, get this shit cleaned up! Come on, Bandit."

As Cruz and Bandit walked into the lobby, Detective Sunset and his partner Detective Higgins stood next to the receptionist desk with smug looks on their faces.

"Yes, Officers, how may we help you?"

"Mr. Conrad Cruz, is it?" the younger detective said as if he had just solved the biggest case of his short career.

"Yes, it is and you are?"

"I'm Detective Higgins, and this here is my partner, Detective Sunset."

"Well, what can I do for you, Officer?"

"You can tell us who killed the Locklords," the young detective said with somewhat of an attitude. Nevertheless, the look on Cruz's face was one that did not give up a clue one way or the other.

"Okay," Detective Sunset said as he joined in the conversation, "it's clear to see that you don't want to talk about the murders, but maybe you want to talk about who raped and killed your mother. Or about who killed your wife's mother?"

This time, Cruz's facial expression spoke volumes.

"I think we hit a nerve on that one, rookie," Detective Sunset said as he smiled at Detective Higgins, who was smiling as well.

So Bandit broke in, "Look, Detective, we don't know what you're talking about. My man here just lost his mother, so shouldn't your department be out looking for the bad guy right now?"

"The bad guys? You hear this shit, Higgins?"

"Yes, Lieutenant, I'm hearing it, but I'm not liking it one fucking Bit. The way I see it, we're talking to the bad guys. And who the fuck is he, your lawyer?" Detective Higgins said as he pointed at Bandit.

"No! But I am!" Sandy said as she abruptly entered the room and conversation.

"I'm the president of this company, and yes, along with that, I do have a law degree."

The detectives just stood there looking at Sandy as if she had just lost her mind by trying to dismiss them with that "lawyer" shit. Knowing that the detectives didn't have anything, Sandy went big on them. "Well, then, it's clear that you officers do not have any paperwork that allow you to be here, so Mr. Cruz, would you and my VP show these gentlemen to the door?"

"It would be my pleasure, Mrs. Cruz."

Cruz and Bandit waved their hands toward the door at the same time.

"You three little pigs don't even realize that the big badass wolf is standing at your door, do you? Well, you will, when he blows this house of cards down on top of your heads," Detective Sunset said sarcastically.

"Well, until then, detectives, you both have a nice day!"

Both men walked out the door with Cruz and Bandit hot on their heels as if to show them the way. But just as all four men stepped out the door, a black four-door sedan came to a screeching halt with bad intentions. Both Bandit and Cruz had seen the car in time. Neither wanted to pull his gun in front of the police, so all they could do is run back into the building. The detectives, however, made a play for their guns. Nevertheless, neither one of them would even get their pistols out of their holsters. It was like something from out of the movies, as the man in the passenger side of the car got off first with his automatic weapon. The two detectives tried to split up in order to take the shooter out, but this only gave the driver and the men in the back seat a chance to do their thing. Higgins was hit first, but the first shot did not put him down. Nevertheless, the rookie panicked as more shots whizzed past his ears. He tried to make a move for cover but was hit once more, and this time he went down. Higgins wasn't dead yet. However, he was no longer a threat, which gave the shooters the time they needed to focus on Detective Sunset, who had taken cover behind Baby Gangbanger's car. It was then that the man on the passenger side of the car exited with a .45 automatic in one hand and a grenade in the other. And as he walked passed Higgins's half-dead body, he pumped at least five more bullets into the back of the desperate man, finally killing him this time. Without slowing down his brisk walk, he headed for the building where Cruz and Bandit stood in the doorway with guns in hand this time. However, this didn't stop the shooter as he got as close to the double glass doors of the studio as he could. With that, a new gun battle erupted. As the first shots shattered the double glass doors, the gunman's standard military-issued .45 ran out of gas. *Click, click, click!* But Cruz and Bandit's guns were still spitting thunder at him, and before long one of their bullets found its target, hitting the gunman in the shoulder and knocking him to the ground. With the instinct of the cold-blooded killers they were, Cruz and Bandit began to move in on their fallen foe. But as if the fallen man was the undertaker from *Friday Night Smackdown*, he sat up on his back pockets, pulled the pin out of the grenade at the same time, and hurled it in to the lobby of the recording studio. In what seemed like slow motion, the grenade bounced…one, two, three times on to the lobby floor as Cruz and Bandit ran in different directions. Then without warning—BOOM! Both men went airborne just barely escaping with their lives.

"Officer down! OFFICER DOWN! Damn it! I'm under fire!" Detective Sunset cried out over his two-way radio, which at that very moment he heard a big ass explosion coming from the lobby of the studio.

"Shit!" he almost screamed out like a desperate woman. Now he was looking around wildly like a man surrounded by wild wolves. All kinds of fear began to take hold of him, as he wondered if he would make it out alive on this one. But it only got worse when he looked up and saw another gunman walking away from the explosion, slipping what seemed to look like another clip into his already-smoking gun. Before Sunset could think clearly, he was under fire from yet another angle.

"Higgins, get them off me!" he cried, not knowing that his partner was already dead.

As the bullets hailed down on him, he had only one chance, and he took it. He stood up and tried to dump on the man that was trying to pin him down, but a bullet from one of the other gunman's weapon hit him in the neck. "I'm hit, I'M HIT!" he cried into his radio, but as the blood spit out of his neck like waterholes, Sunset ducked back behind the car, thinking that the end had finally found him out. The fourth gunman knew that he had to finish the cop off, so he pulled out another hand grenade. But before he could pull the pin on this one, the sirens in the near distance warned him otherwise. So he calmly walked back to the waiting car with the sounds of Detective Sunset crying behind him. "Oh God, please, please help me, I don't want to die!"

Jonathan let out a sinister laugh as he thought to himself, *There must be a God (because this nigga was as good as dead).*

As Jonathan got back in the car, each man removed their ski masks and tossed them along with their guns out of their windows, leaving the scene of the crime. With that, Solo pulled slowly into traffic. It was only seconds before the police passed them going in the opposite direction. Each of the men smiled at one another as

Five-0 passed them on their way to the scene of the crime they had just committed.

Four blocks away from the drama that had taken place, Solo ducked into an alley where another car was waiting. The men took off their gloves and tossed them into the car they pulled up in, and Jonathan poured gasoline all over the car and set it ablaze. With that, the four men got into the car that Tim was waiting for them in. Jonathan looked at his Rolex as Tim pulled off. It seemed like forever, but the whole ordeal had only taken six minutes.

Now that's that gangsta shit, he thought to himself. "Keep the pressure on a muthafucka until he can't breathe no more, now that's how we're rolling up in this bitch!"

*****

"Oh my god, Conrad! Are you okay?" Sandy shouted as she made her way through the mayhem, disorder, and havoc caused by the hand grenade and shooting.

"Look, get my gun and Bandit's, put that shit in the safe along with any other drugs and guns that may be up in this muthafucka. Be quick about it, baby, because Five-0 gon' be all over this bitch sooner than later."

"But baby, let me check on Bandit."

"Bitch! Fuck Bandit! Just do what I told you to do."

"Are you sure you all right?"

"I will be as soon as you do what you're told, Sandy! We can't afford to get caught slipping, now do what I asked you to do, damn it!"

"Okay, Daddy!"

Sandy took his gun and stepped over the receptionist's body who looked dead with the blood flowing from her head. As she made her way to where Bandit's unconscious body lay, a single tear rolled down her face. That is, until he moved. She found his gun still hot to the touch, which he had been firing moments earlier. She smiled, thanking God under her breath that he was still alive. People were moving slowly as they were trying to make sense of what just happened. Nevertheless, she ran past them back to the conference room and collected the rest of the drugs and guns as those in the room hurled question after questions at her.

"Look, damn it! We just been hit up, and Five-0 is all over this bitch! As of now, I know as much as y'all do, which is really *nothing*! But! If you do not want to go to jail, y'all gotta give me them guns and shit now!"

After everyone complied, Sandy took control again. "Now, let's walk up out of this muthafucka like we ain't nothing more than victims of a violent crime. Is that understood?"

No one said a word, but all understood and followed her.

*****

"We got a dead officer here!" one of the cops cried out to the others.

"Come out with your hands up," the sergeant commanded over the bullhorn as he faced the blown-out doorway of the studio. With that, Detective Sunset pulled himself together and stumbled out of his hiding place. "Freeze! Goddamn it, FREEZE!" the cop yelled at the bloody man until he identified Sunset to be one of their own.

"Oh my. It's Detective Sunset!" the sergeant yelled out through his bullhorn once again.

But as the people filed out of the building, some were holding up others while some were dragging dead bodies out of the establishment. It became clear to see that these people were victims as well.

"None of them had anything to do with the shooting," Detective Sunset said in a weak voice. With that said, the detective passed out due to the vast amount of blood lost.

"Where's that fucking medic at?" the sergeant yelled out one more time even as he, along with everybody else, could hear the ambulance in the distance.

*****

Back at the hospital, Sandy and Cruz sat in the waiting room until the nurse wheeled Bandit out in a wheelchair. "Look at this nigga, Sandy!" Cruz said jokingly. "Anytime he can get a free ride, he'll take it."

But Bandit wasn't in a joking mood. The explosion had fucked him up. One of his arms was broken, and a piece of metal had hit him in the right eye. The whole right side of his face was swollen, and by the doctor's account, he was most likely going to lose sight in the damaged eye. Nevertheless, he was still banged the fuck out as ever.

"What the fuck y'all looking at?" were the first words that came out Bandit's mouth. "Let's go dump on them muthafuckas!"

As much as Cruz wanted to do so, he knew that they couldn't. It was hard to attack an enemy you couldn't see, especially when you have no knowledge whatsoever of where their hiding place was.

"We're still try'na find out where the Locklords' rest at, Loco."

"Then let's go kill someone close to them, Cruz!"

"Like who, Bandit? His mother? His grandmother? Who? We already killed everyone close to the kid, so who else can we possibly slaughter for it to really matter? Him and that bitch, Maria: like Bonnie and Clyde, if one ride they both gon' ride. Oh, and to make matters worse, it seems the kid has come up on an army of killas! In addition to this, they also got whatever Businessmen niggas that's left and stayed on. That's the shit that adds insult to the injury," Cruz expressed himself.

"The shit they hit us off with today was some military shit. Now he's rolling with niggas that don't give a damn about killing cops. It's a whole new ball game, Bandit. It's a whole new muthafuckin' ball game."

"So what's our next move, Cruz?"

"We're too visible, Bandit. His ass is all over us, when it should be the other way around!"

"And why is that, Conrad?" Sandy said with more than a hint of anger in her voice.

"I'll tell you why that is! It's because he's sleeping with a bitch you used to trust. A bitch you gave all your information to. First, she rob us, then she starts sleeping with your firstborn son, and if that wasn't enough, she also helped kill our mothers! So what's next, Cruz, our kids?"

Cruz looked at her as if she had just spit on him.

"Yeah, Daddy, I know that look. But before you kick my ass, please know this. We done killed everyone in his family, what would you do, Cruz, if you was him? You would kill everyone in his family too, wouldn't you? Well, Daddy, that little son of a bitch gon' stay true to the blood of the madman. That's right, Conrad, he got the blood of a madman running through his veins. That madman is you! So why should I not be worried about our kids?"

"Cruz," Sandy said, this time softly to remove some of the sting of the words she could not take back. "Jonathan don't have anything to lose, Daddy! We've had a man watching Rose's grave site for almost the last three months now. And you know why Jonathan has not visited his own mother's grave yet? No, of course you don't, so I'll tell you. There was another lot purchased right next to where Rose is planted, and there's nobody lying in it yet. It's empty! But it does have a headstone on it, Daddy! And I bet you that you don't know whose name it is, Cruz. Ten will get you twenty, you don't know. Tell him whose name it is that's on it, Bandit!"

Bandit sighed. "It's got your name on it, dog," Bandit said, hoping not to have to intervene if Cruz decided to kick Sandy's ass.

"You heard that? It's your name, Daddy! YOUR NAME! Now what the fuck is that all about, baby? Who's next?"

For the first time in a long time, Cruz did not have an answer to her question. Deep down he knew that this was a war he had not counted on, so the cost was at this time unknown to him. He wanted to tell her that it was going to be all right, but in his heart of hearts, he knew that it would be a lie. So he just pulled her to himself and held on to her. At that moment an old Mazda RX-7 passed by and the muffler backfired, *Pow! Pow!* This caused all three of them to jump. Both men reached for their guns as their hearts raced, only to realize that they weren't strapped.

"Nigga, fuck this shit, I can't live like this. Cruz, we got to pull that bitch-ass muthafucka out of whatever hole he hiding in, like yesterday."

Cruz looked into Sandy's eyes and said, "Do you really think I'm going to let my seed beat me, Mommy?"

Their eyes locked, and Sandy wondered for the first time if her man had what it would take to withstand this new challenge. However, his eyes told her he did, and as always she believed in him.

"No, Daddy. It's only one winner in this city and that's you. But we got to make that punk muthafucka pay, Conrad. Baby, we got to make him feel it."

"And so we will, Sandy, that's on my life that we will! Now take the kids home, call yo' sister and tell her to meet you at our house, and I'll be there shortly.

"Then what, Cruz?" Bandit said with war in his voice.

"Then we go for broke, dogg! We let the blue steel choke from the smoke."

*****

Back at Tim's Harley Store, the men prepared to go their separate ways. As Jonathan looked each man over, he still could not grasp the fact that Tim had persuaded some of the dudes from his old Naval Seal Unit to back them up. Those cats were down with it, but no average man would know that just by looking at their appearance. They were the kind of old dudes that you would see kickin' it at the park with their grandkids and shit like that. You know, the kind of dudes that some stupid muthafucka might underestimate and end up with their wig split back till the fatty meat was hanging out. He recalled sitting with Tim and them as they put the plan together to hit Cruz up. Jonathan knew then that these were the type of killers that you would never see coming. He also knew that it was better to have them with him than against him.

"What's the damage?" Jonathan asked, being ready to pay the men off. They all just looked at Jonathan and laughed at the same time. Then the one they call Cannibal spoke up. "Look here, young-blood, we gon' help you bury that sick muthafucka, and we gon' place you on that ghetto throne. Okay, somebody say it with me—all hail the new king!"

The men repeated and were clowning around as they pointed at Jonathan. Cannibal continued, "Don't get it twisted, crime is not going away. Don't think of us to be a bunch of old fools. However, muthafuckas like Cruz that hang out in front of high schools and junior highs are not criminals, they're cockroaches that need and must be exterminated. That's it and that's all. You want to know how you can pay us back? You pay us back by ridding the city of sick muthafuckas like your dad, that's how you pay us back, young kingpin!"

With that said, the man extended his hand to Jonathan, and Jonathan took it. "Until we ride again, youngblood, you be easy." Cannibal nodded at Solo as he and the rest of his crew exited the shop.

As Jonathan and Solo walked over to where Tim was listening to a police scanner, they could hear the bad news reaching Tim's ears before they had a chance to tell him. Tim looked up from the radio at them and said, "Was there any other course you could have taken other than killing that detective and wounding another?"

"Do you really want me to answer that, Tim?" Jonathan said with a hint of hurt in his voice. Tim just looked at him and shook his head.

"Well, J, you really got to let your nuts hang now because you have just catapulted us to the next level of the game. In any event, let's get that bullet out of your shoulder. Solo, I'm going to need you to put some hot water on, and go get me some clean towels from one of my bitches upstairs."

"Hold the fuck up!" Jonathan protested. "You gon' tell me that you gon' try to pull this shit out on yo' own? Look, big dog, you a lot of things but I know one thing for sure, you ain't no muthafuckin' doctor. So unless there's a muthafuckin MD up them stairs, you best be getting me to a hospital, damn it!"

Tim handed Jonathan a bottle of Bacardi 151 and said, "Here, drink this."

"What? Tim, I ain't some fuckin' cowboy out on the range. I need a doctor, dude!"

"The cops are all over this shit, J! There ain't no way you gon' go in and out of a damn hospital without someone calling the police. Now this is the shit I'm talking about when I say you gon' have to let your nuts hang. Now drink that shit, so we can do this."

Jonathan just looked at him for a moment, forgetting that he wasn't much of a drinker. He turned the bottle of 151 up. Within a half an hour he was sloppy drunk. The next thing he knew, he was waking up with Maria and Shannon sitting on either side of the bed.

"How did I get home?" was all he could say. "My head," he said as he held it in his hand, "is spinning out of control."

"Awww, the poor baby, him head hurting," Maria said playfully. But Shannon was on some other shit.

"Who the fuck shot you, Baby Locklord? And if they not already dead, then when we gon' kill them?"

"Damn bitch!" Maria said. "Give the nigga some air, and let him rest before you send him on yet another mission."

But Shannon was not feeling what Maria was talking about as her next words made that very clear. "Maria, fuck what you going through! If I have to get on some solo shit for our nigga, this shit ain't gon' go unanswered. Now who the fuck shot you, Jonathan Baby Locklord?"

Both women stared each other in the eyes with anger, as both had ready-for-war looks on their faces. After a moment, Shannon looked away, but Maria did not break her gaze from Shannon when she said, "Well, Daddy, seeing as this bitch done put it all out there bluntly and shit, tell us who did it so we can go flat line their asses."

"How did I get home, damn it?"

"Solo dropped you off, Daddy. He told us to tell you to call him as soon as you wake up and that it was very important."

"Then what you waiting for, Maria? Give me the goddamn phone, shit!"

But Shannon was already punching up the number. "Here, Baby Locklord."

"What's up, old drunk-ass nigga, you finally woke up, huh?" Solo said on the phone, knowing it was Jonathan 'cuz of his caller ID.

"Yup! What's up, nigga?"

"I'm in front of the house. I'll be up in there in a moment, homey."

"Nigga, you didn't have to sleep in the car, you could have took that shit home."

"Well, Truth, when you hear what I have to say you may feel a little different," Solo said then hung up.

Both women were still looking at Jonathan as if he owed them an explanation for the bullet hole that was in his shoulder, and they were ready to put him through some shit for that explanation too! But Jonathan was not feeling like going through what they were willing to put him through, so he filled them in a little sooner that they had expected.

"We hit the Guns Blazing Recording Studio yesterday as you already know, but the cops got in the way. I had them niggas, Ria, but the shit went all bad. However, we did put in work, but the job is not done."

"So who shot you?" Shannon said to let him know that she had not forgotten.

"I got into a shoot-out with Bandit and Cruz. One of them got me before I got them."

A tear rolled down Shannon's face, so Jonathan hugged her and wiped it away. "I'm sorry that we weren't there to back you up, Daddy," Maria sadly said.

"Don't trip, boo, how did y'all thang go?"

"Daddy, not only did we get the job done, but Shannon here, after she got her mind together and stopped herself from feeling sorry for the victim, had the presence of mind to search the spot for money traps."

"Well?" Jonathan asked.

"Well!" Shannon said in a real sassy kind of way. "There was a floor safe in her office, you know the kind that you need a key to get into, that old-school shit, Daddy. Well, to make a long story short, the Locklord Clan is three hundred grand stronger. I just had a feeling that Cruz and Sandy was hiding money off in that bitch, as on two different occasions I seen that bitch make money drops there," she said as she handed him the briefcase.

"Muthafucka!" Jonathan cried out loud as he looked at all the money. "You bitches are the shit! And trust me, that's meant in a good way. Just to show you where I'm coming from. I want you both to have a hundred Gs apiece, and y'all can do whatever you want with it! The rest we will put in our war chest. Now, who's the muthafuckin' man?"

Both women said it at the same time. "You the muthafuckin' man, Daddy! You the man."

As both women kissed his face in a nonstop manner, Jonathan felt the need to restore the pecking order within the bird's nest but knew he had to be as wise as a serpent and as gentle as a dove with his wording of the situation.

"Maria, Shannon, look I need to talk to you both about some real shit, so get off me and pay attention. What the fuck have I done to bring disorder to a situation that shouldn't have a hair out of place?"

Both women looked at him with stares of dismay, not knowing what to say.

"So now, y'all want to look at a nigga as if he's losing his damn mind, is that it?"

Now you could almost see both women's mind racing to figure out what he was talking about.

"Daddy, what are you talking about?" Maria almost cried out.

"I'm talking about that little exchange you two had moments ago. I'm talking about you two letting your fuckin' emotions get the best of you. A kingdom does not crumble all at once, it's the little cracks over an extended amount of time that causes it to come tumbling down, when one's mind is preoccupied on other matters that might be at hand that don't have anything to do with the big picture. Look, nobody can see the front door and the back one at the same time, so it pays to have one door locked at all times, especially when you can only afford one lock. I said all that just to say this, I love you both, one as much as the other, but in different ways, for different reason. Shannon, there is a chain of fuckin' command in this clan, one that you had said out of your own mouth that you would respect."

Jonathan took a deep breath and sighed. "See, you got at Maria wrong earlier on, so I'm going to need you to fix that shit right now."

He looked at her as if he was daring her not to comply with what he was ordering her to do. Seeing the dander in his eyes, Shannon apologized. "I'm sorry, Maria, I love Baby Locklord and because of that bullet wound in his shoulder I lost my cool. Girl, you know damn well I ain't got no beef with you."

Maria smiled as an expression of her acceptance and forgiveness, so Jonathan continued. "And Maria, yo' shit don't smell like roses, you know better than she do that we can't afford to get at each other in that kind of manner. So, let's get our game on some super tight, untouchable shit, feel me, ladies?"

"Yes, Daddy," both ladies responded with a smile. Shannon looked at Jonathan in a new light and felt the urge to let him know.

"Baby Locklord…"

"What's up, Little Momma?"

"I just want you to know that I recognize," Shannon said.

"Recognize what?"

"That yesterday you was a boy try'na be a man, but that's no longer the case, you're all man now and on some grown-man shit."

She looked toward Maria and continued. "Don't worry, Daddy, we got yo' back, and we won't ever let you down." With each word that come out of her mouth, Jonathan's dick got harder and harder. He desired for her to just straight up suck him off right there in front of Maria and was on the verge of making that request when the doorbell rang.

Buzz! Buzz!

*****

"I smoke the blunt to take the pain away. If I wasn't high I'd probably try to blow my brain away, I'm hopele—" 2Pac sang out Cruz's phone as a ring tone but was rudely interrupted.

"Cruz here."

"What's up, big money? This is Six Guns from that 6-0 gang, we need to meet."

"Cool, meet me at the club," Cruz said.

Click!

"What did he say, Six Guns?"

"He said to meet him at the club, well, not all of us."

The two men looked at Tim, and all three of them began to laugh hard.

My nuts are hangin' so low that I gotta dust 'em off two or three times a day, Tim thought to himself.

His plan to take over the business was quickly slipping away. He had grossly underestimated Jonathan and them bitches. His plan to make Jonathan the puppet that he would control as Jonathan controlled the Businessmen was one that never took root. And when that bitch killed Bo-Pete, the sixties wanted blood, his blood to be exact, for siding with them Compton and Watts niggas being that he was from Westside of South Central, Los Angeles.

Shit? What the fuck could a pimp do? Jonathan's the only bargaining chip I have, Tim started justifying in his own mind. *Man, I love the kid but better him than me. Sunset knows that I know something. It would be better for me to get off now before they put this puzzle together, because once they make the case, the deals that they gon' try to hand out are all going to be fucked up. I ain't got no other choice but to turn State, fuck it! They might as well get their laugh on and clown on now 'cuz if I gotta take Jonathan down to clear my name, I might as well take the sixties down and the Hub and the Dub too! There's always the witness protection program. As much as I feel bad for J, a brotha gotta do what a brotha gotta do! Tim thought.*

"Tim, about five years ago, there was a little nigga with heart that tried to get his dope sacks off up in our hood. I remember you went to bat fo' that nigga and said that he was your family. And that nigga's The Truth, huh?"

Tim did not say a word, 'cuz the truth of the matter was Jonathan had really become his family. Now here Tim was, organizing the triangle that would destroy the kid he looked at like a son. Tim thought to himself, *Jonathan wanted to kill Cruz, the sixties wanted to kill Jonathan, and Cruz and I have to set them all up in order to stay alive.*

"Just go to the club and let Cruz know that you have found out where The Truth and them bitches rest their heads, that's what you do, youngsta! Then find out what it's worth to him, and we'll split it evenly."

The two young men got up with smiles on their faces, and right as they walked out the door, Six Guns looked back and said, "Old-ass nigga, you'll be lucky if we give you bus fare out of town."

With that being said, they walked out the door and Tim made a call. "Detective Sunset, please."

*****

"What it do, Solo?"

"Look, Jonathan, I think we got a big-ass problem."

"Then put that shit in the air, Solo."

"After your man pulled that bullet out of your shoulder, he helped me pour yo' drunk ass into the back seat of your car. Well, as I pulled up outa there, another car pulled up. I didn't really think anything of that shit even when I saw Tim walk up to the ride, but before I got off the block, I remembered that I forgot yo' Desert Eagle. I know that you love that gun, so I went back for that shit. Anyway, when I walked in, I heard voices airing out your name."

"What the fuck do you mean airing out my name?"

"Just like I said, nigga! Some muthafucks was in the room with Tim talking about, 'Give Cruz the Truth's address and let him kill that nigga if you can't do it, Tim. Then we'll lay in the cut and kill Cruz.' Then, at that point, I started backing out of the room, but not before I heard Tim say 'Cool-n-the-game, young blood.'"

Jonathan did not want to believe Solo, so he said, "Nigga, if this is the truth, then time is no longer on my side, so I ain't got time to go back and forth with you. But if in fact you lying to me, for whatever reason, they won't get me before I get you!"

"Jonathan, muthafucka, we Locklords! Everybody else is dead, nigga! We all the fuck we got! What?" Solo said with his hands out stretched.

"Jonathan, I don't think he's lying," Shannon said with a touch of panic in her voice.

Jonathan looked at Maria, and Maria's eyes told him that it was time to go one way or the other.

"Okay," Jonathan said.

"Get the guns and the money. Fuck everything else, and let's roll up out of this bitch, NOW!"

*****

Back at Cruz's club, Six Guns and Little Willie Raw sat drinking as Cruz walked in. Cruz really did not trust these young niggas; it was just something about them that made him feel this way. But then again, Cruz really did not trust anybody. Before him and Bandit got to the bar where the two young men seemed to be enjoying their drinks, Cruz's phone went off with Rose's old cellphone number coming up on the caller ID.

"This can't be Rose, so it must be Jonathan. What you want, nigga?"

"Damn, Dad! Sounds like you still cryin' with feelings. I would call yo' momma so she could dry yo' eyes, but we both know, that ain't gon' happen."

"Anyway, nigga, it's a surprise that you thought of calling. It ain't Father's Day, so what it do, you walking dead man?"

"I'm dealing with a nigga that's try'na set me up, Cruz. Now that may or may not be news to you already. In any event, he's sending some niggas to you to give you my Venice Beach address, but the double-cross is going down, 'cuz while you kill me, they laying in the cut to kill you."

"How do you know that, Jonathan?" was all Cruz could reply.

"Think about it, Cruz, everyone knows that you don't leave witnesses behind, so if they setting me up with a cold-blooded killa like you, they have got to know that you gon' kill them too, so why not set yo' ass up too? It's called two birds with one stone, Dad. The nigga that's setting me up is O. G. Businessman named Tim, you know him?"

"Yeah I know him, Jonathan."

"Then get that name out of them, and you will know that I'm telling you the truth."

"Why you doing this, Jonathan? Why you giving me this information?"

"Because, muthafucka! You killed the only thing I ever loved. What the fuck I look like letting somebody else kill you? Know that when you die, it will be in the hands of the muthafuckin' Truth, nigga!"

Click!

CHAPTER TEN

"Detective sunset is out on sick leave, may I help you?"
Tim wanted to talk to no one else but Sunset. "Do you know when he'll be back?"

"No, sir."

"Well, do you have any other way I can contact him?"

"We cannot give that kind of information out, sir."

"Look, damn it! I got information on the Locklord murders."

"I'm sorry, sir, the best I can do is connect you to another detective."

"Okay, goddamn it! What if I told you that I know who shot Sunset and his partner, how about that?"

"Please hold, sir."

These muthafuckas want to play games, and my life is on the line, Tim thought to himself. He just knew that they were going to connect him to Sunset; he was listening so hard to the classical music for the Detective's voice that he did not hear the Locklords when they came in.

"Put the phone down, Tim," Jonathan said with more hurt in his voice than hate for his longtime friend. But Tim just stood there in shock as he wondered how much Jonathan had heard.

"Put the muthafuckin' phone down, Tim!"

As Tim eased the phone away from his ear, he heard the classical music come to an abrupt halt as the woman said, "I'm putting you through to Detective Sunset, sir."

But it was much too late now.

Click!

All he could do was try to play it off now.

"Hey, J! I didn't even hear y'all come in," he said as he wondered how much they knew and how long they had been listening. He gave Jonathan the key to the shop two years ago, and the kid had never used it until now. As he looked into Jonathan's eyes, he could sense the hurt, but more than that, he also could see that he himself would not live to see another day.

"Nigga, all I want to know is why? After all the shit we been through, why, Tim, why?"

"Come on, J, this is me, it's Tim, baby!"

"Why, muthafucka?" Jonathan said as Maria handed him her TEC-9.

"When you and Rose helped me get this shop, I just wanted to show you both that I had your back in whatever. But I got in too deep, son. How was I to know that you would turn out to be the cold-blooded young muthafucka that you are, kid?"

"Tim, you could have got out at any given time, nigga! We helped you get this shit because we loved you, this wasn't no *Godfather* movie, this wasn't *Blood In Blood Out*."

"Jonathan, you don't get it. Once we cross that invisible line there's no going back to the way it was. Think about it, J. Even if you win against Cruz, what's your exit plan out of the game? Have you even thought about that?"

Tim was try'na buy himself some time, and everyone in the room knew it. He was talking so fast that he took his eyes off Shannon, who made her way behind him.

"Tim, where's my Desert Eagle?"

"That shit's in my safe, J."

"What's the combination to the safe, Tim?"

Tears started building up in Tim's eyes because he knew that his end was at hand.

"Come on, J!"

"Give me the combination, nigga, or I'll kill you right here on the spot!"

Tim was sobbing like a baby now when he spit the combination out. "Ten, twenty-two, sixteen."

"Clean that bitch out, Maria. And get my muthafuckin' gun."

Now Shannon had her .380 in hand, inching even closer to Tim. This even as she saw a tear rolling down Jonathan's face.

"Tim," Jonathan said with noticeable pain in his voice. "If Solo would not have come back here last night to get my gun, I would not have seen this shit coming," Jonathan said as he handed Maria her TEC-9 back. "So I'm going to give you the same chance you was willing to give me."

Jonathan walked up to Tim, both men with tears in their eyes.

"Tim, I'm not going to let you see it coming either," Jonathan said, then kissed Tim on the lips. He then wiped the man's tears away and said, "You know I loved you like a father," and walked away.

Tim tried to follow after him but was unable to do so because of the four .380 slugs Shannon pumped into the back of his head. Tim's body stood in place for a long moment, then all at once the law of gravity did what it was meant to do, and Tim's body came crashing to the ground.

"Burn this bitch down, Solo, and meet us at the house in Newport Beach."

*****

Cruz didn't have time to fill Bandit in on the phone call that Jonathan had just made to him. All he could say was "Take yo' gun off safety, dog. Six Guns, Little Willie." Cruz spoke to both men.

"That's Little Willie Raw, big dog."

Cruz looked at the man and simply said, "What the fuck ever cuzz, Lady Bug."

"Yeah, Cruz?"

"Clear this muthafucka out, I got some business to handle."

"Will do, Boss!"

"Oh and you can have the rest of the day off too, Lady Bug."

"Thank you, Cruz."

When she had cleared the happy hour crowd out of the club, Bandit locked the door and sat back at the table with the men.

"Now, what news you Crips got for a cat?"

"Well, Cruz, we know a dude that know where The Truth rest his head."

"Is that right, Crip?"

"The only thing is, he wants to sell the information."

"So what he want to sell it for?"

"I don't really know, Cruz."

Six Guns looked over at Willie Raw. "I'll tell you what, Cuzz, you get that muthafucka on the phone so we can do business." Six Guns played it off like he was calling somebody.

"And Six Guns" Cruz said. "Tell Tim money's no object."

Six Guns didn't flinch, but his dog Will Raw's face let the cat out of the bag. "You know Tim, Cruz?"

Willie's face showed concern.

"Is that nigga try'na set us up, Cruz?"

"Shut the fuck up, Willie Raw," Six Guns cried out.

But Willie lost his cool. Knowing how Cruz went hard in the paint, Willie went for his gun, but Bandit already had his out under the table. The .44 Magnum kicked off two shots even before Willie could get his hand on the ass of his gun. Six Guns just raised his hands in the air and said, "Please don't kill me, dog."

Willie tried to get up from where he was sitting, only to fall to the floor. Bandit and Cruz never got up from the table. They just observed Willie as he once again got to his feet and tried to make his way to the door, with his gun still in his hand.

"Hey, Willie!" Cruz yelled out. "You gon' leave without saying goodbye?"

Willie just kept on stumbling in the direction of the door.

"Bandit, can you believe this rude muthafucka?"

Bandit didn't say a word.

"Okay, then, show this disrespectful muthafucka how we treat unruly guests."

Bandit stood up, took aim, and noodled Little Willie Raw.

"Damn!" Cruz cried out. "Who gon' clean that shit up?"

"Why don't we make this bitch made muthafucka do it?" Bandit said.

"Sounds like a plan to me," Cruz retorted.

"Bandit, go put the rocket in the car."

Bandit looked at Cruz, and Cruz cut his eyes at Six Guns, and Bandit got the message.

As Six Guns cleaned up the murder scene, all the bitch came out of him. Cruz hated the sixties because they was getting half of downtown LA's money that should have been all his. And now this new shit. Deep down Cruz knew that his whole plan was falling apart. The Crips from Watts had started beefing with the Bloods again, and the Crips in Compton had never really stopped beefing with one another. In all, it was just five sets that was trying to stay true to the plan. And with Cruz fighting two street wars now, he was losing support fast. The DTGs had all but taken their hood back, and shit was going downhill fast. Who would have thought that his own son would have been the reason for his failure? He almost laughed out loud when he thought about how good he had it just working the pimp game. Just then his train of thought was broken.

"Cruz, cuzz? What you gon' do with me?"

"I'm going to kill you, you stupid-ass muthafucka, what do you think?"

Six Guns started sobbing a little harder now.

"Shut the fuck up, you pussy, I'm not going to kill you today."

At that moment, Bandit came back into the room and said, "The rocket's in the car, Cruz, what you gon' do with this nigga?"

"I'm going to let him go. Get up and get yo' bitch ass up outa here!"

Six Guns looked at Cruz and said, "Just like that, Cruz?"

"Just like that, you coward, get out."

Six Guns almost ran to the door. "Is the GPS in place?" Cruz asked Bandit.

"That shit right on top of the rocket."

"Cool, let's go see what we do."

As Cruz and Bandit followed the GPS dot to a burned-out building, it became clear that this was Tim's spot. Six Guns didn't stop to investigate the matter, but Cruz and Bandit looked at each other and said, "Jonathan!"

Cruz smiled to himself as he thought The Truth was really a chip off the old block. They then followed Six Guns to his hood, and as luck would have it they hit the jackpot. It was at least seventeen hoodsta hanging out, and both men smiled as Six Guns pulled to a stop right in front of the crowd.

"Set the rocket off, Bandit," Cruz said in a sinister voice.

Bandit pulled out the remote control and hit the button.

Boom!

The blast killed everyone within fifty feet, blowing away three houses at the same time.

"Now that's the kind of shit that will shut a hood down for two or three months, shit!" Cruz said.

"It's going to take that long just to dig holes for all them dead muthafuckas."

Both men laughed as Bandit backed the car up and pulled into traffic, leaving behind the mayhem that had just taken place.

*****

"Detective Sunset, we seemed to have lost the call."

"Well, do we have a location for the caller?"

"Yes, Detective, please hold. Okay, Detective, it's a Harley Davidson shop at 5401 Broadway Boulevard. However, Detective, that place was blown up this morning."

"Are you sure?" "Yes Detective, one dead; the owner."

"Thank you for your help, dispatch."

"No problem, Detective."

I've been on this case going on four months now. I've lost a partner and an informant as well as a friend. Hell, the shit damn near got me killed, Detective Sunset thought to himself. *The streets are in an uproar but worse than that, there's an unstableness about them. You got gangs getting along with gangs that never got along before, and gangs that had got along for years now trying to take one another out. And now there's this new element being implemented into the streets, as them motherfuckers that tried to murder me are not your everyday gang members. I just don't know, I just don't know! Maybe it's time for me to retire.*

Maybe this Locklord case should be my last case, that is if it don't end up being the death of me, Detective Sunset reasoned within himself. *I've got nothing, it's all smoke and mirrors. The only real lead I got is the teenage kid of one of the victims, and we can't seem to find him. Maybe I should stop by the Newport Beach address again, or maybe I should just let this street war do what it do. I don't know, I just don't know.*

CHAPTER ELEVEN

Cruz and Sandy were busy cleaning their guns in the basement of their Baldwin Hills home, which was the spot that only he, Sandy, and their closest family members knew about. It was cool but nowhere near nice as their Chino Hills home. Sandy's sister had picked up the kids. Still grieving, she looked at Cruz before walking out the door and said, "Don't come get these kids until our mothers can rest in peace, and know that if you two can't get the job done, I'll get it done my goddamn self."

Neither Cruz nor Sandy said a word. Both just looked at the phone as they cleaned their guns. Then it happened, the call they had been waiting for.

"Put the shit on speaker, Sandy!"

"Yeah?" Cruz called out.

"We on Interstate 15, cuzz, looks like yo' boy's on the way to Vegas."

"Just stay on that ass and do what needs to be done, Crip."

"I got you, Loco!"

"Is yo' brother with you?"

"Yeah, Cruz, Get Off's right here with me."

"What it do, Crip?" Get Off sounded off in the background.

"Tell that nigga I said what's up, Tomcat," Cruz said. Tomcat nodded at his brother. "Call me when it's about to go down."

"Will do, Crip!"

Click!

"Them niggas already fucked up once, Daddy, why you put them back on the job?"

"Because they're loyal, fearless, and expendable, boo. If they knock one or two of them out of the box, that will make our job easier."

Sandy looked at Cruz hard. She knew that it had to be more than that, so she asked, "Conrad, shouldn't that be the first-string team on the damn hardwood right now? You can talk to me, boo, what's really going on?"

He looked at her for a long moment before he spoke. And spoke the truth.

"Baby, we *are* the first-string team, Bandit's on some other shit right now. His momma's fuckin' his head up with that Jesus talk. She's like a voodoo lady when it comes to that shit."

"What? He not with us no more, Cruz?"

"He with us, but his mind's somewhere else, Boo."

"Then what about them G niggas from the Hub and the Dub, Conrad?"

"The word on the streets, Sandy, is we hotter then fish grease on a Friday. Niggas think The Truth making a play for my crown, so niggas is steppin' back to see if we can hold on to it. Half of them muthafuckas don't even know who The Truth is, but they low-key respect his work."

"Fuck his work, Cruz! Let's go snatch the muthafuckas breath from him."

"In time, Sandy, in time."

*****

As the S550 dipped down I-15, T.I.'s King CD was banging number 11—"I'm Straight." Maria and Shannon had the car in a fog from the blunt smoke as the Dom P bottles swung from hand to hand.

Life is really a bitch, Jonathan thought to himself. *A year ago, Shannon and I were in high school. Shit! We should still be in high school! But here we are on some black mafia-type shit. Niggas don't even know me, but here I am, the heir to the muthafuckin' kingdom, even if it is a kingdom I don't want. I'm try'na kill my own father, and my own father is try'na kill me! If this is not the kind of shit Hollywood makes movies about, then fuck Hollywood! I'll put the money up myself and film this shit on my own,* he thought to himself as he bobbed his head and turned T.I.'s shit up, "I'm Straight"!

My husband? Now that sounds so good to my ears! Shannon thought to herself. *All I ever wanted was for Baby Locklord to like me with his fine ass. Now here he is in love with me, and I'm never ever gon' let him regret this shit. For God as my witness, what I'm about to say is the truth! Anybody that tries to separate us is going to die. And that includes Maria. So that little sawed-off bitch better think about playing nice. I'm straight!*

My niggas's on some real gangsta shit now. I never really liked Rose, but if she could see her son now, she would really be proud of him. And look at me, bitches! Maria thought to herself. *Is my guy about to turn me into a housewife? I don't give a fuck about what a muthafucka think, there's not a bitch alive that wants to be a hooker! I wonder how the new king of LA gon' feel about becoming a father. I wanted to tell him a week ago that I am with child, but the nigga got too much on his plate right now, so this shit will keep. In any event, this hooker more than ready to become a housewife. I'm straight!*

As they pulled on to the Vegas fast track, Shannon and Maria went crazy. Maybe it was the lights or the fact that none of them has ever been to Vegas before, or maybe both of them were happy that they were finally going to tie the knot, but whatever it was, their happiness quickly became Jonathan's. Both Shannon and Maria paid for their own marriage license. These bitches flipped a coin to see who would get the dick first. They played one hand of blackjack to see who would get to marry Jonathan first, and both wanted to sleep with him alone the first night of the honeymoon. It was crazy that they would even come up with a system such as that, but they had it coming on their special day.

This nigga Jonathan is smoother than the pimping king Iceberg Slim, Solo thought to himself. *And my nigga's not even try'na pimp, nonetheless these bitches giving the nigga* thousands *at a time. Shit! I know I said he could do better than some hoes, but I may have to retract that statement. In any event, meeting Jonathan was one of the best things that has ever happened in my life. The dude don't even really know me, and yet he has treated me as if we have been family from the start. Well, for that I will do or die for this nigga. It's Locklord for life, and I'm straight!*

They found two separate chapels and did what they had to do. This shit was crazy as hell, but like what Solo said, this was some gangsta shit at the same time. As they pulled away from the second chapel, Jonathan thought he seen a dude in a passing car that looked familiar. However, with all that was going on, Jonathan did not have a chance to visit the theaters of his mind's mind to put a time and place with the face. Hopefully he wouldn't live to regret that.

Shannon was the first to get her pussy right on her wedding night, and she really put it on a nigga. By the time it was Maria's turn, a nigga was more than out of gas. But if Jonathan didn't get it together and go hard in the paint for her after what she had just seen, the shit was going to hit the fan. So he had to man up and just do what he had to do. They had a balling-ass room in the MGM Grand, so Maria wanted to get her "look-e look-e" on, as Jonathan and Shannon got it on once again. She was a freak bitch like that, so Jonathan let her and Solo stay. Jonathan even let Solo eat Maria's pussy out as he fucked Shannon. *Why?* You ask him why? Because he could! He's The muthafuckin' Truth and he was feelin" himself, that's why he did it! On top of that, Jonathan really needed to know if he could trust Solo not to do it. But Shannon didn't want to get her look on, so she asked Solo to go to the bar with her to have a drink. Jonathan didn't know why, but he made both of them take their guns with them. Something wasn't right within his person; he had a bad feeling but wasn't sure if he was just trippin' or what. But once Maria started sucking his dick, the only thing Jonathan was trippin' off was the head she was giving him. No wonder why so many niggas got killed behind the monkey that couldn't climb a tree.

"See if y'all can find some weed before you come back," Maria said and tossed the keys to them then continued to suck his dick.

*****

"Let's go try to find the weed first, Shannon," Solo said.

"Whatever, nigga, but you driving!"

"Damn! What's wrong with you, Ms. Thang?"

"Nigga! You is what's wrong with me, why you do that shit?"

"What shit?" he asked.

"Don't play stupid, Solo, don't you know that everything Baby Locklord do there's a reason behind it. Nothing but loyalty is the key with him, he really needs to trust you, but after tonight that nigga's not goin' to ever truly trust you, your stupid ass should have turned that catfish sandwich down."

"But Maria didn't seem to mind, you sure you ain't just trippin, Shannon?"

"Nigga! Maria's a freak bitch! If she can get her pussy ate, she down fo' that, but if he would have asked her to fuck you, that shit wouldn't have happened. It was a test and you failed, nigga."

Solo didn't know how to feel as they rolled down the street.

Fuck! I got love for J. Why would that nigga set me up for a fall? he thought as he made a right turn on Martin Luther King Boulevard. The north side was popping in Clark County as he hit Owens and K Street. "Sit tight, Shannon, let me see if these niggas got any bud."

As Solo got out of the car, niggas mad-dogged him as they tended to do the new face in the hood. Words were exchanged then Solo went into his pocket and handed one of the men some money and started on his way back to the car. Shannon put her gun back down. As Solo was looking the bag over, the niggas that had sold it to him started running real fast. The thing that Shannon had thought to herself at first was that they had just got beat but as Solo looked up from the bag, Shannon saw him going for his gun, and that was when she went for hers. But the car was already coming to a screeching stop as fire came jumping from its window. Solo was hit! But somehow he got his gun out.

"I see you, muthafucka!" he cried out as he fired back at the car. But the driver took a seat on the driver's side window and now was helping the passenger fire on Solo. By now, Shannon had already joined in the gunfight. Running up on the car, Shannon opened the .380 up on the driver of the car. Her first five shots slipped into the night as they missed their mark, but the next five lit his ass up, slumping him as the seatbelt stopped him from falling to the ground outside the car.

"Locklord muthafucka!" Solo screamed as he got hit by the passenger's street sweeper more times than anyone could count. As he went down to one knee, the passenger realized that the driver was not driving off. Solo was still trying to lift his arm to fire the gun, but his arm would not work for him. Shannon tried to fire on the car as the passenger was trying to free the driver, so he could pull off but her gun was empty. So she ran to where Solo was and pulled his gun from his right hand as the passenger was trying to pull away.

Clap! Clap! Clap! Clap! Solo's 9 mm kicked in her hand as she tried to run the car down. It looked like he would get away with the dead body still hanging from the door, but in what must have been luck, one of her bullets hit a tire, causing the car to swing left into a tree. *Clap! Clap! Clap! Clap! Clap!* The 9 mm kicked some more in her hand as she ran full speed up to the driver's side of the car. By that time the gun said *Click! Click! Click!*

Shannon approached the passenger side window with her smoking gun still in her hand. But the dude was dead, just as dead as the man hanging out of the car door still intangled in his seatbelt.

As Shannon turned to run back to where Solo was trying to drag himself back to the car, the phone of the man that was hanging out side of the car door went off.

"Who is it?"

"This Cruz! Who the fuck is this?"

"This is Shannon Locklord, you bitch-made muthafucka! I got a message for you, from yo' boys: they told me to tell you that they dead and that yo' ass is next, nigga!"

Click!

Shannon ran back to where Solo was, and she didn't have to get close to see that he was badly fucked up. She tried to pick him up in order to get him inside the car, but she wasn't strong enough as they both fell to the ground. From afar the police sirens were sounding off, so Shannon ran to the car and drove it to where Solo was lying.

She got out and tried to get him in the car again, but still she wasn't strong enough. Then from out of nowhere a strong hand aided her.

"Get the job done, little lady cuz'. One time is on their way." She looked up to see that it was the nigga that had made the sale to Solo. After he helped Shannon get Solo in the car, not remembering whether she thanked him or not, she was running back to the driver's side of the car and pulling up out of there.

"Solo!" she cried out. "Solo! Hang in there damn it! I'm going to get you some help!"

"Did we get them?" the weak voice whispered out to her.

"Yeah, baby boy! We got them! Now you just hang in there! I'm going to get you some help!"

"I'm not going to make it, Shannon," he said as blood ran out of his mouth like water.

"You gotta get back to Jonathan and tell him I'm sorry for letting him down" was the last words he said before his body slumped over into her lap.

"Solo! Come on, man! Hang in there! Solo! Solo!" Shannon cried out. But it didn't matter how much she cried out, as when death comes it will ignore your concerns. Solo was dead.

*****

Ring! Ring! Ring! Ring!

"Who the fuck can that be on my wedding night?" Jonathan said.

"Well you know you never turn it off," Maria said. "And anyway no one knows that we are married yet."

"I'm just saying, Jonathan!"

Ring! Ring! Ring!

"Yeah? This The Truth!"

"Baby Locklord! It's all bad! You guys got to meet me in the parking lot."

"Can you speak on any of it over the phone?" Jonathan asked.

"No, Baby Locklord! But you need to get down here fast!"

"Okay!"

Click!

"Get up, Maria, we gotta get out of here!"

"What's going on, Jonathan?"

"I don't know but it must be bad. That was Shannon, she wants us to meet her in the parking lot!"

"Shit!" Maria said with a hard whisper. "Here we go again."

When they got to the car, Shannon was standing on the outside of it. As they walked up, one could tell that she was visibly shook up.

"Baby Locklord!" she cried out as she ran up to Jonathan. "It was crazy! Them muthafuckas just came out from nowhere! Slow. Aww! Naw!"

"Shit, Shannon! What the fuck happened?"

"Awww shit, Jonathan!" Maria shouted from the car.

"Solo's fucked up real bad!"

"That's what I'm try'na tell you!" Shannon said. "Solo's dead."

"Slowly, Shannon, tell me what happened."

As she explained the story to Jonathan and Maria, Jonathan could not help but think that he and Maria had played some sort of part in Solo's death. Maria because she was a damn "weedhead" and sent them on that scavenger hunt for some bud. But mostly himself because he seen danger coming but did not do anything about it.

As they pushed through the desert with a dead body in the trunk of the S550, it became all too clear to Jonathan that this shit had to come to an end. Shannon told Jonathan and Maria how Solo had stayed down and how she had killed the two niggas that killed Solo. She also told both of them about Cruz's phone call. When Jonathan had asked her why she had not left Solo's body for the coroner to collect instead of having to have the responsibility of getting rid of it themselves, she looked at Jonathan with teary eyes and said with pain in her voice, "We Locklords, Daddy! I couldn't just leave him behind. Did I do something wrong, Baby Locklord?"

The bitch stayed down by the gangster code that most niggas don't abide by, so what they had to do next was dig a hole in the desert to bury their loved one. The outlaw in Jonathan had to keep it real; Shannon stayed true to a code that died a long time ago.

"No, boo, you did what was supposed to be done!" You a true-blue gangster bitch."

They stopped at a hardware store to pick up a shovel, and the man in the little hick store looked at Jonathan as if to say, "I'm calling the police as soon as your suspicious-looking ass leaves here, nigger!"

Jonathan just looked back at him with a look that told him, "I know you are!"

So they took off in the opposite direction that they had come from and went down about a mile. He then hooked a U-turn and passed right back where he had come from, only to see that there was a cop car pulling off in the direction he had started off in. Jonathan mulled to himself and thought, *Sometimes you just got to follow your instincts.*

After they found a good spot to plant Solo, they dug a hole. Before they took off, the girls asked Jonathan to say some words over the body. *Shit! I don't know what the fuck to say!* Jonathan thought to himself. But just as they did, Jonathan also felt as something needed to be said, so he asked Shannon to say something since she was the last one with Solo. So she did.

"Hey, Solo, we all here, boo! We not gon' forget how you stayed down for the Locklord Clan. I know you may feel lonely right now, but stop trippin', nigga 'cuz that's not the case at all. Rose, Momma Locklord, and yo' brother K-Loc all up there waiting on you. And as for them niggas that got down on you, just take a look over yo' shoulder because they right behind you, boo. I'm looking at Jonathan right now, and I can tell by the look in his eyes we gon' kill the rest of them muthafuckas by the time the sun set tomorrow. So go get with the rest of the Locklord Clan, and keep a eye on us from above as we finish what we began. Until we see you on the other side, boo, know that it's Locklord for life!"

"Well said, girl, well said!" Maria told her as the two hugged.

"Daddy! That's the last of the Locklord that's going to die."

Jonathan looked at the two women and said, "Let's go and smoke that white muthafucka then!"

*****

Ring! Ring! Ring!

"Yeah, what it do?" the female voice came back over the phone.

"This big black dick is what it do if you play yo' cards right, bitch!"

"Who the hell is this?"

"This is Cannibal, baby!"

"No! This is the muthafucka that went big on me in front of his grandkids last night."

"Come on, baby, don't be like that."

"Nigga, what do you want?"

"I want some more of that good-ass pussy, that's what I want!"

"Well, nigga, it's really gon' cost you this time."

"Whatever the price, I got you, baby."

"Where do you want me to meet you at, Big Daddy?"

"The same place, bitch, at my spot in Newport Beach."

"Is that really yo' house, Cannibal?"

"Didn't I tell you that it was, bitch?"

"Yes, Daddy"

"Then get yo' high-yellow ass up here!"

"Okay, Daddy, but I'm gon' drive my van if that's okay with you? I don't like takin' them fuckin' cabs."

"Whatever, bitch, just get that pussy up here!"

"I'm on my way. By the way, Daddy, will we be alone, or will your grandkids be in the way again?"

"They in Vegas, bitch, now will you get your ass on the road!"

"I'll be there in forty-five minutes!"

Click!

"Well, Bandit, that old motherfuck took the bait."

Bandit gave the hooker 25 Gs and said, "I'll give you the rest after we get the job done."

She looked at all the money and said, "I didn't know if I was going to be able to trust you, dude, but I see I was wrong. Do you want anything else before we go, Big Daddy?"

She gave him a "come fuck me" look with her eyes. Bandit just laughed at her and said, "Get yo' shit, you stank bitch and let's go!"

*****

"Cruz," Sandy said softly. "Did them niggas drop the ball, baby?"

Cruz looked at her, and in his eyes she could see that he didn't have an answer to her question. He just picked up the phone and made a call.

"G street Watts, this Big Daddy, what it do?"

"This Cruz, cuzz! I'm going to need to call in a favor."

"Is that right, Crip? Well, it's like this, when you gave the sixties half of downtown LA, you called in the favor when you cut the Watts car out of that drug deal." Cruz just listened in anger.

"But look here, Conrad, this is what a nigga gon' do. I'm gon' let you in on a little something. Yo' plan could have and one day may work. But know this, a white boy will never be able to show the brothas the way. So fight yo' war, Conrad Cruz, but be advised that you're on yo' own. Now, I'm gon' let you get off the phone so you can make yo' other calls. However, niggas laughin' at you, Cruz, and after each call you make, you will hear them clearer and clearer."

Click!

Cruz made call after call, but Big Daddy was right, nobody was fuckin' with him. When he looked up from the phone, Sandy was standing there with her gun in hand and said, "Fuck them, Daddy! We can come up out of this shit even if it's just you, me, and Bandit!"

Cruz hit up Bandit on the phone, and Bandit picked up on the first ring.

"The Outlaw Bandit Loc here!"

"Nigga, where the fuck you been?" Cruz asked, almost happy to hear the man's voice.

"I've been taking care of business, Cruz! I pushed a bitch up under Jonathan's soft-dick rent-a-cop, and I'm all up in that nigga's shit right now!"

"So you got yo' head right again, Bandit?"

"Cruz, I told you I wanted to bark back at them muthafuckas. What? You think I'm playing?"

"Nah, my nigga. So what's the plan?" Cruz was testing him.

"Well, according to the rent-a-cop, they all in Vegas."

Cruz smiled because that's what he wanted to hear.

"And get this," Bandit said, to wipe the smile off his face, "he getting married to Maria and that other little bitch, uhmmm, what's her name? Shannon!"

"You remember the one that slapped you in the mouth with that gun at the club?"

"Yeah, I remember that bitch! As a matter of fact, I just got finished talking to her."

"Then get over here so we can welcome them home!"

"Cool, Crip! I'm on my way!

"Is it all good, Daddy?"

"It's all good, Mommy!"

"Let's get the black bag and roll out."

"I'm on it, Daddy, I'm on it!"

*****

As Jonathan and the girls pulled into the driveway, all looked well, other than the white van that was parked in front of the house.

"Whose shit is that?" Maria asked as they all pulled their guns out. As they exited the car, Jonathan sent the girls around back in case it was some kind of trap. As Jonathan got to the front door, he could see that it was cracked open. He then kicked it in as if he was Five-0 and swung his gun in both directions. He could not believe his eyes. There sitting in his living room was the Grim Reaper himself, The Outlaw Bandit Loc. Jonathan just stood there until Maria hit the room upstairs and Shannon hit the ones downstairs. Once the house was clear, they all stood in the living room looking at Bandit and Cannibal's hooker with Cannibal tied up on the floor.

Jonathan was the first to speak.

"Bandit, you know you ain't gon' get out of here alive, now don't you?"

"Well, Jonathan, I was thinking I might have a fifty-fifty chance. Nonetheless, God has already planned mine as well as your outcome, so if it goes down today, it's as good as any to die."

"What the fuck is going on here?" the hooker shouted out playing her roll, but to her surprise Bandit hit her with two hard elbows that knocked her the fuck out.

"You know this bitch?" Jonathan asked Bandit.

"Yeah," Bandit said calmly, "that's Cruz's wife's sister."

"What?" Maria exclaimed. "That bitch has been inside my house before!"

"That's right!" Bandit responded.

"Okay," Jonathan said. "So Cruz set us up? Now why ain't he here to finish the job?"

"Because he's not the one setting you up, Jonathan, I am!"

"I don't understand, dog, and before I kill you, because I am gon' kill you, that's fo' sho', I do need to understand."

"Well Jonathan, I set you up to set Cruz up!"

"Don't trust this nigga," Maria said softly. "He's the worst kind of snake, Papi."

Jonathan just looked at Bandit for a long moment before he spoke again. "Why, Bandit?" was all Jonathan could say.

"Because he got something I want by the name of Sandy. Surely you can understand where I'm coming from, Jonathan," Bandit said as he looked at Maria.

"What about the bitch on the floor?" Jonathan asked.

"What about this bitch?" Bandit almost spat. "You did kill her and Sandy's mother, the bitch is only up on half of the plan. Let me explain."

Bandit told them all about his mother's dreams she had about Rose, and some other church shit and about how God got some kind of plan for all their lives. The nigga went on and on about how he wanted out of the game, as if setting Cruz up would be his exit pass. Jonathan wanted to believe him, but how could he? So when the hooker came back from being unconscious, Jonathan handed Bandit his gun and told him to do what needed to be done. Bandit looked at Jonathan and said, "Boy, you just like your father."

With that, the nigga took the gun and popped Sandy's sister two times in the head. Her body rolled off the sofa on top of Cannibal, who was try'na scream under his gag.

"Now," Bandit said. "Cruz and Sandy are on their way over here. How's this shit gon' play out, Jonathan?" Jonathan could not believe how cold-blooded this nigga was. These types of niggas can't stop killing. He may want to, but sooner or later he would kill again. At that moment a car was pulling up into the driveway, and Bandit's phone went off.

"It's Cruz, Jonathan, so what's it going to be?"

"Get his gun, Maria. Let's drag these bodies out of the living room. Answer yo' phone, Bandit, then meet the muthafucka at the door."

Bandit went to the door with his phone on his ear. "It's all good, Cruz, get the black bag and come in before they get here. Have Sandy park the car in the back of the house."

As Sandy parked the car at the back of the house, the trust that Cruz had in Bandit would cost him his life on this day, Bandit thought to himself. As Cruz walked into the house behind Bandit, the next thing he knew, he was getting up off the floor in daze with Jonathan holding a gun on him.

"So this is how I'm going out, Bandit Loco? Betrayed by a nigga I trust?"

Bandit did not say a word. Just then Sandy walked through the back with Shannon and Maria holding guns on her.

"Well, Jonathan, the gang's all here," Bandit said as he looked at both Sandy and Cruz.

"What the fuck is this Bandit?" Sandy cried out in fear.

"Sandy," Bandit said. "You don't have to play it off no more, step away from Cruz and step into your destiny."

She did not let any grass grow under her feet. And even as Bandit had already told them what time it was, it was still to their surprise how quickly Sandy moved to his side. Cruz just stood there, and as Jonathan eyed him, a single tear rolled down Cruz's face. Jonathan wanted to laugh and almost did but instead said, "When life gets pissed off at a man, it sure has a way of kickin' him in the ass, doesn't it, Dad?"

"Just do what you gotta do, Jonathan!" Cruz said. "Because I would if I was standing in yo' shoes."

Maria handed Jonathan his Desert Eagle as Jonathan said, "You sure you want me to do what I need to do, you sick muthafucka?"

"Just do it, Jonathan! Where's yo' muthafuckin' heart at, nigga! If you got any of my blood in you, pull the fuckin' trigger and get it over with!" Cruz said with the heart of a lion.

Clap! Clap! The first two shots hit Sandy in the head, removing her whole face. *Clap! Clap! Clap! Clap!* The next four shots sent Bandit spinning off his feet on to the floor, and as he lay there with his eyes still open, the look on his face seemed to almost ask "*Why?*" Everyone in the room was left standing in total shock, and no one dared to move as The Truth spoke.

"It's true that life is a bitch, and then we must die! But nobody should have to die at the hands of betrayal, especially when they're related to me. Cruz! Now tell me, did you see any of this shit coming?"

"No, Jonathan!" he said as he looked at his dead wife who had crossed him for a nigga that he trusted. "I didn't see any of this shit coming at all."

"Maria!"

"Yes, Daddy?"

"Go untie Cannibal!" Jonathan told his wife, who quickly did as she was told. Jonathan continued to speak to Cruz.

"See, Cruz, nothing is ever as it would appear to be.

"Go get the paperwork, Shannon."

She also moved without letting any grass grow under her feet.

"However, Cruz," Jonathan continued, "I got a deal for you. I want the club, the recording studio, and I want my brother and sister."

"*Your* brother and sister?"

"Look, muthafucka!" Jonathan exclaimed. "If you want to live, sign yo' custodial rights over to me, with the rest of the bullshit, that will be Shay Shay's and the boss's when they come to age!"

"You got it all planned out, don't you, Jonathan? What about Sandy's sister? What if she wants the kids?"

"Maria!" Jonathan called out. "Go get Sandy's sister."

Maria dragged the hooker into the room. "As you can see from the bullet holes in her head, Sandy's sister is not thinking about them kids. Now sign the goddamn paperwork!"

This time all three of their guns were pointed at Cruz as he picked up the pen to sign the paperwork that gave Jonathan everything Cruz had ever worked for, including the kids.

"Can I go now?"

"Yeah, Cruz, you can go."

"Don't let him go, Daddy, he'll only come after us." Maria almost pleaded with him.

"I got to, baby, I gave him my word. I gave you my word, Cruz, now get the fuck out."

Cruz walked to the door and then turned around with a deadly look and said, "You taking my kids only means that one day I'll come back around and take yours." He then pointed at Jonathan and pulled the invisible trigger on an invisible gun.

Clap! Clap! Clap! Clap! Clap! Clap! sounded off Maria's TEC-9 as it sent Cruz flying off his feet and out of the door. Shannon moved quickly to pull the corpse back into the house and said, "Now Rose can truly rest in peace."

Maria looked up at Jonathan and said, "I'm two months pregnant with your child, Daddy, and I didn't give this muthafucka my word, so need I say more?"

"No," Jonathan simply replied as he looked at his dead father. His only other words were "Life is truly a bitch, And then we die…"

The End

ABOUT THE AUTHOR

Derrick Spivey was born in Oakland California but raised in South Central Los Angeles, by way of Compton, California. Brought up in a two-parent home where one parent was invisible because he was never there. So as you can imagine, the streets became his father, and against my mother's better wishes, the penitentiary became his home.

He was introduced to the gang life at the tender age of twelve. And just so that the reader will be well-informed, he's a second-generation Crip, under the leadership of Stanley Tookie Williams (may he rest in peace). He could give you more information about him, but all the information you need is already resting in the palm of your hands, as he is The Truth, and The Truth is me (So Let It Be Told).

CPSIA information can be obtained
at www.ICGtesting.com
Printed in the USA
JSHW082206300323
39715JS00001B/69